A SPRINGTIME OF DEVASTATION

When young Timothy decided his moment of recognition and glory had come, the inhabitants of Dynmouth found their lives tragically and irrevocably altered. Adultery, murder, homosexuality, desperate loneliness, and horrifying madness were all brought to light as the villagers were forced to confront the truth about themselves.

"An intriguing psychological study . . . a complex and provocative theme served up in highly readable form"   **—Library Journal**

"Very deftly done"   **—Newsweek**

THE CHILDREN OF DYNMOUTH

WILLIAM TREVOR

A KANGAROO BOOK
PUBLISHED BY POCKET BOOKS NEW YORK

Distributed in Canada by PaperJacks Ltd., a Licensee
of the trademarks of Simon & Schuster, a division of
Gulf+Western Corporation.

This POCKET BOOK edition includes every word contained in
the original, higher-priced edition. It is printed from brand-new
plates made from completely reset, clear, easy-to-read type.
POCKET BOOK editions are published by
POCKET BOOKS,
a division of Simon & Schuster, Inc.,
A GULF + WESTERN COMPANY
Trademarks registered in the United States
and other countries.
In Canada distributed by PaperJacks Ltd.,
330 Steelcase Road, Markham, Ontario.

Published by arrangement with The Viking Press
Library of Congress Catalog Card Number: 76-53741

ISBN: 0-671-81892-9
First Pocket Books printing January, 1978

Trademarks registered in the United States and other countries.

Printed in Canada.

*For
Patrick
and Dominic*

THE CHILDREN OF DYNMOUTH

1

~~~~~~

Dynmouth nestled on the Dorset coast, gathered about what was once the single source of its prosperity, a small fishing harbor. In the early eighteenth century it had been renowned for its lacemaking and its turbot, and had later developed prettily as a watering place. Being still small, it was now considered unspoilt, a seaside resort of limited diversions, its curving promenade and modest pier stylish with ornamental lamp-posts, painted green. At the foot of gray-brown cliffs a belt of shingle gave way to the sand on which generations of Dynmouth's children had run and played, and built castles with moats and flag-poles.

In an unspectacular way the town had expanded inland along the valley of the Dyn. Where sheep had grazed on sloping downs a sandpaper factory stood now and opposite it, on the other side of the river, a tile-works. At the eastern end of the promenade, near the car-park and the public lavatories, there was a fish-packing station. Plastic lampshades were scheduled to be manufactured soon on a site that had once been known as Long Dog's Field, and there were rumors— denied by the town council—that the Singer Sewing Machine organization had recently looked the town over with a view to developing a plant there. There were three banks in Dynmouth, Lloyd's, Barclay's and the National Westminster. There were municipal tennis-courts beside the Youth Center, and a Baptist chapel and a Methodist chapel, the Church of England's St. Simon and St. Jude, the Catholic Queen of Heaven. There were nine hotels and nineteen boarding-houses, eleven public houses and one fish and chip shop, Phyl's Phries, next to the steam laundry on the Dynmouth Junction road. There was the East Street Bingo and Whist-Drive Hall and the ancient Essoldo Cinema in flaking pink, dim and cavernous within. Sir Walter Raleigh Park, enclosed by ornamental railings that matched the promenade's lamp-posts, was rented from the council by Ring's Amusements every summer season. Spreading inland from the cliffs, a golf course had been laid out in 1936.

Winter and summer alike, every Sunday afternoon, the Badstoneleigh and Dynmouth Salvation Army Band marched through the town. Twice a week or so the Dynmouth Hards, a gang of motorcyclists in fringed black leather, rampaged by night, with their black-fringed girl-friends on pillions behind them. In 1969 there'd been a strike at the sandpaper factory. In 1970 an assistant chef at the Queen Victoria Hotel, dissatisfied with the terms of his employment, attempted to burn the building down by soaking curtains and bedclothes in paraffin, an incident that was reported on an inside page of the *Daily Telegraph*. The man, a Sicilian, was stated by Dr. Greenslade to be insane.

A pattern, familiar elsewhere too, prevailed in Dynmouth. The houses of the well-to-do, solitary and set in generous gardens, were followed in order of such esteem by semi-detached villas that stood like twins in Dynmouth's tree-lined avenues and crescents. After which came dwellings that had a look of economy about them, reflecting the burden of rent or mortgage. Far from the sea-front and the centre of the town was the sprawl of council estates and sand-yellow blocks of council flats. In streets near the river there were terraced houses of cramped proportions, temporarily occupied by those who waited for their names to rise to the top of a housing list. So close to the river that they were regularly flooded by it were the cottages of Boughs Lane, which people said were a disgrace. The handsomest dwelling in Dynmouth was Sea House, high on the cliffs beside the golf-course, famous for the azaleas of its garden.

Of the town's 4,139 inhabitants half were children. There were three nursery schools: the Ring-o-Roses, Lavinia Featherston's at the rectory, and the WRVS Playgroup. There was Dynmouth Primary School, Dynmouth Comprehensive and the Loretto Convent. There was Down Manor Orphanage, red-brick and barrack-like, beyond the electricity plant, and Dynmouth Nurseries, a mile outside the town. The Youth Center was run by John and Ted.

The children of Dynmouth were as children anywhere. They led double lives; more regularly than their elders they traveled without moving from a room. They saw a different world: the sun looked different to them, and so did Dynmouth's trees and grass and sand. Dogs loomed at a different level, eye to eye. Cats arched their tiger's backs, and the birds behind bars in Moult's

Hardware and Pet Supplies gazed beadily down, appearing to speak messages. Pairs of Loretto nuns, airing themselves on the promenade, gazed down also, blackly nodding, a crucified body dangling among their black beads. Ring's Amusements were Dynmouth's Paradise.

No longer children, some found office work, others made for the supermarkets, the garages, the hotels, Dynmouth Lace Ltd., the printing-works of the *Badstoneleigh and Dynmouth News*, the laundry. Since the time of Queen Victoria— who visited the town—tea-shops had been a feature: there were twelve now, offering indifferent wages to girls who were nimble on their feet. A few boys became trawler-men, but life was easier and richer at the fish-packing station, and in the sandpaper factory and the tile-works. Some made their careers outside the town when the time came, even though Dynmouth remained home for them and was thought of with affection. Some couldn't stand the town and dreamed, while still children, of being other people in other places.

Lavinia Featherston, who had been herself a child of Dynmouth, remembered when the green ornamental lamp-posts were all of a sudden huge no longer and when the gray-brown cliffs appeared to have been re-cut to size and the Spinning Wheel Tea-Rooms seemed almost tatty. The rectory she lived in now, an ivy-clad building set among ragged lawns, had been a mysterious and forbidding house to her as a child, halfway up the hill called Once Hill, partly hidden from the road by a stone wall and a row of macrocarpa trees. It hadn't changed, yet it was not the same. When she surveyed her nursery school in the

rectory it sometimes saddened Lavinia that everything would become more ordinary for these children as they grew up, that all too soon the birds
in Moul's Hardware and Pet Supplies would cease
to speak messages. She ran her school because
she liked the company of children, though sometimes finding it a strain.

She found it so on the afternoon of a Wednesday in early April, the day, in fact, of St. Pancras
of Sicily, as her husband had remarked at break-
fast-time. Outside, it was blustery and cold. Sheets
of soft rain dribbled on the rectory's window-
panes. The fire in the sitting-room refused to
light.

"I'm really cross," Lavinia said, addressing her
twin daughters, aged four. She regarded them
sternly from the fireplace, out of breath because
she'd been blowing at the charred edges of a
newspaper. All day long, she reminded them,
they'd been nothing but trouble, painting their
hands at nursery school, tearing about Lipton's
when she'd told them to stand by the dog-food,
and now, apparently, throwing jam at the kitchen
window.

"I didn't," Susannah said.

"Fell." Repeatedly Deborah nodded, lending
weight to that explanation. "Fell and fell."

Lavinia Featherston, a pretty, fair-haired
woman of thirty-five, told her daughters to stop
talking nonsense. Jam didn't fall, she pointed
out. Jam wasn't like rain. Jam had to be taken
from a pot and thrown. People were starving in
the world: it wasn't right to throw jam about a
kitchen just because you were bored.

"It fell out of the pot," Deborah said. "Goodness
knows how it got to the window, Mummy."

"Goodness knows, Mummy."

Lavinia continued to look sternly at them. They, too, were fair-haired; they had freckles on the bridges of their noses. Would a boy have looked the same? She'd often wondered that, and wondered it more relevantly just now.

That, at the moment, was the trouble with Lavinia. She was recovering from a miscarriage, feeling nervy and on edge. Everything had been going perfectly until a fortnight ago and then, after the loss of her child, Dr. Greenslade had reminded her that he'd warned her against attempting to have it. The warning had become an order: in no circumstances was she to attempt to have another baby.

This turn of events had upset Lavinia more than she'd have believed possible. She and Quentin had very much wanted a son; Dr. Greenslade stood firm. The disappointment, still recent, was hard to shake off.

"You know what happens to children who tell lies," she crossly reminded her daughters. "It's high time you turned over a new leaf."

The bell at the back-door rang. A stick in the fire began half-heartedly to blaze. Slowly Lavinia gathered herself to her feet. It could be anyone, for the rectory was an open house. It was open to Mrs. Slewy, the worst mother in Dynmouth, a shapeless woman who smelt of poverty and cigarettes, who live in a condemned cottage in Boughs Lane with her five inadequate children. And to the elderly Miss Trimm, who'd been a schoolteacher in the town and nowadays was disturbed in her mind. Children returned for confirmation classes years after they'd left the nursery school, adults came for fellowship discussions. Mrs.

Keble, the organist, came to talk about hymns, and Father Madden to talk about ecumenicalism. Mrs. Stead-Carter came importantly, Miss Poraway for a chat.

Today, though, it was none of these people: it was a figure known in Dynmouth only as Old Ape, who had come a day early for the weekly scraps. The scraps were meant to be for hens he kept, but everyone in Dynmouth knew that he didn't possess hens and that he ate the scraps himself. When he came to the rectory he was also given a plate of meat and vegetables, provided he arrived at six o'clock on the specified day, which was Thursday. "I'll get the scraps," Lavinia said at the back door. "You come back tomorrow for your dinner." Communication with Old Ape was difficult. It was said that he could speak but chose not to. It wasn't known if he was deaf.

In the sitting-room the twins played with the pieces of a jigsaw, squatting on the hearthrug in front of the damply flickering fire. When you interlocked the pieces of the puzzle there was a picture of a donkey, but they'd seen the donkey so many times it didn't seem worth while going to all that trouble yet again. On the lid of the jigsaw box they built the pieces into a pyre.

"Dragons come," Susannah said.

"What's dragons, Susannah?"

"They come if you tell lies. They're burny things. They've flames in them."

But Deborah was thinking of something else. She was thinking of being in the garden, of looking all over the grass and then in the flower-beds and on the gravel by the garage and along by the edges of the paths, until she found a new leaf. She closed her eyes and saw herself leaning down by the edge of a path and turning the new leaf over to see what was on the other side.

In the kitchen their mother made a cup of tea, and in the streets of Dynmouth their father, the vicar of St. Simon and St. Jude's, pedalled through the wind and the rain on a 1937 Rudge, left to him in a parishioner's will. He was an impressive figure on this bicycle, rather lanky, his hair prematurely gray, his face seeming ascetic until cheered by a smile that occurred whenever he greeted anyone. He hoped as he went about his familiar Wednesday duty of visiting the sick among his parishioners that Lavinia wasn't having a time with the twins, cooped inside on a damp afternoon. He thought about his wife as he chatted to old, disturbed Miss Trimm, who had a cold, and to little Sharon Lines, who was on a kidney machine. They'd waited almost nine years for the twins to be born: they had a lot to be thankful for but it was hard to comfort a woman who'd lost a child and couldn't have another. Lavinia's moments of despondency were irrational, she said so herself, yet they continued to afflict her. They made her not at all like what she was.

He rode down Fore Street, where holiday-makers who had taken advantage of the pre-Easter rates looked as though they regretted it as they loitered in the rain. Some took refuge in the doorways of shops, eating sweets or nuts. Others read the list of forthcoming attractions outside the Essoldo Cinema where *The Battle of Britain* was at present showing. In Sir Walter Raleigh Park, beside the promenade, Ring's Amusements were preparing for their seasonal opening in ten days' time, on Easter Saturday.

Machines were being oiled and repaired, staff taken on, statutory safety precautions pondered over with a view to their evasion. The Hall of a Million Mirrors and the Tunnel of Love and Alfonso's and Annabella's Wall of Death were in the process of erection. The men who performed this work were of a muscular, weathered appearance, with faded scarves tied round their throats, some with brass rings on their fingers. Like their garish caravans and pin-tables and the swarthy women who assisted them, they seemed to belong to the past. They shouted to one another through the rain, using words that had an old-fashioned ring.

The promenade was almost empty. Commander Abigail strutted along it toward the steps that led to the beach, with his bathing-trunks rolled up in a towel. The slight, carefully clad figure of Miss Lavant moved slowly in the opposite direction, beneath a red umbrella that caught occasionally in the wind. The wind bustled around her, gadding over the concrete of the promenade and up and down the short pier. It rattled the refuse-bins on the ornamental lamp-posts, and the broken glass in the bus-shelters. It played with cigarette packets and wrappings from chocolate and potato crisps. It drove paper bags into corners and left them there, uselessly sodden.

The sea was so far out you could hardly see it. Seagulls stood like small rocks, rooted to the flattened sand. The sky was gray, shadowed with darker gray.

"Cheers, sir," a voice called and Quentin Featherston turned his head and saw Timothy Gedge standing on the edge of the pavement, apparently hoping for a word with him. Cautiously, he applied the Rudge's brakes.

Timothy Gedge was a youth of fifteen, ungainly due to adolescence, a boy with a sharp-boned face and wide, thin shoulders, whose short hair was almost white. His eyes seemed hungry, giving him a predatory look; his cheeks had a hollowness about them. He was always dressed in the same clothes: pale yellow jeans and a yellow jacket with a zip, and a T-shirt that more often than not was yellow also. He lived with his mother and his sister, Rose-Ann, in a block of council-built flats called Cornerways; without distinction, he attended Dynmouth Comprehensive School. He was a boy who was given to making jokes, a habit that caused him sometimes to seem eccentric. He smiled and grinned a lot.

"Hi, Mr. Feather," he said.

"Hullo, Timothy."

"Nice day, Mr. Feather."

"Well, I don't know about nice—"

"I was meaning for ducks, sir." He laughed. His clothes were wet. His short pale hair was plastered around his head.

"Did you want to speak to me, Timothy?" He wished the boy would address him by his correct name. He had asked him to, but the boy had pretended not to understand: it was all meant to be a joke.

"I was wondering about the Easter Fête, Mr. Feather. Did you know Ring's will be opening up the same afternoon?"

"Ring's always begin on Easter Saturday."

"That's what I'm saying to you, Mr. Feather. Won't Ring's take the crowds?"

"Oh, I don't think so. They haven't in the past."

"I'd say you were wrong, Mr. Feather."

"Well, we'll just have to see. Thank you for thinking of it, Timothy."

"I was wondering about the Spot the Talent comp, Mr. Feather."

"We're having the Spot the Talent competition at two-thirty. Mr. and Mrs. Dass will be in charge again."

More than a month ago the boy had appeared at the rectory one evening, quite late it had been, after nine o'clock, and had asked if there was going to be a Spot the Talent competition at this year's Easter Fête because he wanted to do a comedy act. Quentin had told him he imagined there would be, with Mr. and Mrs. Dass in charge as usual. He'd later heard from the Dasses that Timothy Gedge had been to see them and that they'd written his name down, the first entry.

He was a strange boy, always at a loose end. His mother was a good-looking woman with brassy hair who sold women's clothes in a shop called Cha-Cha Fashions, his sister was six or seven years older than Timothy, good-looking also, employed as a petrol-pump attendant on the forecourt of the Smiling Service Filling Station: Quentin knew them both by sight. In adolescence, unfortunately, the boy was increasingly becoming a nuisance to people, endlessly friendly and smiling, keen for a conversation. He was what Lavinia called a latch-key child, returning to the empty flat in Cornerways from the Comprehensive school, on his own in it all day during the school holidays. Being on his own seemed somehow to have become part of him.

"She's a funny woman, that Mrs. Dass. He's funny himself, with that pipe."

"Oh, I don't think so. I must be off, I'm afraid, Timothy."

"Will it be in the marquee again, sir?"

"I should think so."

"D'you know the Abigails, Mr. Feather? The Commander and Mrs.? I do jobs for the Abigails, you know. Every Wednesday night; I'll be round there tonight. Funny type of people."

Quentin shook his head. He knew the Abigails, he said; they didn't seem funny to him. His right foot was on the pedal, but he couldn't push the bicycle forward because the boy was slightly in the way, his knee touching the spokes of the front wheel.

"The Commander's having his bathe now. I call that funny. In the sea in April, Mr. Feather." He paused, smiling. "I see Miss Lavant's out on her stroll."

"Yes, I know—"

"Out to catch a glimpse of Dr. Greenslade."

The boy laughed and Quentin managed to get the front wheel of his bicycle past the protruding knee. Some other time they'd have a chat, he promised.

"I think I'll call in on Dass," Timothy Gedge said, "to see how he's getting on."

"Oh, I shouldn't bother."

"I think I'd better, sir."

Quentin rode away, feeling he should have stayed longer with the boy, if only to explain why there was no need for him to go bothering the Dasses. There'd been a period when he'd come to the rectory every Saturday morning, sometimes as early as a quarter to nine. He'd had an idea, as he'd explained to Quentin, that when he grew up he'd like to be a clergyman. But when Quentin had eventually tried to persuade him to join his confirmation class, he'd said he wasn't interested and had in fact given up the notion of a clerical career. He hung about the church now, and about the graveyard whenever there was a funeral service. It particularly worried Quentin that he was always around when there was a funeral.

Timothy watched the dark figure of the clergyman pedaling away, thinking to himself that strictly speaking the clergyman was a bit of a fool the way he let himself be taken advantage of. All sorts of tricks people got up to with the man, extraordinary it must be, being a clergyman. He shook his head over the folly of it all, and then he forgot about it and surveyed the promenade. Miss Lavant had gone, the promenade and the pier were deserted. In the far distance, a speck on the beach beneath the cliffs, Commander Abigail ran toward the sea. Timothy Gedge laughed, shaking his head over the folly of that also.

He walked along the promenade, taking his time because there was no particular hurry. He didn't mind the rain, he quite liked it when he got wet. He walked past the small harbor and a row of boats upturned on the shingle. He wandered into the yard of the fish-packing station, to the shed where freshly caught fish was sold to anyone who wanted it. *Dabs*, it said on a slate on one side of the door. *Lemon Sole, Mackerel, Plaice.* If there'd been anyone buying fish there he'd have loitered in order to listen to the transaction, but nobody was. He went into the public lavatories in the car-park, but there was no one there either. He turned into East Street, moving toward the area where the Dasses lived.

"Cheers," he said to a couple of old-age pension-

ers who were tottering along together, clinging to
one another on a slippery pavement, but they
didn't reply. He paused beside three nuns who
were examining a shop window full of garden
tools while waiting for a bus. He smiled at them
and pointed out a pair of secateurs, saying they
looked good value. They were about to reply when
the bus came. "It's the friendly boy Sister Agnes
mentioned," he heard one of them comment, and
from the inside of the bus all three of them waved
at him.

The Dasses lived in a semi-detached house
called Sweetlea. Mr. Dass had been the manager
of the Dynmouth branch of Lloyd's Bank and was
now retired. He was a man with wire-rimmed
spectacles, tall and very thin, given to wearing
unpressed tweed suits. His wife was an invalid,
with pale flesh that had a deflated look. She had
once been active in Dynmouth's now-defunct
amateur dramatic society, the Dynmouth Strollers,
and when Quentin Featherston had decided to
hold his first Easter Fête to raise funds for the
crumbling tower of St. Simon and St. Jude's,
Mrs. Stead-Carter had put forward the idea of a
talent competition and had suggested that Mrs.
Dass should be invited to judge it. The talent
competition had become an annual event, Mrs.
Dass continuing to accept the onus of judgment
and Mr. Dass entering into the spirit of things by
seeing to the erection and lighting of a stage in the
tea marquee that was borrowed annually through
the Stead-Carters, who had influence in the tent-
ing world. The stage itself, modest in size, con-
sisted of a number of timber boards set on con-

crete blocks. There was a wooden frame, knocked
up by Mr. Peniket, the sexton, which supported
a landscape of Swiss Alps painted on hardboard,
and the stage's curtains. Each year the curtains
were borrowed from the stage of the Youth Center, and it was Mrs. Dass, artistic in this direction
also, who had been responsible for the all-purpose
scenery. In his devotion to his wife and knowing
more than anyone else about her invalid state, it
pleased Mr. Dass that the Spot the Talent competition was now an established event at the
Easter Fête: it took her out of herself.

"Only I was passing," Timothy Gedge said,
having penetrated to the Dasses' sitting-room. "I
was wondering how things was going, sir."

Mrs. Dass was reclining on a sun-chair in the
bow-window, reading a book by Dennis Wheatley,
To the Devil, a Daughter. Her husband was standing by the door without his jacket, regretting that
he'd admitted the boy. He'd been asleep on his
bed when the bell had been rung, and the ringing
hadn't immediately wakened him. It had first of
all occurred in a dream he was having about his
early childhood, and had then been repeated
quite a number of times before he could get
downstairs. It had sounded important.

"Things?" he said.

"The Spot the Talent comp, sir."

"Oh, yes."

"Only I was speaking to Mr. Feather and he
said I'd best look in at Sweetlea."

In her sun-chair in the bow-window Mrs. Dass
put down *To the Devil, a Daughter.* For a moment
she watched the sparrows in the small back garden and then she closed her eyes. She'd smiled

a little when her husband had brought Timothy Gedge into the room, but she hadn't spoken.

"Everything's A1," Mr. Dass said. He hadn't thought about the stage or the lighting yet. The stage would be where Mr. Peniket and he had left it last year, in the cellar beneath the church where the coke was kept. The lights were in three cardboard boxes, under his bed.

"We've had quite a few entries," he reported. Stout Mrs. Muller, the Austrian woman who ran the Gardenia Café, went in for the competition every year, singing Austrian songs in her national costume accompanied by her husband on an accordion, in national costume also. A group called the Dynmouth Night-Lifers strummed electric guitars and sang. The manager of the tile-works played tunes on his mouth-organ. Mr. Swayles, employed in a newsagent's, did conjuring. Miss Wilkinson, who taught English in the Comprehensive school, had done Lady Macbeth and Miss Haversham and was down to do the Lady of Shalott this year. Last summer's carnival queen, a girl employed in the fish-packing station, had never before entered the Spot the Talent competition. In her queen's white dress, trimmed with Dynmouth lace, and wearing her crown, she was scheduled to sing "Tie a Yellow Ribbon round the Old Oak Tree."

"Mrs. Dass all right is she, sir?" Timothy Gedge enquired, glancing across the room at her, thinking that the woman looked dead.

Mr. Dass nodded. She often liked to lie with her eyes closed. He himself had moved across the room and was now standing with his back to a small coal fire. He took his pipe from a trouser pocket and pressed tobacco into it from a tin. He wished the boy would go away.

"Only there's not long till the Easter Fête, sir."

To Mr. Dass's horror, the boy sat down. He unzipped his damp yellow jacket, settling himself on the sofa.

"I was saying to Mr. Feather, Ring's is getting ready again. They'll be opening up Easter Saturday."

"Yes, they will."

"Same day as the Easter Fête, Mr. Dass."

"Yes."

"Only I was saying to Mr. Feather they'll take the crowds."

Mr. Dass shook his head. The crowds went from one attraction to the other, he explained. The opening of Ring's Amusements on Easter Saturday brought people from outside Dynmouth: the Easter Fête actually benefited from the co-incidence.

"I wouldn't agree, sir," Timothy said.

Mr. Dass didn't reply.

"It's bad weather, sir."

Mr. Dass said it was, and then asked if he could be of help in any way.

"What's he want?" Mrs. Dass suddenly demanded, opening her eyes.

"Afternoon, Mrs. Dass," Timothy said. Funny the way they wouldn't give you a cup of tea. Funny the man standing there in his shirtsleeves. He smiled at Mrs. Dass. "We were on about the Spot the Talent comp," he said.

She smiled back at the boy. He began to talk about a sewing-machine.

"Sewing-machine?" she said.

"For making curtains, Mrs. Dass. Only the

Youth Center curtains got burnt in December.
New curtains are required is what I'm saying."

"What's he mean?" she asked her husband.

"The Youth Center curtains are apparently un-
available for the Easter Fête, dear. I don't know
why he's come to us about it."

Mr. Dass lit his pipe. He had let the boy in
because the boy had said he had an urgent message. So far no message had been delivered.

"I'm afraid my wife is not in a position to
make curtains," he said.

"We'll have to buy some then, Mr. Dass. You
can't have a stage without curtains on it."

"Oh, I imagine we'll manage somehow."

"I definitely need curtains for my act, sir."

"Mrs. Dass will not be making curtains." A
note of asperity had entered Mr. Dass's voice. As
the manager of the Dynmouth branch of Lloyd's
Bank he had regularly had occasion to call on
this resolute tone when rejecting pleas for credit
facilities. "As a matter of fact," he added, taking
his pipe from his mouth and pressing the smol-
dering tobacco with a thumb, "we are extremely
busy this afternoon."

"I'm worried about the curtains, sir."

"That's really Mr. Featherston's pigeon, you
know."

"Mr. Feather said you'd supply new curtains,
sir."

"Mr. Featherston? Oh, I'm sure you're quite
wrong, you know."

"He said you'd definitely donate them, sir."

"Donate curtains? Now, look here—"

"I think it's a kind of joke," Mrs. Dass said.
She smiled weakly at Timothy Gedge. "We're not
good on jokes, I'm afraid."

Mr. Dass moved from the position he'd taken up by the fire. He leant over Timothy on the sofa. He spoke in a whisper, explaining that his wife liked to rest in the afternoons. It embarrassed him having to say all this to a schoolboy, but he felt he had no option. "I'll see you out," he said.

"All right is she?" Timothy asked again, not that he cared: it was his opinion that Mrs. Dass was a load of rubbish the way she affected herself, lying there like a dead white slug when there was nothing the matter with her.

Mr. Dass opened the hall door of Sweetlea and waited while Timothy zipped up his jacket again.

"You didn't mind me asking about her, sir? Only she looked a bit white in the face."

"My wife's not strong."

"She misses what's-his-name?"

"If you mean our son, yes, she does."

"He hasn't been back in a long time, Mr. Dass."

"No. Goodbye now."

Timothy nodded, not leaving the house. He'd known their son well, he said. He enquired about the work he was doing now and Mr. Dass was vague in his reply, having no wish to discuss his son with a stranger, especially since his son had been at the center of a domestic tragedy. The Dasses had two daughters, both of them now married and living in London. Their son, Nevil, born when Mrs. Dass was forty-two, had taken them by surprise and as a result had been indulged in childhood, a state of affairs that the Dasses now bitterly regretted. Three years ago, when Nevil was nineteen, he had quite out of the blue turned most harshly on both of them and had not been back to Dynmouth since. He'd been particularly the apple of his mother's eye:

his rejection of her had gradually brought about
her invalid state. The Dynmouth doctors had
pronounced her condition to be a nervous one,
but it was no less real for being that, as her
husband in his affection for her realized. The
whole unfortunate matter was never mentioned
now, not even within the family, not even when
the two daughters came at Christmas with their
children and husbands. Every year a place was
laid for Nevil on this festive occasion, a gesture
more than anything else.

"He was very fond of the Queen Victoria Hotel,
sir. I'll always remember him going in and coming out, sir."

"Yes, well—"

"He'd always have the time of day for you."

"Look, I'd rather not discuss my son. If there's
anything else—"

"I need special stuff with lights for the act I've
got, Mr. Dass. I need the stage in darkness and
then the lights coming on. I need that four times,
Mr. Dass, the darkness and the light: I'll give you
the tip by winking. I need the curtains drawn over
twice. That's why I'm worried about them."

"Yes, well, I'm sure we can manage something."

"You're out with a blonde, Mr. Dass, you see
the wife coming?"

Mr. Dass frowned, imagining he had heard in-
correctly. It was cold, standing in the hall with
the door open. "I beg your pardon?" he said.

"What d'you do when you see the wife coming,
sir?"

"Now, look here—"

"The four-minute mile, sir!"

Mr. Dass said he had things to do. He said he'd be grateful if Timothy Gedge left his house.

"I do jobs for the Abigails, Mr. Dass, I'll be round there tonight. If there's anything you had here—"

"It's quite all right, thank you."

"I do the surrounds for Mrs. Abigail, and stuff in the garden for the Commander. I'd clean your boots for you, sir. Mrs. Dass's as well."

"We don't need help in the house. I really must ask you to go now."

"You didn't mind me asking you? I'll pop in again when I'm passing, sir. I'll have a word with Mr. Feather about the curtains."

"There's no need to call here again," Mr. Dass said quickly. "About curtains or anything else."

"I'm really looking forward to the Spot the Talent, sir."

The door banged behind him. He walked down the short tiled path, leaving the garden gate open. It was too soon to go to the Abigails'. He wasn't due at the Abigails' bungalow in High Park Avenue until six o'clock, not that it mattered being on the early side, but it was only five-past four now. He thought of going down to the Youth Center, but all there'd be at the Youth Center would be people playing ping-pong and smoking and talking about sex.

Slowly he walked through Dynmouth again, examining the goods in the shop windows, watching golf being played on various television sets. He bought a tube of Rowntree's Fruit Gums. He thought about the act he'd devised for the Spot the Talent competition. He began to walk toward Cornerways, planning to dress himself up in his sister's clothes.

At Dynmouth Comprehensive Timothy Gedge
found no subject interesting. Questioned some
years ago by the headmaster, a Mr. Stringer, he
had confessed to this and Mr. Stringer had stirred
his coffee and said it was a bad thing. He'd asked
Timothy what he found interesting outside the
Comprehensive and Timothy had said television
shows. Prompted further by Mr. Stringer, he'd
confessed that as soon as he walked into the
empty flat on his return from school he turned
on the television and was always pleased to watch
whatever there was. Sitting in a room with the
curtains drawn, he delighted in hospital dramas
and life at the Crossroads Motel and horse-racing
and cookery demonstrations. In the holidays there
were the morning programs as well: Bagpuss,
Camp Runamuck, *Nai Zindagi Naya Jeevan*,
Funky Phantom, Randall and Hopkirk (deceased), Junior Police Five, Car Body Mainte-
nance, Solids, Liquids and Gases, Play a Tune
with Ulf Goran, Sheep Production. Mr. Stringer
said it was a bad thing to watch so much television. "I suppose you'll go into the sandpaper
factory?" he'd suggested and Timothy had replied
that it seemed the best bet. On the school notice-
board a sign permanently requested recruits for
a variety of departments in the sandpaper factory. He'd been eleven or twelve when he'd first
assumed that that was where his future lay.

But then, not long after this conversation with
Mr. Stringer, an extraordinary thing happened. A
student teacher called O'Hennessy arrived at the
Comprehensive and talked to his pupils about a
void when he was scheduled to be teaching them
English. "The void can be filled," he said.

Nobody paid much attention to O'Hennessy,

who liked to be known by his Christian name, which was Brehon. Nobody understood a word he was talking about. "The landscape is the void," he said. "Escape from the drear landscape. Fill the void with beauty." All during his English classes Brehon O'Hennessy talked about the void, and the drear landscape, and beauty. In every kid, he pronounced, looking from one face to another, there was an avenue to a fuller life. He had a short tangled beard and tangled black hair. He had a way of gesturing in the air with his right hand, toward the windows of the classroom. "There," he said when he did this. "Out there. The souls of the adult people have shrivelled away: they are as last year's rhubarb walking the streets. Only the void is left. Get up in the morning, take food, go to work, take food, work, go home, take food, look at the television, go to bed, have sex, go to sleep, get up." Now and again during his lessons he smoked cigarettes containing the drug cannabis and didn't mind if his pupils smoked also, cannabis or tobacco, who could care? "Your soul is your property," he said.

Timothy Gedge, like all the others, had considered O'Hennessy to be touched in the head, but then O'Hennessy said something that made him less certain about that. Everyone was good at something, he said, nobody was without talent: it was a question of discovering yourself. O'Hennessy was at the Comprehensive for only half a term, and was then replaced by Miss Wilkinson.

It seemed to Timothy that he was good at nothing, but he also was increasingly beginning to wonder if he wished to spend a lifetime making sandpaper. He thought about himself, as Brehon O'Hennessy had said he should. He closed his

eyes and saw himself, again following Brehon
O'Hennessy's injunction. He saw himself as an
adult, getting up in the morning and taking food,
and then reporting to the cutting room of the
sandpaper factory. Seeking to discover an absorb-
ing interest, which might even become an avenue
to a fuller life, he bought a model-airplane kit,
but unfortunately he found the construction work
difficult. The balsa wood kept splitting and the
recommended glue didn't seem to stick the pieces
together properly. He lost some of them, and
after a couple of days he gave the whole thing up.
It was a great disappointment to him. He'd imagined flying the clever little plane on the beach,
getting the engine going and showing people
how it was done. He'd imagined making other
aircraft, building up quite a collection of them,
using dope like it said in the instructions, covering
the wings with tissue paper. It would all have
taken hours, sitting contentedly in the kitchen
with the radio on while his mother and sister
were out in the evenings, as they generally were.
But it was not to be.

Then, on the afternoon of December 4th last,
something else happened: Miss Wilkinson ordered
that the two laundry baskets containing the
school's dressing-up clothes should be carried into
the classroom and she made the whole of 3A
dress up so that they could enact scenes from
history. She called it a game. "The game of charades," she said. "*Charrada*. From the Spanish,
the chatter of the clown." She divided 3A into
five groups and gave each an historical incident
to act. The others had to guess what it was.
Nobody had listened when she'd said that a word
came from the Spanish and meant the chatter

of a clown; within five minutes the classroom was a bedlam. The eight children in Timothy Gedge's group laughed uproariously when he dressed up as Queen Elizabeth I, in a red wig and a garment that had a lank white ruff at its neck. Timothy laughed himself, seeing in a mirror how peculiar he looked, with a pair of tights stuffed into the dress to give him a bosom. He enjoyed laughing at himself and being laughed at. He enjoyed the feel of the wig on his head and the different feeling the long voluminous dress gave him, turning him into another person. It was the only occasion he had ever enjoyed at Dynmouth Comprehensive and it was crowned by his discovery that without any difficulty whatsoever he could adopt a falsetto voice. That night he'd lain awake in bed, imagining a future that was different in every way from a future in the sandpaper factory, *"Charrada,"* Miss Wilkinson repeated in a dream. "The chatter of the clown."

He'd felt aimless in his adolescence before that. After he'd failed with the model-airplane kit he'd taken to following people about just to see where they were going, and looking through the windows of people's houses. He'd found himself regularly attending funerals because for some reason there was enjoyment of a kind to be derived from standing in the graveyard of the church of St. Simon and St. Jude or the graveyard of the Baptist, Methodist or Catholic churches, while solemn words were said and mourners paid respects. He continued to follow people about and to look through windows and to attend funerals, but he also determined to enter the Spot the Talent competition at the Easter Fête with a comic act and he now spent a considerable amount of his spare

time trying to work out what it should be. He
instinctively felt that somehow it should incorpo-
rate the notion of death, that whatever *charrada*
he devised should be of a macabre nature.

In bed at night he thought about this, and continued to do so during geography lessons and
tedious mathematics lessons, staring ahead of
him in a manner that was complained of as vacant. He would smile when he was insulted in
this way and for a moment would pay attention
to a droning voice retailing information about
the distribution of herring-beds around the shores
of the British Isles or incomprehensively speaking
French. He would then revert to his more personal
riddle of how to reconcile death and comedy in
a theatrical act. He wondered about presenting
himself as a female mourner, in a black dress
down to his feet and a veiled black hat, with
cheekily relevant chatter. But somehow that didn't
seem complete, or even right. Then, a month ago,
Mr. Stringer had taken forty pupils to London
and had included in the itinerary a visit to Madame Tussaud's. At half-past eleven that morning
Timothy Gedge had found the solution he was
looking for: he decided to base his comic act on
the deaths of Miss Munday, Mrs. Burnham and
Miss Lofty, the Brides in the Bath, the victims of
George Joseph Smith. All the way back to Dynmouth on the coach he'd imagined the act. To
applause and laughter in the marquee at the
Easter Fête, he rose from an old tin bath while
the limelight settled on the wedding-dress he wore
and his chatter began. He'd never in his life seen
Benny Hill, or anyone else, attempting an act in
a long white wedding-dress, impersonating three
deceased women. It made him chortle so much

in the coach that Mr. Stringer asked him if he was going to be sick.

The rain had increased by the time he reached Cornerways. It dripped from his face and hair. He could feel areas of damp on his back and his stomach. His legs and arms were drenched. In the flat he removed some of the wet clothes in order to practice his act. He didn't turn the television on because he liked the flat to be quiet when he was practicing.

In his sister's bedroom he eased himself into a pair of black tights. A torn toenail caught in the fine mesh of the material, creating an immediate hole. The same thing had happened once before and then he'd felt something else going as soon as he sat down. Rose-Ann had gone on about the damage for quite some time and had eventually taken the tights back to the shop, where she'd been received with hostility.

He regarded himself in the long Woolworth's mirror that Rose-Ann's boyfriend Len had fixed up for her on the inside of her cupboard door. He still wore his own yellow T-shirt; the tights were taut on his calves and thighs. The hole his toenail had caused was round the back somewhere, which was a relief because Rose-Ann mightn't even notice it. He picked up a flowered brassiere and held it for a moment against his chest, examining the effect in the mirror. He had perfected his own method with his sister's brassieres, employing two rubber bands to bridge the gap at the back.

He took off his shirt, selected a pair of Rose-Ann's ankle socks, knotted the rubber bands and attached them securely to the brassiere's hooks. He then slipped the garment over his head, wriggled his way into it, and stuffed an ankle sock into each cup. He put on a dress that was too big for Rose-Ann, which had been given to her by a friend. It wasn't too big for him. It was wine-colored, with small black buttons.

He left his sister's bedroom and crossed the small landing to his room. He stood on a chair and lifted from the top of a cupboard a small cardboard suitcase in which he kept his private possessions. The suitcase itself, reclaimed from the beach, was badly damaged. The brown cardboard was torn here and there, string replaced its handle and only one of its hinges was intact. He opened it on his bed and glanced suspiciously over its contents, as though fearing theft. He kept his money in the suitcase, in an envelope: twenty-nine pounds and fourpence. On his visits to the Abigails' bungalow he'd managed to appropriate some of this, and he'd also managed to filch coins of low denomination from his mother's handbag. Once he'd picked up a purse which he'd noticed an elderly woman dropping in the street and which turned out to contain six pounds and fifty-nine pence. Rose-Ann had left her wage packet on the dresser one Friday evening and when she found it was missing had assumed she'd lost it on the way home from the filling station.

As well as this money, there was a gas-burner in the suitcase—a small smoke-blackened apparatus and a blue cylinder marked "Gaz"—both of which he'd picked up on the beach when the people who owned them were in the sea. There was a glass horse, in blue and green, which Rose-Ann had been given by Len on her twenty-first birthday, and a wooden money-box in the shape of a mug which, strictly speaking, was the property of his mother. *Cuss-box*, it said in poker-work, with a rhyme that began: *Cussin' ain't the nicest thing, friends for you it shore don't bring* . . . There was a vest and a knife and fork in the suitcase, the property of Mrs. Abigail, and a tin box that had once contained lozenges for the relief of throat catarrh and now contained a cameo brooch of Mrs. Abigail's, as well as an imitation pearl necklace of hers and an imitation pearl ring. There was a plastic hand, part of a shop-window model, which he'd found in a rubbish-bin attached to one of the promenade lamp-posts, and the upper section of a set of dentures, which he'd removed from a teacup on the beach while a man was in the sea. There was a narrow, paper-backed volume entitled *1000 Jokes for Kids of All Ages*, legitimately obtained from W. H. Smith's in Fore Street. There was his wig, removed from one of the school dressing-up baskets, and his make-up, from the same source: rouge, powder, cold-cream, lipstick and eye-shadow. The ersatz hair of the wig was orange-colored and tightly curled: it was the one he had worn when he'd dressed up for Miss Wilkinson's charade, to lend verisimilitude to his portrayal of Elizabeth I.

When he'd settled this wig on his head and transformed his face with make-up, he walked about the silent flat, unfortunately having to wear his own shoes since his feet were too large for his sister's. He walked from his bedroom to the kitchen and then into Rose-Ann's room again, into his mother's and the bathroom, and into the room where the television set was, which Rose-Ann and his mother called the lounge. He walked with the short, quick step he'd seen Benny Hill employ when dressed up as a woman for his television show.

Sitting down at the kitchen table, which still had breakfast dishes on it, he opened *1000 Jokes for Kids of All Ages*. He read through the jokes he'd underlined in ballpoint pen, closing his eyes after an initial prompting to see if he could remember them. He laughed as he repeated them in his falsetto voice, jokes about survivors on desert islands, mothers-in-law, drunks, lunatics, short-sighted men, women in doctors' surgeries. "Well, have a plum," he said in his falsetto. "If you swallow it whole you'll put on a stone." His mother wouldn't be back from Cha-Cha Fashions until six. Rose-Ann worked late on the pumps on a Wednesday. Fourteen years ago his father had driven from Dynmouth with a lorry-load of tiles and hadn't ever returned.

He had become used to the empty flat and to looking after himself. Even when he first went to the primary school, when he was five, he would come back and let himself into the flat and wait until Rose-Ann returned from the Comprehensive and his mother from work. Before that he'd spent a lot of time with an aunt, a sister of his mother's who was a dress-maker, who'd since moved to Badstoneleigh. He hadn't cared for this woman. One of his earliest memories was not caring for having to sit in a corner of her work-room while she stitched or cut. All day long she had the radio going and when her husband came in from the sandpaper factory for his mid-day meal he'd say, always the same: "Good Lord, is that boy here again?" It was particularly tedious having to sit in the room for another hour when his mother came to collect him, listening to the two

of them talking. At all other times his mother was
in a hurry, hurrying from the flat in the morning,
hurrying out again in the evenings for a break
in the Artilleryman's Friend or to Bingo. Once
when he'd been waiting for her and his aunt to
stop talking he'd broken a plate. He'd sat on it
pretending he didn't notice it on the sofa, a plate
that his aunt's cat Blackie had had its dinner off.
He'd been three and a half at the time, and he
could still remember the agreeable sensation of
the plate giving way beneath his weight. They'd
both been furious with him.

From time to time, when he was younger, his
mother used to say it was all his father's fault.
If his father hadn't cleared off she wouldn't have
had to go out to work and everything would have
been different. At other times she said she was
glad he'd cleared off. "Shocking, the fights they
had," Rose-Ann used to say. "Horrible he was."
But no matter how hard he tried, he couldn't
remember a single thing about this man. When
he was at primary school and Rose-Ann was still
at the Comprehensive he'd often asked her because it was something to talk about in the afternoons, but Rose-Ann said curiosity killed the cat
and would close herself into her bedroom. His
mother and Rose-Ann were pally, sharing all sorts
of conversational intimacies, rather like his
mother and his aunt. "Three's a crowd," Rose-Ann
had had a way of saying when she was younger.

He'd become used to three being a crowd and
at least he was glad that he no longer had to
spend days in his aunt's work-room. Every Sunday
now his mother went over to Badstoneleigh to
visit her sister and at one time Rose-Ann had
always gone with her, but this arrangement had

changed when Rose-Ann's Len arrived on the
scene. Timothy declined to go on these excursions
himself, plainly to his mother's relief.

There had, over the years, developed in Timothy
a distrust of his mother, and of his sister also.
He didn't speak much in their company, having
become familiar with their lack of response. He'd
be the death of her, his mother used to reply
when he asked her something, although he'd never
been able to understand why he could be. "You're
a bloody little dopey-D," Rose-Ann had a way of
saying when she wasn't saying three was a crowd
or curiosity killed the cat. It was all half joking,
all quick and rushy, his mother laughing her
shrill staccato laugh, Rose-Ann laughing also,
neither of them listening to him. In the end
he'd come to imagine that the atmosphere in the
flat was laden with the suggestion that there'd
be more room if he wasn't there, more privacy
and a sense of relief. Occasionally he felt that this
suggestion peered at him out of their eyes, even
when they were smiling and laughing, smoking
their cigarettes. He listened to them talking to
one another about things that had happened at
the clothes shop and the Smiling Service Filling
Station, and once he'd had a most peculiar dream:
that sitting there listening to them he'd turned
into his father, which was why, so he said to
himself in the dream, they kept sticking forks into
the backs of his hands. Whenever he could, he
lay in bed in the mornings until they'd left the
flat.

At Dynmouth Comprehensive the distrust continued. He had never thought much of the place,
nor of its staff and pupils. He couldn't see the
point of having hair halfway down your back,

which was the fashion among the boys, and it seemed to him that neither staff nor pupils had a sense of humor. Once during break he had sawed through the leg of a chair on which a heavily-built girl called Grace Rumblebow usually sat. Unfortunately, when the chair gave way, Grace Rumblebow struck the side of her forehead on another chair and had to have seven stitches in it. On another occasion he'd mixed up everyone's books and pencils, muddling the contents of one desk with another. He'd set a piece of paper alight during a history lesson. He'd attached a needle to the end of his ruler with Sellotape and had prodded Grace Rumblebow with it. He'd put his mother's alarm clock in Raymond Tyler's desk and set it to go off during the worst lesson of the week, double physics. He'd wiped away the calculations that Clapp, the mathematics man, had taken twenty minutes to work out on the black-board and was going to explain in detail after break. No one had thought any of it funny, not even when Grace Rumblebow screeched like a cat the time the needle went into her. No one laughed, even tittered, until Miss Wilkinson ordered that the dressing-up baskets should be carried into 3A, until he put the wig and the clothes on, and discovered he could do the voice. Fantastic, they kept saying then, suddenly aware of him. Everyone in the room stopped dressing up and turned round to look at him. Better than Morecambe and Wise, Dave Griggs said. Beverly Mack said he was a natural. Afterward, unfortunately, they seemed to forget about it.

But all that was in the past now. At the moment what was more to the point was that he needed, and had no intention of purchasing, a bath and a wedding-dress, and a suit for George Joseph Smith. There was a tin bath, badly damaged by rust, in the yard of Swines' the builders. He had asked if it was wanted and the foreman had said it wasn't. It was just a question of persuading someone to transport it for him. He knew where there was a wedding-dress: it was just a question of appropriating it. There was a dog's tooth suit, ideal for the purpose, hanging in Commander Abigail's wardrobe.

Ever since he'd planned to go in for the Spot the Talent competition he'd been affected by a pleasant fantasy. Having been successful in the competition, he found himself going in for *Opportunity Knocks* on the television. Sometimes, if he let his thoughts drift, it seemed that Hughie Green was staying in the Queen Victoria Hotel, in Dynmouth for the golf, and having nothing better to do had wandered up to the Easter Fête in the rectory garden and had wandered into the Spot the Talent competition. "That's really good!" he proclaimed with great delight, excited when he saw the act, and the next thing was the act was being done in the *Opportunity Knocks* studio.

Timothy walked about the flat again, from one room to another, practicing in front of the bathroom mirror, telling jokes in his falsetto, smiling at himself. "You're easily tops, lad," Hughie Green was enthusing, putting an arm round his shoulder. The applause and the laughter gave off warmth, like a fire. The clapometer was bursting itself, registering 98, a record. "You're bringing the house down," Hughie Green said.

2

That afternoon, while Timothy Gedge practiced
his act and the Featherston twins continued to
be bored in the rectory, Stephen and Kate Fleming, aged twelve, returned to Dynmouth by train
from London. At eleven o'clock that morning their
parents—Stephen's father and Kate's mother—
had been married in a register office, making the
children, in a sense, brother and sister. Their
parents were now on their way to London Airport,
to honeymoon in Cassis. For the next ten days
the children were to be on their own with Mr.
and Mrs. Blakey in Sea House.

"Let's have tea," Kate said, putting down a
book about three children who surreptitiously kept
a turkey as a pet.

Stephen was reading last year's Wisden. He
had once scored seventeen runs in an over, against
the bowling of a boy called Philpott, A. J. His
ambition, unuttered, was to go in Number 3 for
Somerset. He supported Somerset because it was
next door to Dorset and because it had once
looked as though Somerset might win the county
championship. That hadn't happened, but he'd
remained loyal to the county and believed he
always would be. He also believed, but did not
often say, that Somerset's captain, Close, was the

most ingenious cricketer in England. Cricket interested him more than anything else.

In the empty dining-car they sat down at a table for two. They were still in their school uniforms—Stephen's gray with touches of maroon, Kate's brown and green—for the marriage had been arranged to coincide with the end of the Easter term. That morning Stephen had traveled down from Ravenswood Court in Shropshire and Kate from St. Cecilia's School for Girls in Sussex, two days before she should have.

Of the two, Kate was the less matter-of-fact. Her mind had a way of wandering, of filling sometimes with day-dreams. At St. Cecilia's she had been designated both idle and slap-dash. Romantic she had not been called, although that, more essentially, was what she was. *Kate's imagination can be fired,* a sloping hand had once pronounced on an end-of-term report. At the moment she knew by heart "The Lord of Burleigh," having recently been obliged to learn it as a punishment for firing imaginations herself: with the seven other inmates of the Madame Curie dormitory, she had been caught at midnight by Miss Rist performing rituals culled from a television documentary about the tribes of the Amazon. Her face was plump, with brown hair curving round it and eyes that were daubs in it, like blue sunflowers.

"Home for the hols?" a stout waiter waggishly enquired in the dining-car. "Tea for two, madam?"

"Yes, please." Kate felt her face becoming warm, the result of being addressed so jauntily without warning.

"I've seen him before," Stephen said when the man had gone. "He's all right actually." He wasn't a tall boy; he had a delicate look, although physically he wasn't delicate in the least. His eyes were a dark shade of brown and remained serious when he smiled. His smooth black hair was an inheritance from his mother, who had died two years ago.

Kate nodded uneasily when he said the waiter was all right. She felt embarrassed because her face had gone red like that. Several times at the party that had taken place after the ceremony in the register office it had gone red, especially when people had jocularly enquired if she approved of the marriage. The party, in a lounge of a hotel, had been almost unbearably boring. She felt it had been unnecessary as well: after the ceremony there should immediately have been the journey back to Dynmouth, to the house and the dogs and Mr. and Mrs. Blakey. Ever since half-term, when she'd first heard about the marriage arrangements, she'd been greedily looking forward to being alone with Stephen in Sea House with only Mr. and Mrs. Blakey to look after them. In the Madame Curie dormitory it had seemed like a form of bliss, and it still did. No other friendship was as special for Kate as the friendship she felt for Stephen. She believed, privately, that she loved Stephen in the same way as people in films loved one another. When they walked along the seashore at Dynmouth she always wanted to take his hand, but she had never done so. She often imagined he was ill and that she was looking after him. She'd once dreamed that he had lost the use of his legs and was in a wheel-chair, but in her dream she loved him more than ever because of that. In her dreams they agreed that they would marry one another.

For Stephen the friendship was special too,

though in a different way. Since the death of
his mother it was with Kate more than anyone
that his natural reticence most easily evaporated.
At school he had never found it easy to initiate
friendships and often did not want to. He was on
the fringes of things, or even in the shadows, not
unpopular with other boys and not aloof, but
affected by a shyness that hadn't existed in his
relationship with his mother and didn't with Kate.
He found it easy to drift in and out of conversations with Kate, as it had been with his mother.
It wasn't necessary to make an effort, or to be
on guard.

Other people sat down in the dining-car, a
sprinkling at the empty tables. The stout waiter
carried round a tray of metal tea-pots. The children talked about the terms they'd spent at Ravenswood Court and St. Cecilia's, and about the
people at these two similar boarding-schools. The
headmaster of Ravenswood Court, C. R. Deccles,
was known as the Craw, and his wife as Mrs.
Craw; Miss Scuse was the headmistress of St.
Cecilia's. At Ravenswood Court there was a master
called Quiet-Now Simpson, who couldn't keep
order, and a master called Dymoke—Geography
and Divinity—who was known as Dirty Dymoke
because he'd once confessed that he had never in
his life washed his hair. Quiet-Now Simpson had
kipper feet.

At St. Cecilia's little Miss Malabedeely taught
History and was fifty-four, bullied by Miss Shaw
and Miss Rist. Miss Shaw was moustached and
had a hanging jaw, all teeth and gums; Miss
Rist was forever knitting brown cardigans. They
were jealous because Miss Malabedeely had once
been engaged to an African bishop. They often

spoke of Africa in a disparaging manner, and when they were speaking of something else they had a way of abruptly ceasing when Miss Malabedeely entered a room. "We'll go on with that later," Miss Rist would say, sighing while she looked at Miss Malabedeely. There were other teachers at St. Cecilia's, and other masters at Ravenswood, but they weren't so interesting to talk about.

In the dining-car Kate imagined, as she often had before, Quiet-Now Simpson's kipper feet and Dirty Dymoke. And Stephen quite vividly saw the fortitude on the face of little damson-cheeked Miss Malabedeely let down by an African bishop, and Miss Shaw's landscape of teeth and gum and Miss Rist forever knitting cardigans. He imagined the bullying of Miss Malabedeely, the two women breaking off their conversation whenever she entered a room. That term, he said, a boy called Absom had discovered Quiet-Now Simpson and Mrs. Craw alone in a summer-house, sitting close to one another.

"You pour the tea," he said.

They went on talking about the schools and then they talked about the party that morning in the lounge of the hotel, at which there'd been champagne and chicken in aspic and cream cheese in bits of celery stalks and smoked salmon on brown bread.

"Toasted tea-cake, madam?" the stout waiter offered.

"Yes, please."

The conversation about schools and the wedding party was a way of filling in the time, or of avoiding what seemed to Kate to be a more important conversation: was Stephen as happy as

she was about their parents' marriage? It was
more of an upheaval for Stephen, having to move
with his father to Sea House, where she and her
mother had always lived. As they ate their toasted
tea-cakes it occurred to her that Stephen might
never refer to the subject at all, that this single
conversation might be difficult between them. His
mother was dead: did he resent someone else
in her place? Did he resent all of a sudden having
a sister? Being friends was one thing; all this
was rather different.

They added raspberry jam to brown bread and
butter. They watched a station going by, in a
heavy, dismal downpour. Leaning on a brush, a
damp porter looked back at them from the plat-
form. *Machine Engraving*, it said on a poster,
Archer Signs Ltd.

"D'you think you'll like living in Sea House,
Stephen?"

He was still looking out of the window. "I don't
know," he said, not turning his head.

"It'll be all right."

"Yes."

Already his father had sold Primrose Cottage;
already their furniture had been moved to Sea
House. Going to live there was apparently the
best arrangement, or so his father had explained
when telling him about the forthcoming marriage.
Kate's mother had actually been born there and so
had Kate. The house was much bigger than Primrose Cottage and more suitable for the four of
them in other ways as well. But Primrose Cottage,
a mile from Dynmouth, on the Badstoneleigh road,
was what Stephen still thought of as his home,
with its banks of primroses, and buddleia full of

butterflies in the small back garden, and the memory of his mother.

"You'll like it, Stephen. The Blakeys are nice."

"I know the Blakeys are nice." He smiled again, his eyes remaining somber even though he didn't want them to. "I'm sure it'll be all right."

The train rushed through the dismal afternoon, the silence between them had an edge to it. Stephen was often silent, but she knew he was thinking now of their parents' marriage, and wondering about it. Two facts had made it possible: the divorce of her own parents and the death of his mother. The divorce had happened before she or Stephen could remember. Now and again her father came back to Dynmouth, or to see her at St. Cecilia's, but the visits made her unhappy because his presence caused her to sense the trouble and the pain there'd been. She couldn't help not liking him, sensing as well that it was he who had been cruel, that he had deserted her mother for the wife he was now married to.

The waiter brought sandwiches and more hot water and then a tray full of cellophane-wrapped pieces of fruitcake and slices of Swiss roll. Kate took a slice of Swiss roll and the waiter told her to have another because the slices were small. Stephen took a piece of fruitcake. He undid the cellophane, carefully remembering the past, wanting to because it was relevant on this particular day: the details were preserved, behind some screen in his mind, always available. A time would never come when he'd forget it had been autumn, or forget the slight foreboding he'd felt at being summoned. The undermatron, Miss Tomm, had come into the dormitory and asked him to come with her to the study. The half-past eight bell had just gone. Lights-out was in a quarter of an hour. "Eee, what's Fleming done?" Cartwright shouted out, standing by his bed in a checked dressing-gown, with a towel in his hand. He flicked the towel at Stephen, and Miss Tomm sharply told him to leave off.

His father was in the study, sitting in the chair in front of the Craw's desk, the chair the Craw asked you to sit in when he was going to give you a row. His father hadn't taken off his overcoat or his scarf.

"Ah," the Craw said when Stephen entered.

The Craw found another chair and drew it up to the desk. He told Stephen to sit on it, in a voice that wasn't as scratchy as usually it was. His eyes kept darting about. Fingers like sticks were restless on the desk in front of him.

"Shall I?" he suggested, raising gray eyebrows at Stephen's father. "Or would . . . ?"

"I'll do it, please."

His father was different also. His cheeks were pale, quite noticeably so in the hard glare of the room's electric light. Stephen thought he was ill. In the confusion of being so abruptly called out of the dormitory and then finding his father in the study, he could think of no better reason for his father's presence than that he should have come to Ravenswood Court to tell him that he was ill.

"Mummy," his father said in a peculiar, stuttering kind of voice, quite unlike his usual one. "Mummy, Stephen. Mummy . . ."

He did not go on. He wasn't looking at Stephen. He was looking down at his open overcoat, at its buttons and the brown and green of its tweed.

"Is Mummy ill?"

His father controlled himself. When he spoke

it was no longer with a stutter. He said: "Not ill, Stephen."

Blood spread into Stephen's neck and face. He could feel its warmth, and then he felt it draining away.

"Mummy has died, Stephen."

The clock on the mantelpiece ticked busily. The Craw moved a paper on his desk. There was a knock on the door, but the Craw didn't answer it.

"Died?"

"I'm afraid so, Stephen."

"You must be brave, old chap," the Craw said, his voice beginning to make its scratchy sound again.

The knock on the door was repeated. "Not now," the Craw shouted.

"It would be better if you didn't come home. It would be better if you could stay at school, Stephen. I thought at first you should come home."

"Best to stay at school, Stephen," the Craw said.

"Died?" Stephen said again. "*Died?*"

His lips began to quiver. He felt the bones of his shoulders shaking uncontrollably. He could hear his own breathing, a noisy panting he couldn't control either.

"Died?" he whispered.

His father was standing beside him, holding him.

"It's all right, Stephen," he said, but it wasn't all right and the other two in the room knew it wasn't either. It was unbelievable, it was something that could not be true. He felt the tears on his face, a wetness that came warmly and then was chill. He struggled, as he often did in nightmares, trying to reach a surface, struggling to wake up from horror.

"You must be brave, old chap," the Craw said again.

She had a way of comforting, holding you differently from the way his father was holding him now. There was the softness of her hands, and her black hair, and a faint scent of perfume. "Eau de Cologne," she said. She smiled at him, her eyes lost behind sun-glasses.

The Craw was no longer in the room. His father had a handkerchief in his hand. Stephen wept again, closing his eyes. He felt the handkerchief on his face, wiping away the tears. His father was murmuring but he couldn't hear what he was saying.

He couldn't prevent himself from seeing her. She stood by the edge of the sea, a rust-colored corduroy coat pulled tightly around her; he could see her breath on the icy air. He watched her making drop-scones in the kitchen of Primrose Cottage.

Mrs. Craw came in with a cup of chocolate, with the Craw behind her, carrying a tray of tea things. They didn't say anything. The Craw put the tray on the desk, and Mrs. Craw poured a cup of tea for his father. They both went away again.

"Try and drink your chocolate," his father said.

A skin had already formed on the surface. "Disgusting!" he used to cry when she brought him chocolate in bed, and she'd laugh because it was a joke, because he was only pretending to be cross.

He drank the chocolate. His father repeated that it would be better if he remained in the school rather than return to Primrose Cottage. "I'm sorry to be so little help," his father said.

When he'd finished the chocolate the Craw and Mrs. Craw returned. Mrs. Craw said: "We're going to put you in the san for the night. In Miss Tomm's room."

There were awkward silences then, but they were only awkward afterwards, looking back on them; they were nothing at all at the time. His father put his arms round him again, and then Miss Tomm came into the study with his clothes and shoes for the morning, and his wash-bag. The wash-bag was dangling from one of her fingers, yellow and blue and red. "Here's a nice one," he'd said in Boots in Dynmouth the time they'd bought it. "This one."

He walked with Miss Tomm across the quadrangle and then along the path by the playing-fields, to the sanatorium. Leaves squelched beneath their feet, it was windy and drizzling slightly. He couldn't help shivering, even though it seemed wrong to be affected by the cold.

It seemed wrong to fall asleep, but he did fall asleep. He was in a camp-bed beside Miss Tomm's bed, and when he woke he didn't know where he was. Then he remembered, and lay in the darkness sobbing, listening to Miss Tomm breathing. Once or twice she spoke in her sleep, once saying something about spoons, and once saying she loved someone. There was a smell of powder in the room, a smell that wasn't like the smell of eau de Cologne and yet reminded him of it. When the dawn began to come he could see the outline of Miss Tomm in bed and when the light was better he could see her open mouth and the hairpins in her hair and her clothes on a chair quite close to him.

An alarm clock went off at half-past seven and he watched Miss Tomm waking up and being surprised when she realized he was there. He watched her frowning, peering at him.

"My mother died," he said.

He wasn't going to cry. He wasn't going to shiver like that. If he cried, it would be in the middle of the night again, quietly and to himself. He felt an emptiness in his stomach when he thought about it, an actual pain that came and went. But he did not want to cry.

He walked with Miss Tomm back to the school, carrying his pajamas and dressing-gown and slippers. They would be late for breakfast, he said, because the bell had stopped ringing more than a minute ago. Mr. Deccles had promised it wouldn't matter, Miss Tomm said, and when they entered the dining-hall together he knew that the Craw had told the whole school what had happened. There was a silence when they entered the dining-hall, which continued while Miss Tomm went to the sideboard where the cornflakes were given out, while he himself pushed his way to his place.

The boys at his table looked at him, and although talk had begun again at other tables the boys at his remained silent. Quiet-Now Simpson, who was at the head of the table, didn't know what to say.

Afterward, during the day, boys said they were sorry. And much later on he was told that when the Craw had informed the school he'd said it would be better if boys didn't mention the matter.

"Just be kind to Fleming," apparently he'd admonished.

He went to see the Craw and said he wanted to go to his mother's funeral. He didn't want to remain at home after it, or to go home immediately. He just wanted to return to Dynmouth for the funeral.

The headmaster shook his head, and for a moment Stephen thought he was going to say that this request would be impossible to grant.

"Your father," the Craw said instead. "I just wonder what your father . . ."

"Could you telephone my father, sir? Please, sir."

"Well. Well, yes, I dare say."

There and then the telephone call was made. Impatiently, the headmaster's stick-like fingers rapped the surface of the desk while he waited to be connected. It was clear he would have preferred not to telephone. It was clear that he considered it a nuisance, a boy having to go to a funeral, special arrangements made.

"Ah, Mr. Fleming. Deccles here." His voice, softened by an injection of mournfulness, was less scratchy than it had been a moment ago. He repeated the request that had been made. He listened for a moment. He nodded and then he said, handing Stephen the receiver:

"Your father'd like to speak to you."

Stephen took the receiver from him, unable to avoid contact with the fingers that generations of boys hadn't cared to touch either.

"Are you really sure, Stephen? Mummy wouldn't have—"

"I'd like to come."

Miss Tomm put him on a train, his father met

him at Dynmouth Junction and drove him back
to Primrose Cottage. Later they drove from the
cottage to Dynmouth, to the church of St. Simon
and St. Jude, where Mr. Featherston conducted
the service. The clergyman gave an address, referring to the death as a tragedy. "Forasmuch as
it hath pleased Almighty God of His great mercy,"
he said softly, "to take unto Himself the soul of
our dear sister, we therefore commit her body to
the ground."

It was sunny in the graveyard. Yellow and
brown leaves were scattered everywhere. It was
unbelievable that she was lying in the gleaming
coffin which four men were lowering on ropes.
It was unbelievable that her body was going to
rot, that never again would she be seen or heard,
that never again would she kiss him. He wasn't
able to prevent himself from crying. The more
he held it all back the worse it became. He wanted
to cry loudly, to run to the coffin and embrace it,
to speak to her even though she was dead.

"Come now, Stephen," his father said, and the
people standing about—relations and friends,
strangers some of them—turned away from the
grave.

The clergyman put his hand on Stephen's
shoulder. "You're a brave little boy," he said.

His father drove him all the way back to
Ravenswood Court, and the silence of the journey
made him realize why his father hadn't wanted
him to come home for the funeral "I've got a few
sweets," Miss Tomm whispered in the hall of
Ravenswood "Lime and lemon sherbet. D'you
like sherbet, Stephen?"

Miles of landscape had gone by, the silence in

the dining-car had been a lengthy one. The stout waiter broke it by asking if everything had been all right. He flicked a page of the pad he held and swiftly wrote them out a yellow bill. "Obliged to you, sir," he said, giving it to Stephen.

They each placed money on the table, and the waiter collected it up and thanked them. Out of the ugliness of the divorce and the death it seemed only fair to Kate that there should come this happy ending. Her mother had been deserted. Stephen's father had suffered a horrible tragedy. She loved her mother, and she liked Stephen's father better than her own. She liked him because he was quiet and gentle. He had a smile she liked, he was clever: an ornithologist with a passion for the birds he wrote books about. With Stephen, she'd watched him cleaning oil from the feathers of seagulls. He'd shown them how to set a stone-chat's broken wing.

In the house they were to share all four of them deserved their happy ending: an idyll, Kate had said to herself ever since she'd known about the marriage that had been planned, repeating the word because she loved the sound of it. All the pain there'd been would be soothed away, since that was what idylls were for.

There were two approaches to Sea House, one from the road that rose steeply from Dynmouth and led to Dynmouth Golf Course and then on to Badstoneleigh, the other from the seashore, by a path that rose more steeply still, sharply winding around the contours of the cliff-face. The latter surfaced at the eleventh green and continued by the turf's edge until the turf gave way to a high wall of weathered brick, touched with

Virginia creeper. This bounded a garden that was uniquely rich, a streak of acid soil in the surrounding lime, a fluke of nature that generations in Sea House had taken advantage of. Set in an archway in the wall, a white wrought-iron gate led to a path through the shrubbery of azaleas for which the garden was reputed but which, in April, was only a mass of green. Magnolias and tree mallows stood starkly, with dripping leaves; rhododendrons glistened, heavy with buds. Ahead, the garden inclined upward, stretching extensively over three levels, with steps and banks of heather separating one surface from the next. Only daffodils and crocuses were in bloom now, and spring heathers and some winter jasmine. In the distance, to the left of the house and behind it, glass-houses leant from the high brick wall, with vegetable-beds around them; nearer, a paved herb garden had box hedges and a sundial. There were rose-beds and a white summer-house. A monkey-puzzle stood solitary on a wide expanse of lawn.

Sea House itself was a long, low Georgian manor, two storeys of old brick. A row of six French windows opened directly on to grass, beneath twice as many windows upstairs. The window-frames were white.

Two dappled English setters nosed about the garden on this damp Wednesday afternoon, their huge frilled tails thrashing the air, their gray and white coats wet, their mouths exposing handsome fangs and long pink tongues. They ran and sniffed by turn, looking for frogs in the long grass beneath the tree mallows. They settled for a while by the summer-house, leonine, eyeing one another. They rose and stretched, and nosed their

way around the house and down the gravel drive
that curved between further lawns to iron entrance gates. They returned with their tails less
vigorous, satisfied that all was in order on their
territory. In front of the white hall-door they
settled again, between two pillars and urns containing tulips

Within the house Mrs. Blakey made raisin-and-
stout cake in the kitchen. Her husband had gone
to Dynmouth Junction to meet the children off
the six-forty train. They'd be on the way back
by now, she reflected, glancing at the clock on
the dresser, and for an instant she imagined the
two contrasting faces of the children, and the
children themselves sitting in the back of the old
Wolseley, and her husband silently driving because silence was his way. She tipped the brown
cake-mixture into a baking tin, scooping the last
few spoonfuls out of the bowl with a wooden
spoon. She placed it in the top oven of the Aga
and set a timer on the dresser to buzz in an hour.

Mrs. Blakey, with busy eyes and cheeks that
shone, possessed a nature which had been formed
by a capacity for looking on the bright side. Clouds
were there for the harvesting of their silver lin-
ings, despair was just a word. The kitchen of Sea
House, where she spent the greater part of her
day, seemed quite in keeping with all this: the
Aga burning quietly, the lofty, panelled ceiling,
flowered plates arranged on the dresser, the com-
modious wall-cupboards, the scrubbed wooden
table. The kitchen was comfortable and comforting, as in many ways Mrs. Blakey herself was.

The Blakeys had come to live at Sea House in
1953, the year their daughter Winnie married, the
year after their son had emigrated to British

Columbia. Before that they'd come up from Dynmouth every day, to work in the garden and the
house. The work was part of them by now, and
they were part of the house and garden. They
remembered the birth of Kate's mother. There'd
been the deaths, within six months, of Kate's
grandparents. Although he never said it, Mrs.
Blakey knew that her husband sometimes felt,
through his affection for it, that the garden was
his. He had dug more soil in it than anyone else
alive now, and year by year had watched more
asters grow. He had changed the shape of the
herb garden; forty-one years ago he had created
two new lawns. He knew the house as well, and
felt a similar affection for it. It was he who
cleaned the windows, inside and out, and cleared
the gutters in the spring and repainted, every
three years, the white woodwork and the drain-
pipes and the chutes. He replaced slates when
storms blew them from the roof. He knew the
details of the plumbing and the wiring. Five years
ago he had re-boarded the drawing-room floor.

The tires of the Wolseley crunched on gravel,
a sound which carried faintly to Mrs. Blakey and
caused her face to crinkle with pleasure. She left
the kitchen and moved along a corridor with
springy green linoleum and green walls. She
passed through a door that had baize of the same
green shade on the side that faced the corridor.
In the hall she could hear Kate's voice telling
the dogs not to jump up. She opened the hall-door
and descended three slender steps to greet the
children.

〰〰〰〰〰〰〰〰〰〰〰〰〰〰〰〰〰〰〰〰〰

3

"Cheers, Mrs. Abigail," Timothy Gedge said, stepping into the Abigails' bungalow in High Park Avenue. "Rain's started up again."

She made a fuss, saying that the rain had soaked through his jacket. She made him take it off and hang it on a chair in front of the electric fire in the sitting-room, two bars glowing above an arrangement of artificial coal. She made him stand in front of the fire himself, to dry his jeans.

Mrs. Abigail was a slight woman, with soft gray hair. Her hands and the features of her face were tiny; her eyes suggested tenderness. It was she who had knitted Timothy Gedge a pair of ribbed socks one Christmas, feeling sorry for him because he had turned out awkwardly in adolescence. Feeling sorry for people was common with Mrs. Abigail. Her compassion caused her to grieve over newspaper reports and fictional situations in the cinema or on the television screen, or over strangers in the streets, in whom she recognized despondency. When she'd first known Timothy Gedge he'd been a child with particularly winning ways, and it seemed sad to her that these ways were no longer there. He'd called round at the bungalow a week after she

and her husband had moved in, nearly three
years ago now, and had asked if there were any
jobs. "Boy scout are you?" the Commander had
enquired. "Bob-a-job?" And Timothy had replied
nicely that he wasn't actually a boy scout, that
he was just trying to make a little pocket money.
He'd seemed an engagingly eccentric child, solitary in spite of his chattering and smiling, different from other children. He'd spent that first
morning helping to lay the dining-room carpet,
as cheerful as a robin.

In every way Mrs. Abigail had found him a
delightful little boy, and in the transformation
that had since taken place it sometimes seemed
to her that a person had been lost. The sol-
itariness which had lent him character made her
wonder, now, why it was that he had no friends;
his chatterbox eccentricity struck a different note.
But on Wednesday evenings he still came to do
jobs, and in fact to share the Abigails' supper.
Under the Commander's supervision he worked
in the small front garden and in the back garden
also. He'd assisted the winter before last in the
painting of the larder. Mrs. Abigail believed it
was not impossible that the loss which had occurred might somehow be regained.

"Commander still out on his swim, is he, Mrs.
Abigail?"

"Yes, he's still out." She wanted to say that it
was foolish of her husband to stay out in all
weathers, that it was foolish to go bathing at this
time of year in the first place, but of course she
couldn't, not to a child, not to anyone. She smiled
at Timothy Gedge. "He won't be long."

He laughed. He said: "Good weather for ducks,
Mrs. Abigail."

Steam rose from his yellow jeans. Soon he would be shaving. Soon he'd have that coarse look that some youths so easily acquired.

"Care for a fruit gum?" He held out the Rowntree's tube, but she declined to accept one of the sweets. He took one himself and put it in his mouth. "I see Ring's setting up in the park," he said.

"Yes, I noticed this morning."

"I don't expect you and the Commander would ever fancy the Amusements, Mrs. Abigail. Slot machines, dodgems, type of thing?"

"Well, no—"

"Rough kind of stuff, really."

"It's more for young people, I think."

"Slot machines is for the birds."

He laughed again, imagining for a moment Mrs. Abigail and the Commander playing on a slot machine, or in a dodgem car, being pitched all over the place by the Dynmouth Hards, who were notorious in the dodgem rink. He mentioned it to her and she gave a little laugh herself. He began to talk about the Easter Fête, saying it was a pity that Ring's Amusements opened for the first time on the afternoon of Easter Saturday, the very same time as the fête. It would take the crowds, he said. "I was saying that to the Reverend Feather and to Dass. They didn't take a pick of notice."

She nodded, thinking of something else. When Gordon returned from his swim he would offer the boy sherry. He'd done it before, the last three Wednesdays. She'd said she didn't think it was a good idea. She'd said that tippling away at glasses of sherry wasn't going to help the boy through a difficult adolescence, but Gordon had told her to learn sense.

Timothy went on talking about the Easter Fête because he didn't want her to suggest it was time for him to begin on his jobs. One Wednesday he'd managed to go on talking for so long that the jobs hadn't got done at all and she'd forgotten they hadn't when the time for payment came. He said he was really looking forward to the Spot the Talent competition, but she didn't seem to hear him. He was disappointed when a moment later she said that this week she wanted him to clean the oven of the electric cooker and to scour a saucepan that had the remains of tapioca in it. He far preferred to perform tasks in her bedroom because he could go through various drawers.

"When the Commander offers it just say no, Timothy." She spoke in the kitchen, while he sprayed the oven with a cleaning agent called Force. "Just say your mother'd rather you didn't."

"What's that then, Mrs. Abigail?"

"When the Commander offers you the sherry. You're under age, Timothy."

He nodded, with his head partly in the oven. He said he was aware he was under age, but the law, he reminded her, applied only to persons under age being supplied with alcohol in a public house or an off-license. He didn't himself see any harm in a glass of sherry.

"One thing I'd never touch, Mrs. Abigail, and that's a drug."

"Oh, no. Never, never take drugs. Promise me, never, Timothy."

"I'd never touch a drug, Mrs. Abigail, because I wouldn't know how to get hold of it." He laughed.

She looked down at him kneeling on a *Daily*

Telegraph in front of the stove. His jacket was still drying in front of the sitting-room fire. There was a smudge on one of his wrists, where it had brushed against the half-congealed gravy in the oven. Laughing had caused the skin of his hollow cheeks to tighten. The laughter drifted away. His mouth still smiled a little.

"Do it for me, dear," she whispered, bending down herself and smiling back at him. "Don't take the sherry, Timmy."

He sniffed her scent. It was a lovely smell, like a rose garden might be. At her neck a chiffon scarf in powder blue blended with the deeper blue of her dress.

"Please, dear," she said, and for a moment he thought she was maybe going to kiss him. Then the Commander's latch-key sounded in the lock of the front door.

"Remember now," she whispered, straightening up and moving away from him. "Timothy's here, Gordon," she called out to her husband.

"Oh, well played," the Commander said in the hall.

Commander Abigail, who had served at that naval rank for five months during the Second World War, was a scrawny, small man, bald except for a ginger fluff at the back of his head and around his ears. A narrow ginger moustache grew above a narrow mouth; his eyes had a staring quality. He was sixty-five and hampered in damp weather by trouble in the joints of the left side of his body. When he'd retired from a position in a London shipping firm he'd decided to come and live in Dynmouth because of his devotion to the sea. As well, he'd hoped the air would be bracing and with a tang, cold rather than wet.

His wife had pointed out that the area had one of
the highest rainfall records in England, but he had
argued with her on the point, categorically stating
that she had got the facts wrong. When an estate
agent sent him a notice of the bungalow in High
Park Avenue he'd announced that it was just what
they wanted, even though he'd in the meantime
discovered that she was right in her claim that
the Dynmouth area was one of the wettest in
England. You must never admit defeat was one
of Commander Abigail's foremost maxims: you
must stick to your guns even though the joints
on the left side of your body were giving you
gyp. It was sticking to your guns that had made
England, once, what England once had been.
Nowadays it was like living in a rubbish dump.

"Cheers, Commander," Timothy said when the
Commander came into the kitchen with his swimming-trunks and towel, and his sodden brown
overcoat on a coat-hanger.

"Good afternoon, Timothy."

The Commander unhooked the ropes of a
pulley and released a wooden clothes-airer from
the ceiling. He placed the coat-hanger on it and
hung out the swimming-trunks and towel. He
returned it to its mid-way position. The overcoat
began to drip.

Mrs. Abigail left the kitchen. A pool of water
would spread all over the tiles of the floor. Gordon
would walk in it and Timothy would walk in it,
and when the dripping had ceased, probably in
about an hour and a half, she'd have to mop
everything up and put down newspapers.

"And how's Master Timothy?"

"All right, Commander. Fine, thanks."

"Well played, boy."

Timothy rinsed the sponge-cloth he was using, squeezing it out in his bowl of dirty water. He wiped the inside of the oven, noticed that it was still fairly dirty, and closed the door. He rose and carried the bowl and the sponge-cloth to the sink. He was thinking about the acquisition of the wedding-dress and the bath and the Commander's dog's-tooth suit. No problem at all, he kept saying to himself, and then he tried not to laugh out loud, seeing himself rising up out of the bath as Miss Munday when she should be dead as old meat.

"Sherry when you're ready," the Commander said, placing glasses and a decanter on a small blue tray. "In the sitting-room, old chap."

Timothy scratched with his fingernails at the burnt tapioca in the saucepan that had been left for him. "Only fifteen years of age!" cried the voice of Hughie Green excitedly.

He reached for a scouring cloth on a line that stretched above the sink. He rubbed at the tapioca with it, but nothing happened. He scratched at it again with his fingernails and rubbed at it with a Brillo pad. He then filled the saucepan with water and placed it, out of the way, on the draining-board. He'd explain to Mrs. Abigail that in his opinion it needed to soak for a day or two.

"Big hand!" cried Hughie Green. "Big hand for Timothy Gedge, friends!"

To Stephen none of it was strange. For as long as he could remember he'd been coming to this house to play with Kate. The brown, bald head of Mr. Blakey was familiar, and his slowness of movement and economy with speech. So

were the dogs and the garden, and the house itself, and Mrs. Blakey smiling at him.

He watched while Mr. Blakey undid the ropes
that secured their two trunks in the open trunk
of the car. It wasn't raining any more, but the
clouds were dark and low, suggesting that the
cessation was only a lull. The air felt damp, a
pleasant feeling that made you want to shiver
slightly and be indoors, beside a fire. It was something his mother used to say about cold days in
spring and summer, that it was a different kind
of coldness from winter's, pleasant because it
wasn't severe.

A fire was blazing in the hall. It was the only
house he knew that had a fireplace in the hall.
Kate said the hall was her favorite part of the
house, the white marble of the mantelpiece, the
brass fender high enough to form a seat of up-
holstered red leather, Egyptian rugs in shades of
brown and blue spread over stone flags. On the
crimson hessian of the walls a series of water-
colors was set in brass frames: eighteenth-century
representations of characters from plays. Neither
of them knew what plays they came from, but
the pictures were quite nice. So was the wide
mahogany staircase that rose gently from the hall
at the far end, curving out of sight at a window
that reached almost to the wainscotting. He wondered if, in time, the hall would become his
favorite part of the house too.

Mrs. Blakey paused before passing through the
door to the green-linoleumed passage, calling to
them that supper would be ready in fifteen minutes. Stephen watched the door closing behind
her and for a moment it seemed wrong that he

should be here, standing in this house when his mother was dead. But the moment passed.

In the rectory the twins sat at the kitchen table with their parents, all of them eating poached eggs.

"Horrible," Susannah said.

"I said horrible," Deborah said. "I said horrible when Mummy."

"I said horrible when Mummy."

"I looked round and saw Mummy. Soon's Mummy's in the room I said horrible. You weren't even looking, Deborah."

"When Mummy bringed the eggs I said horrible, Susannah."

"Mummy, Deborah'll get dragons after her."

"Dragons and dragons and dragons and dragons and—"

"You eat up your egg, Susannah."

"Too tired, Mummy."

"Now, now," Quentin said, finishing his own egg.

"Too tired, Daddy. Mouth too tired, Daddy. Terribly, terribly tired. Terribly, terribly, terribly." Susannah closed her eyes, clenching the eyelids tightly. Deborah closed hers also. They began to giggle.

Lavinia felt weary. She snapped at her daughters, telling them not to be tiresome.

"Supper," Mrs. Abigail announced in Number Eleven High Park Avenue, entering the sitting-room and discovering that Timothy had taken no notice whatsoever of her request about the sherry. He'd put his zipped jacket on again and was sitting on the sofa on one side of the electric fire. Gordon was in his usual armchair, on the other. The curtains were drawn, the fire threw out a powerful heat. Only a table-lamp burned, its weak bulb not up to the task of fully illuminating the room. The effect of this half-gloom was cozy.

"Oh, time for another." Commander Abigail gave a brief little laugh, expertly aiming the sherry decanter at Timothy's glass and speaking to his wife as he did so. "Sherry, dear girl? Take a pew, why don't you?"

She stood by the door, one foot in the hall, the other on the patterned sitting-room carpet. "Don't mind if I do, sir," she heard Timothy saying after Gordon had refilled his glass, as though he had totally forgotten what she'd said to him. He even smiled at her through the gloom. "Yes, take a pew, Mrs. Abigail," he even said, the words sounding foolish on his lips. The very sight of him was foolish, a child with a glass of Cyprus sherry in his hand, awkwardly holding it by the stem.

"It's just that it'll all be overcooked," she said quietly, and her husband replied—as she knew he would—that they wouldn't be more than another five minutes. She also knew that he'd enjoyed inviting her to take a pew in that casual way when everything was ready to eat. He gave the child sherry in order to irritate her. It was a pity he was like that, but it couldn't be helped.

She closed the door and returned to the kitchen. She turned on the wireless and washed up some dishes. Voices were chatting their way through a word game. An audience laughed noisily at what was being said, but Mrs. Abigail didn't find any of it funny. Quite a few times in their marriage it had been suggested that she didn't possess a sense of humor.

Mrs. Abigail had married her husband because of his need of her and because, in her sympathy and compassion, she had felt affection for him. There was an emptiness in her marriage but she did not ever dwell on it. For thirty-six years he had been at the center of her life. She had accepted him for better or for worse: in no way did she permit herself to believe that she was an unhappy woman.

She ladled pieces of chicken and vegetables on to three plates and placed them in the oven. On the wireless the word game came to an end and a play began. By the time she'd strained the peas and scooped the mashed potatoes from the saucepan into a dish she heard her husband's voice in the hall, talking about pride.

"A certain pride," he repeated as he sat down at the dining-room table. He smoothed the ginger of his small moustache with the forefinger and thumb of his right hand. "You were proud to be an Englishman, Timothy, once upon a time."

"Cherryade?" she offered, poising the bottle over Timothy's glass.

"How about a glass of ale?" the Commander suggested. "Watney's Pale all right for you, old chap?"

She thought at first she had misheard him, but knew of course that she hadn't. Never before had he brought beer into the house. He claimed not to like beer. At Christmas he purchased a bottle of Hungarian wine in Tesco's. Bull's blood he called it.

"Nothing like a drop of ale." He opened the sideboard, took from it two large bottles marked

Watney's Red, Pale Ale and removed the caps. "Fancy a little yourself, dear?"

She shook her head. She could tell from the size of the bottles that they each contained a pint. With that amount of beer on top of two glasses of sherry the child could hardly be expected to remain sober. She voiced this fear, knowing it was unwise to do so.

"Oh, no, no, dear girl." He laughed in a way he had. Filling his glass, Timothy laughed also.

"A sense of peace," the Commander said, sitting down again. "In towns like Dynmouth you felt a sense of peace in those distant days. On Sundays people went to church."

Timothy listened, aware that familiar developments were taking place around the table. Extraordinary couple they were. Extraordinary of the Reverend Feather to say they weren't a funny type of people. Bonkers, the pair of them.

"You'd find a shilling in your pocket, Timothy. Enough to take you to the pictures. *Fire Over England!*, *Goodbye, Mr. Chips*. First-class fare. You'd pay for a seat and you'd have enough left over for a bag of fish and chips. God's own food, the way they cooked it before the War."

"So I heard, sir." He spoke politely because he wished to please. The man like to be addressed like that, and she liked you to smile at her. She was grumpy at present, but she'd soon cheer up.

"Delicious potatoes, Mrs. Abigail," he said, smiling widely at her. "Really nice they are."

She began to say something, but the Commander interrupted her.

"You'd go out hiking at the weekend. You'd take an early-morning train from London, you'd be in the middle of Bucks in half an hour. Packet

of Woodbines in your back pocket, wet your
whistle in a nice old pub. You wouldn't meet a
soul, except some ancient laborer maybe, who'd
raise his cap to you. Damned interesting, some of
those old chaps were."

"So I heard, sir." He was feeling really good.
Faintly, he was aware of applause, as though it
were actually in the room. He closed his eyes,
savoring the sensation of hearing something which
he knew wasn't really there. He concentrated on
the sound. It flowed, softly and warmly, like a
tepid sea. In the darkness behind his eyelids
lights pleasantly flashed. He felt a hint of pressure on his left shoulder, as though someone had
placed a hand there, in all probability Hughie
Green. He was surprised when he heard the voice
of Mrs. Abigail, talking about steamed pudding.
He opened his eyes. More time than he imagined
appeared to have passed.

"Fig, Timmy?" she was saying. "Steamed fig
pudding? You liked it last time."

She held a knife above a brown lump of stuff
on a plate, asking him how much he'd like.

"D'you know what a york is?" the Commander
was enquiring.

"Timmy?"

"Delicious, Mrs. Abigail. Really good, fig pudding is. A town is it, sir?"

"It's a strap that used to be worn by a farm
laborer, around his trouser-leg."

"Custard, dear?"

"Great, Mrs. Abigail."

She poured custard on to his pudding for him,
fearing he would spill it if she handed him the
jug. He wasn't sober. Even before he'd taken
more than a few sips of the beer she'd noticed

that his movements weren't coordinating properly. Sweat had begun to form on his forehead.

"Time was," the Commander said, "when you could go into a grocer's shop and there'd be a round-bottomed chair up by the counter for a customer to sit on. What d'you get now? Some child in a filthy white coat picking the dirt out of her nose while she's working a till in a supermarket. No, I'll not have any of that, dear girl."

"All right, Timmy?" she whispered.

"Cheers, Mrs. Abigail."

"Some of those girls press half a million buttons a day," the Commander said.

Timothy drank more beer, washing down a mouthful of fig pudding and custard with it. He remembered a time when he was eight or so, walking along the wall of the promenade and Miss Lavant coming up to him and saying he shouldn't because it was dangerous. She was a beautiful woman, always fashionably turned out: you wouldn't mind being married to Miss Lavant. When he'd climbed down from the wall in order to please her she'd given him a sweet, holding out a paper-bag so that he could choose, Mackintosh's Quality Street. The one he'd taken had green silver paper on it, a chocolate-covered toffee. All you had to do was to smile at women like that and it pleased them, like it pleased this woman now. He tried not to laugh, thinking of Miss Lavant in her expensive clothes, going up and down the promenade, giving people sweets. But he was unable to keep the laughter back and had to say he was sorry.

After that he lost track of time again. He noticed that she was on her feet, clearing their pudding plates away, putting them on the tray she always used, a brown tray made of imitation wood. She put the remains of the steamed pudding on it, and the custard. She was still looking grumpy, not smiling, not even trying to smile. Miss Lavant did that sometimes because for all her beauty she had bad teeth. He wondered if Miss Lavant was her sister. They were both small women, neither of them possessed children.

Timothy sat back in his chair and finished his beer. She'd be back in a few minutes with flowered cups and saucers and a flowered tea-pot, and cake. She'd sit down, trying not to listen to the Commander going on with his rubbish. She'd offer him a piece of McVitie's fruitcake, and there was no reason why he shouldn't ask her if Miss Lavant was her sister. It would please her, a question like that. It would please her if he told her a couple of funnies from *1000 Jokes for Kids of All Ages*. He laughed and saw the Commander looking across the table at him, laughing himself, a tinny sound as though the man had something wrong with him. "Cheers, Commander," he said, waving his glass at him. "Any more Watney's Pale, sir?"

"My dear fellow, of course there is. Well played, old chap." The Commander rose at speed and crossed to the sideboard, from which he withdrew two further pint bottles. He was feeling sunny, Timothy guessed, because it would annoy her when she came in and found more beer on the table. "Forgive my inhospitality," the Commander said.

"Ever read books, Commander? *Embarrassing Moments* by Lucy Lastick?" He laughed vigorously, wagging his head at the Commander. He could have sat there forever, he said to himself, telling funnies where they were appreciated. "Lucy Lastick," he said again. "D'you get it, sir? *Embarrassing Moments* by Lucy Lastick? Bloke in a cafe, Commander: 'Waiter, what's this fly doing in my soup?' 'Looks like the breaststroke, sir.' D'you get it, Commander? This bloke in a cafe—"

"Yes, yes, Timothy. Very amusing."

"This woman goes into the kitchen and says to her kid she should have changed the gold-fish water. 'They haven't drunk the last lot yet!' the kid says. D'you get it, Commander? The kid thinks—"

"I understand, Timothy."

"D'you know Plant down in the Artilleryman's Friend, Commander?"

"I don't know Mr. Plant. Well, I mean I know him to see. I've seen him out with his dog—"

"I was in the car-park of the Artilleryman's one night and Plant comes out of the Ladies. Two minutes later this woman comes out. I saw him up to it a few times. D'you get it, Commander?"

"Well, yes—"

"Another time I got up at two A.M. to go to the toilet and there's Plant in our lounge in his shirt. Paying a visit to my mum, taken short in the middle of it." Again he was unable to prevent himself from laughing, thinking of Plant's wife blowing her top if she ever heard about any of it. A big Welshwoman she was, with a temper like a cat's. Disgusting Plant had looked, with his legs and his equipment showing.

She came into the sitting-room and placed a tray of tea things and the McVitie's fruitcake on the table. He smiled, wagging his head at her.

"It's green and hairy and goes up and down, Mrs. Abigail?"

She didn't understand the question. She frowned and shook her head. She was beginning to add that she wondered if Timothy could manage a slice of cake when she noticed the newly opened bottles of beer.

"Gordon! Are you out of your mind?"

She couldn't help herself. She knew it was wrong, she knew it was ridiculous to speak like that when he had opened the two fresh bottles purely in order to upset her. He smiled narrowly beneath his narrow moustache.

"Mind?" he said.

"He's had a pint of beer already. And sherry. Gordon, he's fifteen. No child's used to it."

"The boy asked for a little more ale, Edith."

Timothy was red-faced, his lips wetly glistening, the upper one speckled with foam. His eyes were stupid-looking.

"A gooseberry in a lift," he said.

"I told you not to take the sherry," she cried, suddenly shrill.

He laughed, wagging his head. "D'you get it, though? Up and down in a lift. A gooseberry in a lift."

She asked him to try and be sensible. He looked absurd, sitting there with his head wagging.

"Bloke in a cafe: 'Do you serve crabs?' 'Sit down, mister, we serve anyone.' This bloke goes into this cafe, see, and says do they serve crabs—"

"Yes, yes, of course, Timothy."

"Ever read books, Mrs. Abigail?"

She didn't reply. He couldn't see if she was smiling or not. He couldn't see her teeth but she could easily be smiling and not showing her teeth.

Her sister hadn't shown her teeth for an instant, the time she'd given him the choice of her Quality Street. Funny thing, really, a woman handing out sweets on a promenade just because she met someone else. "I met the boy," Plant had whispered that night when he'd returned to the bedroom, and then a giggling had started even before Plant closed the bedroom door. Plant was the type who was always coming out of toilets, the Ladies in the car-park, anywhere you like. Another time Rose-Ann and Len had been on the job, on the hearthrug in the lounge, when he'd walked in after the pictures. They hadn't turned a hair.

The room moved slightly. On the other side of the table the Commander slipped about, to the left and then to the right, overlapping himself so that he had more than one pair of eyes and more than one moustache. "You've gone and got him drunk," her voice said, sounding distant, as though she were on the other end of a telephone.

Feeling that a further drink of beer would settle his vision, Timothy finished what was in his glass. He liked beer very much. Alone in the Youth Center one afternoon, the first time he'd ever tasted beer, he'd found two bottles which someone had hidden at the back of a cupboard. No beer was permitted on the premises, only Coca-Cola or Pepsi, but often for a special occasion some was smuggled in. He'd taken the two bottles to the Youth Center lavatory and had drunk the beer they contained, not expecting to like it but drinking it because it didn't belong to him. He'd left the bottles sitting in the lavatory-pan in the hope that someone would use it before noticing they were there. He'd walked out into a sunny afternoon feeling tip-top. Ever since, he'd drunk what beer he could manage to get hold of.

He poured more now. He was aware that she was asking him not to. The liquid reached the top of his glass and over-flowed on to the table-cloth because when he'd been smiling at her he'd forgotten to stop pouring it.

"Whoa up there, old chap," the Commander protested with his tinny laugh.

"Is Miss Lavant your sister, Mrs. Abigail?"

He felt her fingers on his, taking the bottle from his hand. He said it didn't matter, she could have it if she wanted it, he wouldn't deprive her of a drink. Her sister was always fashionably dressed on account of the thing with Dr. Green-slade. Her sister had no children either, he re-minded her, and fashionable though she was she didn't like to show her teeth.

The Commander was amused again. He was pointing at his wife with his thumb, only the thumb kept slipping about, like a bunch of thumbs. He was shaking his head and laughing.

"I haven't a sister," she said quietly.

"My dad scarpered, Mrs. Abigail."

"Yes, I know, Timothy."

"He couldn't stand it, a squawking baby around the place. If they'd taken precautions I wouldn't be sitting here."

He saw her nodding. He smiled across the table at her.

"This woman goes into the kitchen, Mrs. Abi-gail, and the kid's there with the gold-fish bowl—"

"Oh, for heaven's sake, Timothy!"

She was trying to take the glass away from him, but he didn't want her to. He held on to it, smiling, with one eye closed in order to see properly. He heard her saying he'd better have some hot tea, but as soon as she released her hold on the glass he lifted it to his mouth and drank some more beer. The Commander was saying something about a young man growing up. She was trying to seize the glass again.

He began to laugh because it was really funny, the way she would keep pulling at the glass and the way the Commander's face was sliding all over the place, and the way he himself was dying to go to the bog. His fingers slipped from the glass and some more of the beer got spilt, which caused him to laugh even more.

"I need to go toilet," he pointed out, endeavoring to get to his feet and finding it difficult. "Toilet," he repeated, suddenly recalling the two beer bottles sitting in the lavatory-pan in the Youth Center.

"Come on then, old chap." The Commander was standing beside him, not sitting across the table any more. "Steady up, old chap," the Commander said.

Odd as square eggs they were. Standing up or sitting down, it didn't matter a penny: really funny they were, funnier than the Dasses by two million miles. Ridiculous it was, the woman saying she hadn't a sister. "*Charrada,*" he said, up on his feet, with the Commander's arm supporting him. "You're out with a blonde, Mrs.—"

"Manage now, old chap?" the Commander interrupted. "All right on your own, eh?"

The room was moving again, going down at one end and then coming slowly back again. She was on about giving alcohol to a child. The Commander was saying to have sense.

"We did charades at the Comprehensive," he told them because as far as he could remember he hadn't told them before. "Only the Wilkinson woman let the whole thing out of control. They had me done out as Elizabeth the First, jewelry, the lot. I must go to the bog, Commander."

He felt better now that he'd got the hang of being on his feet. He crossed the room, opened the door without assistance and closed it behind him. He moved toward the lavatory, resolving that when he'd finished there he'd slip into the sitting-room and have another glass of sherry since she wasn't keen on his taking any more Watney's Pale. He whistled in the lavatory, saying to himself that he was as drunk as a cork. He felt really fantastic.

In the dining-room, meanwhile, there was silence. Mrs. Abigail poured two cups of tea and handed one across the table to her husband.

"Dear girl, it's not my fault if the boy had a drop too much."

"Then who's fault is it, Gordon?" She knew it was as wrong to say that as it had been to ask him if he was out of his mind. Yet she still couldn't help herself. No one could just sit there.

"The boy asked for it, you know. I told you he asked for it."

"He asked for it because you've given him a taste for it. It's silly, Gordon. Drinking sherry with a schoolboy, bringing beer. You never bought beer in your life before, Gordon."

"No harm in a glass of ale, dear girl. Prince Charles takes a glass, the Duke of Edinburgh—"

"Oh, nonsense, Gordon." She spoke in a way that was most unlike her, not caring what she said now because it had all become so silly. "And another thing. All that talk about going into a grocer's shop. What on earth interest d'you think it is to a boy of fifteen?"

He delighted in her agitation. There was pleasure in a fleeting little smile that came and was quickly banished. He said snappishly:

"It's of historical interest, for a start. Are you saying it's wrong for a lad to know the facts about his country?"

Mrs. Abigail did not reply. Two small red spots had developed in her face, high up on either cheek.

"I've asked you a question, Edith." His head was poked out across the table at her, his shoulders aggressively hunched. "I've asked you a question," he repeated.

She indicated that she was aware she'd been asked a question. Speaking quietly, she said that in her opinion the fact that there were once chairs in grocers' shops was hardly of historical interest. In Mock's in Pretty Street, she pointed out, a chair was still put out for customers but nobody ever sat on it.

"That's not true." His voice was controlled, matching her calmness. "I sit on that chair myself."

"Then what are you on about, Gordon? One minute you're talking about chairs in grocers' shops as though they were a thing of the past, the next you're saying you sit on one yourself when you go into Mock's. Besides," she added quietly, "it's all irrelevant."

"It's hardly irrelevant that the country for which men were prepared to give their lives has become a rubbish dump."

"It's irrelevant at this moment, Gordon."

"Oh, for heaven's sake have sense, woman!"

He was losing his temper, which he loved
doing. His eyes flashed, his lips quivered, causing
the ginger moustache to quiver also.

"That boy's all part of it," he snapped. "D'you
think he'd be the same, for God's sake, if he
was at Charterhouse or Rugby? Have a titter of
sense, Edith."

She sighed, vaguely moving her head about,
shaking it at first and then nodding it. It was
no time for arguing. There was the problem
of an inebriated boy, and she was being as silly
as anyone, making matters worse by pursuing a
pointless disagreement.

She watched him drinking his tea with victory
in the gesture of lifting the cup. The flare of
temper had died away; he had inflicted the defeat
he had wished to inflict without having to throw
a milk-jug at the wall, as he'd had to do once,
early on in their marriage. He would be compli-
menting himself on his restraint: she could even
see a reflection of that in his gesture of victory
with the tea-cup. It had often occurred to her
that marriage was all defeat and victory, and
worked better when women were the defeated
ones since men apparently could not bear to be
and had no philosophy for that condition.

"What shall we do with Timothy, Gordon?"

He drew back his lips, displaying a small array
of teeth that were appropriately tinged with
gingery brown.

"Leave Master Timothy to me," he said, his
tone of voice confirming what she already knew:
that he had created the situation in order to display his prowess by sorting it out, just as he had
goaded her into an argument in order to experience the thrill of winning it. She was reflecting

upon all that, and at the same time worrying
about the condition of the child who was being
such a long time in the lavatory, when the door
opened and Timothy entered. To her astonishment, he was wearing one of Gordon's suits.

"My God!" the Commander murmured.

He smiled at them, holding on to the back of
a chair, swaying a bit. He said he wanted to show
them the thing about the charades. He had invented a comic act, he said, which he was going
to do at the Easter Fête. He had to dress up as
three different brides. He had to dress up as
George Joseph Smith as well: he was trying the
suit on for size. He'd chosen the dog's-tooth one
because he reckoned it was the kind the man
would possess.

"Stringer took us into Tussaud's, down to the
Horror Chamber. Did you ever see Miss Lofty,
sir?"

"You've had too much to drink, Timmy," she
whispered.

He nodded at her, saying that once upon a time
he'd searched high and low for her wedding-
dress. When he couldn't find it he'd remembered
where there was another one. A wedding-dress
wasn't an easy garment to come by.

"Get into your clothes immediately, boy. Cut
along now." The Commander's voice was sharp,
like a splinter of something.

Timothy laughed because the voice sounded
funny. Bloody ridiculous it was, going into the
sea every day in bathing togs.

"Could you make a pair of curtains, Mrs. Abigail?"

She shook her head, not knowing what he was
talking about.

"I was saying it to Mr. Feather and he said to ask you."

"We'll talk about it another time, Timothy."

"Have you got a sewing-machine? Only you couldn't make curtains without a machine."

"No, of course not—"

"D'you think your sister has a sewing-machine?"

She nodded, trying to smile at him.

"No problem then."

"I've made a request of you," the Commander said in the same splintery voice. "Take off my suit immediately."

"It would please us if you put on your own clothes again, dear."

Children did dress up, she thought, trying to think calmly. It was a children's thing, they enjoyed it. And yet it wasn't like that at all. It wasn't a child dressing up just for the fun of it. It was a child made drunk, his mouth pulled down at the corners, his eyes glassily staring, sweat all over his neck and face. In the dog's-tooth suit he was grotesque. What was happening was like something you'd read about in a cheap Sunday newspaper.

He mentioned *Opportunity Knocks*, and Hughie Green, who might be staying in the Queen Victoria Hotel, in Dynmouth for the golf. Nobody had ever done a show like that on *Opportunity Knocks*. There were acts with pigeons on *Opportunity Knocks*, and family acts, and trick cyclists and singers and kids of three who could dance, and dogs smoking pipes, but he'd never yet seen a show that was comic and also about death. You'd have each of the brides acting like she was struggling against George Joseph Smith and all the time George Joseph Smith would be winning, only you wouldn't actually see him, you'd have to imagine him. And when she went under the water the lights would go black and George Joseph Smith would appear a few seconds later in the dog's-tooth suit. He'd tell jokes, standing beside the bath with the bride in it. You'd know she was in it because a bit of her wedding-dress would be draped over the side, only of course she wouldn't be there at all because it was a one-man act. "Ah well, best be getting back to work," George Joseph Smith would say when he had them bringing the house down. The lights would go black and the next thing you'd see would be another bride struggling against the murdering hands of the man. After he drowned each bride George Joseph Smith had gone out to buy the dead woman her supper, fish for Miss Munday, eggs for Mrs. Burnham and Miss Lofty. It was a peculiarity with him, like his passion for death by the sea. George Joseph Smith had once stayed in Dynmouth, in the Castlerea boarding-house.

While she listened to all this, Mrs. Abigail repeatedly believed she was dreaming. It was like a dream, a nightmare that held you and held you, not letting you wake up. A child had perpetrated a comic act about three real and brutal murders. In a marquee on the lawn of a rectory he expected people to laugh. He appeared to believe that some television personality might by chance be there to see him.

"D'you ever see Benny Hill, Mrs. Abigail? Really funny, Benny Hill. And Bruce Forsyth. D'you like Bruce Forsyth when he gets going?"

"Please." She still spoke softly, with a reason-

ableness that suggested the plea was being made
for the first time.

"Benny Hill was an ordinary milkman with
pint bottles on a dray, cream and yoghurt and
carrots, anything you wanted at the door. Opportunity knocked for Benny Hill. It could happen to you, Mrs. Abigail. It could happen to anyone."

"Quickly now," the Commander limply ordered.
"Get a move on, Gedge."

But Timothy didn't get a move on. He wagged
his head, not attempting to rise from the chair
he was sitting on. He mentioned the teacher
called Brehon O'Hennessy and the drear landscape and how there were people like last year's
rhubarb walking about the streets. You had to
smile, he said, but you could see the man's point
of view. Mad as a hatter he'd been, a real nutter,
yet you couldn't help getting the picture. He
laughed. He spent a lot of time himself, he said,
following people around, looking in windows.

"Is Miss Lavant her sister, sir? Only Lavant's
fancied Dr. Greenslade for twenty years and he
won't lift a finger in case he'd be struck off. Isn't
it awful, Miss Lavant wasting herself on a married man? Isn't it a terrible story, Mrs. Abigail?
Your sister in a predicament like that?"

She nodded, not knowing what else to do.

"There's worse than that in this town. The time
she gave me the sweet I thought maybe she was
going to kidnap me. I thought she was after a
ransom, two or three thousand—"

"My wife has no sister. Will you kindly cease,
boy."

"Miss Lavant's the one I mean, sir. She gave
me a sweet—"

"Miss Lavant is not her sister."

Mrs. Abigail dragged her eyes away from the child, startled by the note of panic in her husband's voice. He wasn't enjoying being angry any more. His face was blotchy, his lips quivered as he shouted, his eyes were quivering also. Something was happening in the room, something that had more to do with Gordon than with the child dressed up in his clothes. She could feel it gathering all around her, cloying and thick and heavy. Gordon was hunched, appearing to be terrified, his eyes staring. Timothy Gedge was smiling pathetically. She wanted to weep over both of them, to ask Gordon what on earth the matter was, to ask Timothy the same question in another kind of way.

Still smiling, he spoke again. He'd witnessed all sorts, he said: the dead buried, kids from the primary school lifting rubbers out of W. H. Smith's, Plant on the job with his mother, his legs as white as mutton-fat. He'd witnessed Rose-Ann and Len up to tricks on the hearth-rug, and others up to tricks in the wood behind the Youth Center, kids of all ages, nine to thirteen, take your pick. He'd seen the Robson woman from the Post Office buying fish and chips in Phyl's Phries with Slocombe from the Fine Fare off-license, and Pym, the solicitor, being sick into the sea after a Rotary dinner in the Queen Victoria Hotel. He'd seen the Dynmouth Hards beating up the Pakistani from the steam laundry in a bus-shelter, and spraying *Blacks Out* on the back wall of the Essoldo. He'd seen them terrorizing Nurse Hackett, the midwife, swerving their motor-cycles in front of her blue Mini when she was trying to go about her duties at night-time. There was wife-swapping every Saturday night at parties on the new estate, Leaflands it was called, out on the London road. He'd looked in a window once and seen a man in Lace Street taking out his glass eye. He'd seen Slocombe and the Robson woman up on the golf-course. In Dynmouth and its neighborhood he'd witnessed terrible things, he said.

He appeared to be rambling again, but it was hard to be certain. He had seemed to be rambling when he'd first mentioned a wedding-dress and when he'd referred to Miss Lavant as her sister and to a gooseberry in a lift.

"You've no right to spy on people," the Commander began to say. "You've no right to go poking—".

"I've witnessed you down on the beach, sir. Running about in your bathing togs. I've witnessed you up to your tricks, Commander, when she's out on her Meals on Wheels."

He smiled at her, but she didn't want to look at him. "I wouldn't ever tell a soul," he said. "I wouldn't, Commander."

She waited, her eyes fixed on the flowered tea-pot, frowning at it. Whatever he was referring to, she didn't want to hear about it. She wanted him to stop speaking. She felt herself infected by her husband's panic, not knowing why she felt like that. They would keep the secret, the boy said. The secret would be safe.

"There's no secret to keep," the Commander cried. "There's nothing, nothing at all."

She wished he hadn't said that. If he hadn't said it, they might have glossed over all the boy had said already. They might have pretended they were trying to help the boy, humoring him by agreeing there was some secret that affected them. They had been married thirty-six years, she said to herself, puzzled that that fact should have occurred to her now.

"He's talking nonsense." The Commander's voice had dropped, his words were almost unintelligible.

She was a happy woman: she told herself that. She'd been perfectly happy making the supper, the chicken and the fig pudding. It didn't matter if Gordon wanted to win arguments. It didn't matter if his clothes dripped all over the kitchen. She'd devoted her life to Gordon. She didn't want to hear. Whatever there was, she didn't want to know.

"Please don't," she said, looking up from the tea-pot, looking across the table at Timothy Gedge. "Please don't say anything more."

Timothy smiled at her. It was a secret between himself and the Commander, he said. He rose unsteadily from his chair and moved around the table to where Gordon was sitting. Her instinct was to put her hands over her ears, but she couldn't bring herself to do it because it seemed so silly. One Sunday afternoon, watching suburban cricket in Sutton, he had asked her to be his wife, telling her he loved her.

Timothy whispered, but the whisper was clumsy because of the sherry and the beer: she heard distinctly, as though he were shouting. They would keep the secret, he said, he would never tell a soul that her husband went after Dynmouth's cub scouts, intent on committing indecencies.

A storm blew through the town that night. The narrow streets were washed with rain, the canvas of Ring's Amusements flapped in Sir Walter Raleigh Park, breakers crashed against the wall of the promenade. The town was deserted. The pink Essoldo was dead as a doornail, Phyl's Phries had shut up shop at half-past ten, the night-porter of the Queen Victoria Hotel, slept undisturbed in his cubby-hole. The police-car that sometimes slipped through Dynmouth's night streets was parked with its lights off in the yard of the police station. The Dynmouth Hards weren't abroad, nor was Nurse Hackett in her blue Mini. Only the shop windows showed signs of life. Television sets recorded the soundless mouthing of a late-night newsreader. In harsh white light figures without eyes displayed twin-sets and dresses or sat on G-plan furniture. A cardboard couple smiled joyfully, drawing attention to a building society's rates.

The rain rattled on the slated roof of the Artilleryman's Friend, beneath which its proprietor lay, drowsily fulfilled. Half an hour ago Mr. Plant had engaged in sexual congress with his stoutly built Welsh wife, and in the ladies' lavatory of the public house car-park he had earlier indulged himself with the trimmer form of Timothy Gedge's mother. As always, he had enjoyed the contrast, both in anticipation during his conjunction with Mrs. Gedge and in retrospect while involved with his wife. For their parts, the women had appeared to be satisfied.

In the ivy-clad rectory Lavinia Featherston lay awake, sorry she'd been so cross all day. It was wrong to be upset by circumstances, by a fact of your life that could not be altered. She'd been cross again after she'd put the twins to bed.

She'd protested quite sharply to her husband about the people who came so endlessly to the rectory, the town's unfortunates, the dirty, the ugly, the boring, the mad. She was tired of listening to Mrs. Slewy complaining about the social security man, Mrs. Slewy with a cigarette perpetually on the go, leaning against the back door, asking for the loan of a pound. She was tired of Old Ape arriving on the wrong day for his meal. She must have made a thousand cups of Nescafé for Mrs. Stead-Carter, being bossed all over the place while she did so. It was a relief that crazy old Miss Trimm had a cold, a respite at least from her belief that she'd mothered a second Jesus Christ. Miss Poraway made you want to scream. Quentin had listened to her quietly, saying it was all understandable, and in greater irritation she'd replied that it was typical of him to say that, and then she'd cried. "Sorry," she murmured at his sleeping form, knowing that tomorrow she'd probably be edgy too.

She lay there, thinking of her nursery school. Little Mikey Hatch getting his arms wet. Jennifer Droppy looking sad. Joseph Wright pushing. Mandy Goff singing her song. Johnny Pyke laughing, Thomas Braine interrupting, Andrew Cartboy being good, Susannah and Deborah throwing dough. She forced herself to think of them, and then to think about prices and to work out figures in her mind because one of these days a new Wendy house was going to be necessary. Her mind attempted to reject these calculations and to return to its brooding, but she refused to permit that. Mandy Goff's father might offer to make a new Wendy house if she paid for the materials and offered to pay for his time. With hardly any prompting he'd made the rack for hanging coats on, and the slide. She dropped into drowsiness, thinking of the gray wooden slide and the children sliding down it.

In the room next door the twins looked happy in their sleep, their limbs similarly arranged. Two miles away, in the Down Manor Orphanage, the orphans without exception dreamed, frightening themselves and delighting themselves. So did the children of Lavinia's nursery school, scattered all over Dynmouth, and the children of the Ring-o-Roses nursery school and the WRVS Playgroup, and the children of Dynmouth Primary and of Dynmouth Comprehensive and of the Loretto Convent, and the traveling children of Ring's Amusements, and Sharon Lines who owed her life to a machine.

In the house called Sweetlea Mrs. Dass lay sleepless in the dark, remembering the son who'd been the apple of her eye, a child she'd painfully borne, who had painfully rejected her. In her bedsitting-room in Pretty Street the beautiful Miss Lavant, who wished in all the hours of her wakefulness that she might have borne the child of the man she hopelessly loved, pored over the day's blank space in her diary. *Wet*, she wrote and could think of nothing else to record: the day had passed without a sight of Dr. Greenslade.

In Sea House Kate dreamed of the bedroom she slept in, its orange-painted dressing-table and orange-painted chairs, its blinds and wallpaper of a matching pattern, orange poppies in long grass. She dreamed that the stout waiter from the dining-car was standing in this room, offering her a toasted tea-cake, and that Miss Shaw and Miss Rist were bullying little Miss Malabedeely.

A wedding took place in the room: an African bishop swore to honor Miss Malabedeely with his black body. He had the marks of a tiger's claw on his cheeks. He said the toasted tea-cake was delicious.

Stephen slept also. He'd lain awake for a while, remembering his bedroom in Primrose Cottage, wondering who was sleeping there now. He'd been going through the Somerset batting averages for last season when he fell asleep.

Mr. Blakey, awake above the garage, listened to the crash of breakers. Sudden gusts fiercely rattled the windows, driving the rain in sheets against the panes. Beside him, his wife was content in her unconsciousness.

Mr. Blakey slipped out of bed. Without turning a light on he drew a brown woolen dressing-gown around him and left the room. Still in darkness, he passed through a small sitting-room and down a flight of stairs to a passage that led to the kitchen. He brewed tea and sat at the table to drink it.

In the outhouse where they slept the dogs barked, a distant sound that Mr. Blakey paid no attention to, guessing it to be caused by the storm. He left the kitchen and passed along the green-linoleumed passage, into the hall. A window might be open, a door might be banging in the wind on a night like this. There was no harm in looking about.

He switched a light on in the hall, illuminating the theatrical figures on the red hessian walls. He listened for a moment. No sound came from the house, but the dogs still faintly barked and the sea was louder than it had been in his bedroom. Drawn by the sound of rain on the French win-

dows, he moved into the drawing-room. Enough
light to see by filtered in from the hall, though
not enough to draw color from the gloom. Wallpaper and curtains were grayly nondescript, pictures and furniture were shadows.

The sea was noisier in this room than anywhere else in the house, yet through the wide
French windows there was nothing to be seen of
the storm. He strained his eyes, peering into the
dark for the familiar shapes of trees and shrubs,
wondering what damage was being wrought. But
when a shaft of moonlight unexpectedly flashed
it wasn't damage to his garden that startled his
attention. A figure moved beneath the monkey-
puzzle. A child's face smiled at the house.

4

The storm died out in the night. At breakfast Mrs.
Blakey asked the children what they were going
to do that day and Kate said that if Mrs. Blakey
would agree to have lunch early they'd like to
walk the eight miles to Badstoneleigh. The attraction was *Dr. No* and *Diamonds Are Forever*
at the Pavilion. Mrs. Blakey, while quite agreeable
to providing an early lunch, pointed out that this
double bill was due at the Essoldo the following
week, but Kate said they'd rather not wait.

It was quite nice, Stephen thought, having

breakfast without any fuss in the big lofty-ceil-
inged kitchen, with Mr. Blakey not saying anything while he ate his sausages and bacon and
an egg. He thought it might be quite nice to be
like Mr. Blakey, slow and silent and looking after
a garden. It would be nice to have played cricket
for a county first, so that you could think about it
when you were growing dahlias and lettuces, fifty-
seven not out against Hampshire, ninety against
Lancashire, four for forty-one in a one-day Gil-
lette Cup final versus Kent. Mr. Blakey was happy,
the way often people weren't: you could tell by
the way he sat there at the table. "You must try
and be happy again," his father had said to him.
"She'd want us both to be."

It was a long time ago now; there wasn't really
a reason not to be happy. He knew there wasn't.
He knew it was easy to feel resentful just because
his father had married again. But unhappy people
were a bore and a nuisance, like Spencer Major
who cried whenever there was fish, who was
afraid of Sergeant McIntosh, the boxing instruc-
tor.

In the garden after breakfast they played with
the setters, throwing a red ball and a blue ball
on the damp grass of the lawns. There was no
way of telling if you'd ever be good enough to bat
for a county. You just had to wait and see, pretending a bit in the meanwhile.

"Nice morning, Mr. Plant," Timothy Gedge said
on the promenade, where the publican was taking
his ritual morning outing with his dog, Tike. Mr.
Plant was a large, red-fleshed man, the dog a
smooth-haired fox-terrier, hampered by the ab-
sence of a back leg.

"Hullo," Mr. Plant said. His spirits, which had been high, sank. Because of his relationship with the boy's mother, Timothy Gedge embarrassed him.

"Nice after the storm, sir." He was carrying an empty carrier-bag with a Union Jack on it. He'd woken up at a quarter to eight with his mouth as dry as paper. He'd lain in bed, waiting for Rose-Ann and his mother to leave the flat, waiting for the two flushes of the lavatory and his mother's hurrying feet and her voice telling Rose-Ann to hurry up also, and the smell of their after-breakfast cigarettes that always penetrated to his bedroom, and the abrupt turning-off of the kitchen radio, and the bang of the door. He'd got up and taken four Aspirins from his mother's supply and drunk nearly two pints of water. He'd gone back to bed and lain there, going over the events of the night before, trying to remember. When eventually he'd got up he'd had to iron his jeans and his zipped jacket because they'd become creased when they were damp. He was feeling a bit better now, but if he received an invitation to step down to the Artilleryman's Friend so that he might restore himself further with a glass of beer he would accept it eagerly. No such invitation was forthcoming.

"Only I thought the storm might last a few days, Mr. Plant."

Mr. Plant nodded, not interested in what this boy might have thought about the weather. He whistled at his dog, who was sniffing at the boots of two old men on a seat. The dog limped hurriedly back to him, its head slung low in anticipation of punishment.

"Lovely dog, that," Timothy said. He had

dropped into step with Mr. Plant, to Mr. Plant's discomfiture. "Like a gum, sir?" He offered the tube he'd bought yesterday. Mr. Plant shook his head. "Tike like one, would he, sir?"

"Leave the dog be, son."

Timothy nodded agreeably. He placed a black-currant-flavored gum in his mouth and returned the tube to his pocket. He wanted to laugh because he'd suddenly remembered, rather faintly, that in his confusion last night he'd kept insisting that Miss Lavant was Mrs. Abigail's sister. He lifted a hand to his lips and kept it there for a moment, holding the laughter back. Mr. Plant surveyed the sea, his eyes vacant and a little blood-shot, as they always were. Timothy said:

"You're out with a blonde, Mr. Plant, you see the wife coming?"

"What?"

"What would you do, sir?"

"Eh?"

"The four-minute mile, Mr. Plant!"

Timothy laughed, but Mr. Plant didn't. A silence developed between them. Then Timothy said:

"Only I was anxious to have a word with you, sir."

Mr. Plant grunted, still surveying the sea.

"I need your assistance, Mr. Plant."

It surprised the publican to hear this. He considered it a strange statement for a boy to make, and he wondered for a moment—without knowing quite why he wondered it—if the boy was going to ask him about the facts of life. Uncomfortably, he recalled the occasion when he'd been discovered in the Cornerways flat with only a shirt on.

"I'm going in for the Spot the Talent, Mr. Plant. At the Easter Fête."

Mr. Plant frowned at the horizon and then slowly turned his head and looked down at the sharply-featured face of Timothy Gedge. Beneath the short, nearly-white hair the eyes were earnest, the mouth smiled slightly beneath the suspicion of a pale moustache. As Mr. Plant watched, the lips parted in a greater smile.

"I'd like to tell you about it, Mr. Plant," Timothy said, and did so as they walked. He went into detail, as he had for the Abigails, although in a different manner because he hadn't had sherry and beer. He spoke of the brides of George Joseph Smith, and George Joseph Smith himself, who had bought fish for the dead Miss Munday, and eggs for Mrs. Burnham and Miss Lofty. He explained about how each of the brides would be struggling against the invisible hands of George Joseph Smith and how the stage would go black and when the light went up George Joseph Smith would be standing there, with jokes, in a dog's-tooth suit.

"You're bloody mad," Mr. Plant said, staring at the boy.

"There's an old bath down in Swines' yard. I asked the foreman about it. Only we'd need your van to convey it, sir."

"Van? Who'd need the van? What're you on about?"

"Your little brown van, Mr. Plant. If we could erect the bath up in the marquee on the Saturday morning. We could cover it with a sheet so's nobody'd guess. We can get hold of a wedding-dress, no problem at all."

"You're a bloody nutcase, son."

Timothy shook his head. He sucked on his fruit gum and said he wasn't a nutcase. All he wanted to do, he explained, was to go in for the Spot the Talent competition.

Mr. Plant did not reply. He turned and began to walk back toward the town. His dog had gone to sniff a lamp-post. He called him to heel.

"Shall I do you a woman's voice?" Timothy Gedge suggested.

Mr. Plant wondered if she'd dropped the boy when he was a baby. You heard of that kind of thing, a kid's head striking the edge of something when the kid was a couple of months old and the kid never being normal. Then, as Mrs. Abigail had, he recalled that dressing up and putting on shows was an activity that was popular with children. He'd often sat with his wife watching his own two boys and two girls enacting a playlet they'd made up by themselves, some fantasy set in a country house or a railway station. The Gedge boy seemed to be intent on something like that only with a gruesome flavor, murders taking place in a bath. Sick they called it nowadays, and sick it most certainly was. In his entire life, he estimated, he'd never heard anything like it.

"It's in the yard on the left, Mr. Plant, behind the timber sheds. I told the foreman you'd be coming for it. Today or whenever you had a minute."

"You did what, son?" His voice was quiet, with a threat in it. He was staring at Timothy Gedge again. "No one's going getting baths out of Swines' yard. Today or any other time."

"I'm anxious for your assistance, Mr. Plant."

"Hop it, son. Go on now."

"I said some time, Mr. Plant. I didn't say today

specially. The Saturday morning, Easter Saturday—"

"You're up the chute, son."

For the first time Timothy noticed that there was red hair growing out of the publican's ears and nose. The hair was coarse and wiry, like the hair on his head. Women the age of his mother couldn't pick and choose, he supposed. Nor could the women who let Plant get on the job in the Ladies in the Artilleryman's car-park. He'd followed him in once and had listened to the sound of clothes being removed, and whispering. On another occasion, when he was watching *A Man Called Ironside*, he'd heard whispering and knew that his mother had taken Plant into her bedroom. He'd left the television on and gone to listen at the bedroom door. He'd looked through the key-hole and seen his mother without a stitch left on her, taking off the man's socks. He reminded him now of this occasion, and of the occasion in the middle of the night.

"You bloody young pup!" Mr. Plant exclaimed hotly.

"All I mean is, we'll keep the secret, Mr. Plant. We have the secret between us, sir. I wouldn't open my mouth to Mrs. Plant."

"You bet your bloody life you wouldn't. If you opened your bloody mouth you'd get a hiding that would cripple you."

"I'm saying I wouldn't, Mr. Plant. I'd never do a thing like that, sir. So if we could fix it for Saturday A.M. and if you could get the bath in your little van, and don't tell a soul so's it's a surprise. I've got the whole thing planned, Mr. Plant—"

"Well, get it unplanned if you don't want to end up in a borstal."

They had ceased to walk. Timothy listened, still sucking his fruit gum, while Mr. Plant told him that he'd never heard anything as stupid or as pathetic in his life. No one was going to watch the kind of stuff that had been described to him, in a marquee or anywhere else. He spoke of a borstal again, he denied that he was an immoral man. He denied emphatically that the scene during *A Man Called Ironside* had ever taken place; or if it had, it had been some other man in the bedroom. On the night Timothy had seen him in a shirt he had come round to the Cornerways flat because Timothy's mother had wanted his advice about a notice she'd had from the council regarding rent. He'd caught his trousers on a nail and had had to remove them in order that she could repair them. There was nothing wrong in that beyond what a dirty mind would make of it. "You want to be careful of that, son. Keep a clean nose on your face."

Timothy mentioned the Ladies in the car-park, adding that he had repeatedly observed Mr. Plant emerging a few minutes after a woman. He mentioned the time he'd heard clothes being removed, and the whispering. Mr. Plant said he was mistaken. Then, suddenly, he laughed. He told Timothy not to poke about in things he didn't understand. If he'd emerged from the toilet, he said, then maybe he'd been in there fixing a ball-cock, and there was no crime in removing an article of clothing in a toilet. Still laughing, he said it could happen to anyone, a pair of trousers catching on a nail.

"You mind your own bloody business, son," he

said, not amused any more, "unless you want a fat lip." He lifted a large hand in the air and held it up in front of Timothy Gedge's face. He told him to look at it and to remember it. It would thump him to a pulp. It would thump the living daylights out of him if he ever again dared to open his mouth as he had just now, to anyone.

"You don't get the picture, Mr. Plan—"

"I bloody do, mate. You'll be left for dead, son, and when they get you to your feet you'll do five and a half years in a borstal. All right then?"

Mr. Plant walked away with his dog hobbling beside him. Timothy did not follow him. He stood on the promenade, watching the publican and his three-legged pet, bewildered by the man.

"Ashes to ashes," intoned Quentin Featherston in the churchyard of St. Simon and St. Jude's. A small piece of clay, dislodged from the side of the grave, clattered on the brash new wood of a coffin containing the remains of an aged fisherman called Joseph Rine. Attired in black, the elderly wife of the fisherman wept. A sister, bent with rheumatics, wept also. The old man's son considered that his father had had a good innings.

Quentin shook hands with them at the end of the service and walked to the church with the sexton. Quietly, Mr. Peniket remarked that the Rines were a good family, even if they didn't go to church much. He'd had to order more coke, he added, although he'd hoped not to have to do so until the autumn. He hoped that was all right.

"Yes, yes, of course, Mr. Peniket."

"Better to be safe, sir."

Mr. Peniket was a conscientious bachelor of

late middle age, devoted to St. Simon and St. Jude's. He polished the pews and the brass and personally washed the tiles. He was in no way hostile to Quentin, but he often spoke of the time when old Canon Flewett had been the rector, when many more people had come to church and church life had thrived. He was aware that times had changed, yet somehow when he spoke about Quentin's predecessor Quentin always felt that he believed that if old Canon Flewett were still in charge the change would not have been so drastic.

"I'll just tidy around," the sexton said now, and Quentin nodded, stepping into the vestry.

"Really good that was," Timothy Gedge said, entering the vestry a minute or so later with his carrier-bag. "Really nicely done, Mr. Feather."

Quentin softly sighed. The boy had recently developed this habit of walking into the vestry without knocking, usually to announce that a funeral service had been nicely conducted.

"I'm disrobing, Timothy. I like to be alone when I'm disrobing, you know."

"I've come in for a chat, sir. Any time you said. Isn't it a pity about Mr. Rine, sir?"

"He was very old, you know."

"He wasn't young, sir. Eighty-five years of age. I wouldn't like to live as long as that, Mr. Feather. I wouldn't feel easy about it."

Quentin began to disrobe since it was clear that the boy wasn't going to leave the vestry. He removed his surplice and hung it on a peg in a cupboard. He unbuttoned his cassock. Timothy Gedge said:

"A very nice man, Mr. Rine, I often had a chat with him. God's gain, sir."

Quentin nodded.

"The son's in the fish-packing station. An under-manager. Did you know that, Mr. Feather? There's fish in the family."

"Timothy, I wish you wouldn't call me by that name."

"Which name is that, Mr. Feather?"

"My name is Featherston." He smiled, not wishing to sound pernickety: after all, it wasn't an important point. "There's a ston at the end, actually."

"A ston, Mr. Feather?"

He hung the cassock in the cupboard. There was a Mothers' Union tea that afternoon, an event he had to brace himself to sustain. Nineteen women would arrive at the rectory and eat sandwiches and biscuits and cake. They'd engage in Dynmouth chatter, and he would call on God and God would remind him that the women were His creatures. Miss Poraway would say it would be a good thing if something on the lines of a Tupperware party could be arranged to raise funds, and Mrs. Stead-Carter would coldly reply that you couldn't have anything on the lines of a Tupperware party unless you had a commodity to sell. Mrs. Hayes would suggest that not all the funds raised at the Easter Fête should go toward the church tower, and he'd have to point out that if salvage work didn't start on the church tower soon there wouldn't be a church tower to salvage.

"What's it mean, ston, sir?"

"It's just my name."

He lifted his black mackintosh from a coat-hanger and locked the cupboard door. The boy walked behind him when he left the vestry and by his side on the aisle of the church. Mr. Peniket was tidying the prayer-books in the pews. It embarrassed Quentin when Timothy Gedge came to the church and Mr. Peniket was there.

"This bloke in a restaurant, Mr. Feather. 'Waiter, there's a rhinoceros in my soup—' "

"Timothy, we're in church."

"It's a lovely church, sir."

"Jokes are a little out of place, Timothy. Especially since we've just had a funeral."

"It's really good the way you do a funeral."

"I have been meaning to mention that to you, Timothy. It isn't the best of ideas to hang round funerals, you know."

"Eh?"

"You seem always to be at the funerals I conduct." He spoke lightly, and smiled. "I've seen you in the Baptist graveyard also. It's really not all that healthy, Timothy."

"Healthy, Mr. Feather?"

"Only friends of the dead person go to the funeral, Timothy. And relatives, of course."

"Mr. Rine was a friend, Mr. Feather. Really nice he was."

Mr. Peniket was listening carefully, doing something to a hassock. He was bent over the hassock in a pew, apparently plumping it. Quentin could feel him thinking that in Canon Flewett's time schoolboys wouldn't have come wandering into the church to discuss the recently dead.

"What I mean about going to funerals, Timothy—"

"You go to the funeral of a friend, sir."

"Old Mrs. Crowley was hardly a friend."

"Who's Mrs. Crowley then?"

"The woman whose funeral you attended last Saturday morning." He tried to speak testily but did not succeed. It annoyed him when he recalled the attendance of Timothy Gedge at Mrs. Crowley's funeral, a woman who'd been a resident in the town's old people's home, Wisteria Lodge, since before Timothy Gedge's birth. It annoyed him that Mr. Peniket was bent over a hassock, listening. But the annoyance came softly from him now.

"I'd rather you didn't come to funerals," he said.

"No problem, Mr. Feather. If that's the way you want it, no problem. I wouldn't go against your wishes, sir."

"Thank you, Timothy."

At the church door Quentin turned and bowed in the direction of the altar and Timothy Gedge obligingly did the same. "Goodbye, Mr. Peniket," Quentin said. "Thank you."

"Goodbye, Mr. Featherston," the sexton replied in a reverent voice.

"Cheers," Timothy Gedge said, but Mr. Peniket did not reply to that.

In the porch, full of missionary notices and rotas for flower-arranging, Quentin bent to put on his bicycle-clips.

"Funny fish, that sexton," Timothy Gedge said. "Ever notice the way he looks at you, sir? Like you were garbage gone off." He laughed. Quentin said he didn't think there was anything funny about Mr. Peniket. He wheeled his bicycle on the tarred path that led, between gravestones, to the lich-gate.

"I went up to see Dass, sir. Like you said."

"I didn't actually say you should, you know."

"About the Spot the Talent competition, Mr. Feather. You said the Dasses was in charge."

"I know, Timothy, I know."

"Only the curtains in the Youth Center got burnt, Mr. Feather. Two boys burnt them in December."

"Burnt them?"

"I think the boys had been drinking, sir."

"You mean, they just set light to them?"

"They put paraffin on them first, sir. They were making an effort to burn the place down, sir."

He remembered. There had been an attempt to burn the Youth Center down, but he hadn't known that the curtains of the stage had been at the point of ignition. It was true, though: the curtains hadn't been there for ages. He'd wondered why a couple of times.

"Only I need curtains for my act, Mr. Feather. I need darkness in the marquee and the curtains drawn twice. I explained to Dass. I have quick changes to do."

"I'm sure Mr. Dass can rig something up."

"He says he can't do curtains, Mr. Feather. No way, he says."

"Well, we'll find something somewhere." He smiled at the boy. He pushed his bicycle across the pavement and on to the road. He had a list of shopping to do for the Mothers' Union tea.

"Dass says he couldn't supply curtains on his own, sir, on account of the expense. Only I think he's maybe in financial trouble—"

"Oh, we couldn't have Mr. Dass spending money on curtains. I'm sure we'll find some somewhere. Don't worry about it."

"You can't help worrying, sir."

Astride the saddle of his bicycle, the tips of his

toes touching the ground in order to retain his balance, Quentin said again that curtains would be found for the Spot the Talent competition. He nodded reassuringly at Timothy Gedge. He felt uneasy in the presence of the boy. He felt inadequate and for some reason guilty.

"You're out with a blonde, sir, you see the wife coming—"

"I'm sorry, Timothy, I really must be on my way now."

"It's a joke when I call you Mr. Feather, sir. Like a feather in a chicken, if you get it."

Quentin shook his head. They'd have another chat soon, he promised.

"I don't think that sexton likes us, sir," Timothy Gedge called after him. "I don't think he cares for either of us."

At half-past eleven that morning a man and a woman on a motor-cycle asked the way to the Dasses' house, Sweetlea.

"Name's Pratt," the man said when Mr. Dass answered the doorbell. Beneath a street-light that was still flickering from the night before the motor-cycle was propped up by the curb. A woman in motor-cycling clothes and a helmet was standing beside it.

The man said he'd heard about the Spot the Talent competition at the Easter Fête. He was new to the neighborhood, he and his wife had come to live in Paltry Combe, eighteen miles away. They'd ridden over on the bike as soon as they'd heard, on the chance that they wouldn't be too late to fill in an entry form. He did imitations of dogs, he said.

He was a stocky man with a crash-helmet on

his head and leather gloves tucked under his arm. He gestured with his head in the direction of the woman by the motor-cycle, confirming that she was his wife. He went in a lot for competitions, he said, villages, resorts, it didn't matter to him. He asked about the prize money when he'd finished filling in the entry form, and wrote down the amounts on the back of an envelope. "An old pro," Mr. Dass remarked in the sitting-room after he'd gone. "Makes eleven in all. Two up on last year." Yesterday had officially been the last day for entries, but he'd seen no reason to turn away the man's fifty p.

The doorbell of Sweetlea rang again, and Mr. Dass said if it was someone else who wanted to enter he'd again stretch a point. Imitations of dogs weren't exactly going to set Easter Saturday alight, and everything else looked like yesterday's buns with a vengeance. Contrary to his speculations, however, their visitor wasn't another late entrant.

"Cheers," Timothy Gedge said, and then reported that he'd spoken to the clergyman about the curtains and that the clergyman had been at his wits end to know where to lay his hands on some.

Mr. Dass looked at the boy, determined not to let him into his house. It was intolerable, having your privacy invaded at all hours, for no reason whatsoever.

"Is that all you came about, curtains?"

"I thought you'd like to know, sir."

Mr. Dass, about to ejaculate angrily, did not say anything. He peered at the boy through his spectacles, thinking that he seemed to be off his head.

"Funny the way your son doesn't ever come back to Dynmouth any more, sir. Funny he wouldn't want to see his mum. I remember the night he cleared off, sir."

"Now look here, boy—"

"Mr. Feather said definitely come over to you, Mr. Dass. There isn't a curtain to be had in the place, sir. Nor high nor low, sir, the church, the rectory—"

"I told you," Mr. Dass said in a level voice. "I told you not to come calling at this house. You're a damned pest, if you must know. Will you kindly get it into your head that I do not intend to supply curtains for that stage? If there are no curtains on that stage, then we must manage without. Now will you please go away?"

The boy smiled at him and nodded. He'd followed his son, he said, on that particular night. He'd followed him from the Queen Victoria Hotel, interested in him because he'd been staggering. He'd followed him all the way to this house. He'd listened at the window of the dining-room and had overheard the conversation that had taken place.

"Who is it?" Mrs. Dass called gently from the sitting-room and, quite unlike himself, her husband did not reply. For nineteen years Nevil had seemed fond of them, fonder than most sons in a way, and then in a matter of moments he'd spurted out his awful truth. She'd had a sardine salad ready in the dining-room for supper, and instead of watching Nevil enjoying it she had heard herself despised. Nevil had always found it difficult to work and had spent long periods at home, doing nothing. They'd known even then that he'd perhaps been a little indulged by both of them, but on that awful evening he'd turned their indulgence into a crime, bitterly referring to the long periods he'd spent at home, eating their food and accepting pocket money. They'd ruined him. They'd wanted to keep him for ever in the house they boringly called Sweetlea. They'd made him fit for nothing, they'd made allowances for his failures when they should have told him to get on with it. It had been tedious beyond words, he said, living with all that: all his life, for as long as he could remember, he'd been bored by them. He had no love for her, he said to his mother; no love had been bought. They'd treated two daughters in a sensible manner; why couldn't they have been sensible with him? In a matter of moments he had broken his mother's heart.

"It would upset her to know a stranger heard," the boy said, smiling as though in sympathy before he turned to go away. Any mother would be upset, he added, to know that a stranger had overheard remarks like those. "But we could keep the secret, Mr. Dass. We could keep it from her. Only I couldn't perform the act on a stage without curtains."

5

〰〰〰〰〰〰〰〰〰〰〰〰〰〰〰〰〰〰〰〰〰

They clambered down the cliff-path from Sea House and set off in a western direction along the beach to Badstoneleigh. They wore fawn corduroy jeans, sandals and jerseys, Kate's red, Stephen's navy-blue. Mrs. Blakey had spoken of anoraks, and the children had obediently collected these from their rooms. But not wishing to have the bother of carrying them, they'd left them on a chair in the kitchen.

The sea was out. It pattered quietly in the distance, each small wave softly succeeding the next. Near its edge the dark, wet sand was a sheen on which footsteps kept their shape for only a minute or two. Closer to the shingle, the children walked on sand that was firmer.

Kate related her dream about little Miss Malabedeely being bullied again by Miss Shaw and Miss Rist and then Miss Malabedeely's marriage to the African bishop, who'd promised to worship her with his body. He couldn't remember if he'd dreamed, Stephen said.

They might have exchanged, again, the people of their two schools, but to Kate these people seemed for the moment irrelevant. So were the Blakeys and her mother and Stephen's father honeymooning in Cassis. Only she and Stephen were relevant. She wanted to ask him if he liked being alone with her, as he was now, on the quiet seashore on a nice day, but naturally she did not.

"I'd say we'd gone two miles," Stephen said.

There were worms of sand where they walked, and here and there embedded shells. Fluffy white clouds floated politely around the sun, as though unwilling to obscure it. Far out to sea a trawler was motionless.

For a moment she had a day-dream. They were in a sailing boat, as far out as the trawler, both of them older, eighteen or nineteen. Stephen wasn't different except for being taller; she was prettier, not round-faced. He said she was inter-

esting. She made him laugh, he said, and in any
case prettiness didn't matter. She was witty; she
had an interesting mind.

"Further," she said. "More than two miles, I'd
say." She asked him to test her on fielding positions, and he marked out on the sand the two
sets of stumps and the ten fielding positions around
them. "Silly mid-on," she said. "Silly mid-off,
square leg, slips, long-stop. Wicket-keeper, of
course."

He told her the others and she tried to mem-
orize them, the positions and the titles. He explained how the positions would change according
to the kind of bowler, fast, slow, medium, or according to whether leg-breaks were being bowled
or off-spin employed. They would also change according to the caliber of the batsman, and whether
or not a batsman was left-handed, and the state
of the wicket. Some batsmen, included in a team
because of their bowling, might find themselves
crowded by close slips. Others, in powerful form,
would force the fielders to the boundary. Kate
found it all difficult to understand, but she wanted
to understand it. She only wished she was any
good at the game herself, which unfortunately she
wasn't. She'd always preferred French cricket,
although she'd naturally never told Stephen that.

They walked on, and after what they reckoned
to be another mile they paused again and looked
back at Dynmouth. It was now a cluster of houses
with the pier protruding modestly into the sea
and, unimpressive on the cliffs, the house they
lived in themselves. On the beach a speck moved
in the same direction as they did.

There was a second figure, which they didn't
see: high above them, Timothy Gedge gazed down

from the cliff-top path. For a moment he ceased his observation of them and instead gazed out to sea, at the trawler on the horizon. The Commander was fond of saying it was the sea on which the Spanish Armada had been defeated, the sea that Adolf Hitler had not dared to cross. Timothy nodded to himself, thinking about the sailing ships of the Spanish Armada and the severe face of the German Führer, of which he'd seen pictures. On the golf-course behind him a foursome of players shouted to one another as they approached the fourteenth green.

He watched the children from Sea House again, becoming smaller on the sand. He guessed they were on their way to Badstoneleigh because of the double bill at the Pavilion. He'd seen it himself but he'd see it again just to keep latched on to them. They'd be at a loose end when it was over, which would be the time to approach them. He'd mention something about when Bond was in the sewer or whatever it was meant to be, load of rubbish really. With one hand he grasped the string handle of the carrier-bag with the Union Jack on it. In the other he clutched a fifty-p piece, a coin he'd discovered the evening before in Mrs. Abigail's purse, which carelessly she'd left on top of the refrigerator.

The children were dots on the sand, well ahead of him now, getting smaller all the time. In the other direction, becoming larger, the figure of Commander Abigail slowly advanced.

Mrs. Abigail took round Meals on Wheels with Miss Poraway as her assistant, or runner, as the title officially was. Miss Poraway wore a mauve coat and a mauve hat that clashed with it. Mrs. Abigail was neat, in blue.

They collected the food—each meal on two covered tin plates and the whole lot contained in large metal hot-boxes—from the old people's home, Wisteria Lodge. Mrs. Abigail drove the blue WRVS van, Miss Poraway sat beside her with a list of the names and addresses they were to visit that morning, the diabetics marked with a "D," as were the corresponding dinners in the metal hot-boxes. Those who didn't like gravy were indicated also, for there was often trouble where gravy was concerned.

"Roast beef and rice pudding," Miss Poraway remarked as Mrs. Abigail steered the van through the morning traffic. She went on talking about roast beef. They always liked it, she declared, and rice pudding too, come to that, though heaven alone knew why, the way they cooked it in Wisteria Lodge. She examined the list of names and addresses. Mr. Padget, 29 Prout Street, who was usually the first to receive his meal, had been struck off. "Oh dear," Miss Poraway remarked.

Mrs. Abigail nodded vaguely. The last thing she'd have chosen to listen to this morning was Miss Poraway's conversation. When she'd lain awake in the night realizing how upset and worried she was by Timothy Gedge's visit, she'd thought the one thing she wouldn't be able to do was Meals on Wheels with Miss Poraway. She'd planned to telephone Mrs. Trotter, who organized everything, and explain that she wasn't feeling well. But when the morning came it had seemed disgraceful to pretend illness and let everybody down. She had reminded herself that once or twice recently Miss Poraway hadn't been able to come because of her nasal complaint, and Mrs. Blackham, who was at least efficient, had taken her place.

"Well, I do like that," Miss Poraway was saying, pointing at a cartoon cut from the WRVS News that someone had stuck with Sellotape to the dashboard of the van. It showed an elderly couple being given their meal by a uniformed WRVS woman who was asking them if the food had been all right the last time. "Meat were luvely," the elderly wife was enthusing. "But gravy were tough," her ancient partner toothlessly protested. Since Mrs. Abigail, intent on driving, was unable to benefit from this, Miss Poraway read it out. She also read the message in italics printed beneath the cartoon, to the effect that the cartoonist responsible had for many years been officially connected with a provincial newspaper and was now, in the sunset of his life, himself the recipient of twice-weekly Meals on Wheels.

"Well, I do call that amusing," Miss Poraway said, "the whole thing."

The van drew up in Pretty Street and Miss Poraway and Mrs. Abigail got out, Miss Poraway still talking about the cartoon, saying it would tickle her brother when she told him about it. Mrs. Abigail carried the two covered plates, one on top of the other, using a tea-towel because they were hot. She opened the gate of Number 10, the terraced house of Miss Vine, whose budgerigar was unwell. Miss Poraway clattered noisily behind her, with her list and a tobacco tin for collecting the money in.

"Morning, Miss Vine!" Mrs. Abigail called out, forcing cheefulness as she opened the front door.

"Morning, dear!" Miss Poraway called out behind her.

They made their way to the kitchen, where Miss Vine was sitting on a chair beside the budgerigar cage. Usually she had a saucepan of water simmering on the electric stove, with two plates warming on top of it, waiting to receive the meal. But this morning all that had been forgotten because the budgerigar had taken a turn for the worse.

"He'll not last," Miss Vine said gloomily. "He's down in the mouth worse'n ever today."

"Oh, he'll perk up, Miss Vine," Mrs. Abigail said, mustering further cheerfulness as she emptied roast beef, potatoes, brussels sprouts and gravy onto a cold plate. "They often pine for a day or two."

Miss Poraway disagreed. She was peering through the bars of the cage, making sucking noises. She advanced the opinion that the bird wouldn't last much longer, and recommended Miss Vine to think about the purchase of a new one.

"Pop your rice pudding in the oven, shall I?" Mrs. Abigail suggested, opening the oven door and lighting the gas.

Miss Vine did not reply. She had begun to weep. Nothing would induce her, she whispered, to have another bird in the house after poor Beano had gone. You got to love a bird like a human. You got so that the first thing you did every day was to go into the kitchen and say good morning to it.

Mrs. Abigail took a soup-plate from a cupboard and emptied the rice pudding on to it. Miss Poraway should by now have collected twelve pence from Miss Vine. She should have ticked off Miss

Vine's name on her list and been ready to carry
the empty plates and covers back to the van. Two
minutes in any one house was as long as you
dared allow if the last half-dozen dinners weren't
to be stone cold. She placed the plate of rice
pudding in the oven and drew Miss Vine's attention to it. "Cub scouts," the voice of Timothy
Gedge whispered again, like some kind of echo.
All night long he'd been saying it.

"That chap that has the hardware," Miss Poraway said. "Moult, isn't it? Brings paraffin round
in a van. He's got birds. He'd really fix you up,
dear."

"Have you got your twelve p, Miss Vine?" Mrs.
Abigail asked. "Don't forget that rice pudding's in
the oven now."

"Shame really," Miss Poraway said, "when little
creatures die."

Unable to help herself, Mrs. Abigail made a
vexed noise. It was quite pointless having a runner who saw the whole thing as a social outing
and had once even sat down in a kitchen and said
she'd just rest for a minute. Half-past three it
had been when they'd arrived at Mr. Grady's, the
last name on the list, his fish and chips congealed
and inedible. As she collected up the plates and
covers herself and went without Miss Vine's twelve
p, the face of Timothy Gedge appeared in her
mind, causing her to feel sick in the stomach.
God knows, it was bad enough having to poke
your way along in the van, peering at the num-
bers of houses because your runner was incapable
of it. It was bad enough having to do every single
bit of the work, rushing like a mad thing because
the person who was meant to help you couldn't
stop talking. It was bad enough in normal cir-

cumstances, but when you hadn't slept a wink, when you'd lain there suffering from shock and disgust, it was more than any normal person could bear. Of course she'd been wrong not to telephone Mrs. Trotter. She should have told Mrs. Trotter that she was in no condition to deliver forty dinners, obstructed at every turn by Miss Poraway. She should have told her that after thirty-six years of marriage she'd discovered her husband was a homosexual, the explanation of everything.

She drove to the Heathfield estate, to Mr. and Mrs. Budd's bungalow, and to Seaway Road, to Mrs. Hutchings', and then to the elderly poor of Boughs Lane. All the time Miss Poraway talked. She talked about her niece, Gwen, who had just married an auctioneer, and about the child of another niece, who had something the matter with his ears. When they arrived at Beaconville, where three elderly people lived together, Mrs. Abigail gave her one dinner to carry but she dropped it while trying to open the hall-door. In every house they called at she forgot to collect the money. "It's dangerous, a cold when you're your age, dear," she said to Miss Trimm. "Don't like the look of her," she remarked loudly in the hall, forgetting that despite her other failings Miss Trimm's hearing had sharpened with age. They'd buried old Mr. Rine that morning, she added, and old Mrs. Crowley on Saturday.

As Mrs. Abigail struggled through the morning, she was repeatedly reminded, as though this truth sought to mock her, that she had never wished to come to Dynmouth. In London there were the cinemas she enjoyed going to, and the theater matinees. There were Harvey Nichols and Harrods to browse through, not that she ever bought anything. In Dynmouth the antiquated and inadequately heated Essoldo showed the same film for seven days at a time and the shops were totally uninteresting. With Miss Poraway chattering beside her, she reflected upon all this and recalled, as she had in the night, the course of her virginal marriage.

They had been two small, quiet people; he'd been, at twenty-nine, a gentle kind of man. She hadn't known much about life, nor had he. They'd both lived with their parents near Sutton, he already in the shipping business from which he'd retired when they came to Dynmouth, she working in her father's estate agency, doing part-time secretarial duties and arranging the flowers in the outer office. Both sets of parents had been against the marriage, but she and Gordon had persisted, drawn closer by the opposition. They'd been married in a church she'd always gone to as a child and afterward there was a reception in the Mansfield Hotel, nearby and convenient, and then she and Gordon had gone to Cumberland. She'd been trim and neat and pretty. She'd powdered her face in the lavatory on the train, examining her reflection in the mirror, thinking she wasn't bad-looking. Twice before she'd had proposals of marriage and had rejected them because she couldn't feel for the men they came from.

She hadn't known what to expect of marriage, not precisely. They'd shared a bed in Cumberland and she had comforted Gordon because nothing was quite right. Everything took getting used to, she said, saying the same thing night after night, softly in the darkness. You had to learn things, she whispered, supposing that the

activity which Gordon found difficult required
practice, like tennis. It didn't matter, she said.
They went for long, pleasant walks in Cumberland. They enjoyed having breakfast together in
the hotel dining-room.

She remembered clothes she had then, on her
honeymoon and afterward: suits and dresses,
many of them in shades of blue, her favorite
color, coats and scarves and shoes. They had
friends, other couples, the Watsons, the Turners,
the Godsons. There were dinner-parties, bridge
was played, there were excursions to the theater,
and dances. Once a man she'd never met before,
a man called Peter who didn't seem to have a wife,
kept dancing with her in the Godsons' house,
holding her very close, in a way that quite upset
her and yet was pleasurable. A year later, when
the war had started and Gordon was already in
the Navy, she'd met this Peter in Bond Street
and he'd invited her to have a drink, reaching for
her elbow. She'd felt quite frightened and hadn't
accepted the invitation.

After the war she and Gordon moved to another part of London. They didn't see their pre-
war friends again and didn't replace them, it was
hard to know why. Gordon seemed a little different, hardened by the war. She was different
herself, looking back on it: she'd lost a certain
naturalness, she didn't feel vivacious. It was a
disappointment not having children, but there
were millions of couples who didn't have children,
and of course there were far worse things than
that, as the war had just displayed.

At no time had she ever felt that Gordon was
perverted. At no time, not even vaguely, had such
a notion occurred to her, nor did she even think

that he was not as other men. Since other marriages were without children she presumed that other couples, in their millions, shared their own difficulty. And it was theirs, she considered, not simply Gordon's. They were both at fault if fault it could be called, which she doubted: more likely, it was the way they were made. She didn't think about it, it was not mentioned.

But now it was everywhere, clamoring at her, shouting down the years of her virginal marriage. The bungalow they'd come to end their lives in was rich already with this new and simple truth, with a logic any child could understand. That Timothy Gedge, so awful in his drunkenness and apparently in himself, should have released it was even fitting. In his drunkenness he had seemed like something out of a cheap Sunday newspaper: her marriage was like that also, as her husband was, underhand and vicious in a small town. Only the truth had passed from Timothy Gedge, the unarguable strength of it, the power and the glory of it. She didn't want to think about Timothy Gedge, to dwell on him or to consider him in any way whatsoever. Nothing could change the truth he had uttered, and that for the moment was enough.

"Well, I do think it's a lot, you know," Miss Poraway was remarking. "Forty dinners for just two pairs of hands."

Mrs. Abigail, taking another couple of plates from the back of the van, was aware only that her companion was speaking; the content of her statement did not register. All during the night, over and over again, she had found it absurd that she'd ever considered herself a happy woman. And in the same repetitious way she had recalled the scene she'd interrupted the evening before by announcing that supper was ready: Gordon and the boy seated in the sitting-room before the cozy glow of the electric fire, drinking sherry.

"Oh, for heaven's sake, Miss Poraway!" she cried as another rice pudding slipped from Miss Poraway's fingers. "What kind of fool are you?"

On his walk, in his brown overcoat, not carrying his towel and swimming-trunks, Commander Abigail was upset also. At breakfast nothing had been said, which perhaps wasn't unusual, but afterward she'd left the house without saying anything either. On a Thursday there was invariably some instruction about the lunch she'd left him, since Thursday was her day for doing her charity with the elderly. Yet not only had she not said anything but as far as he'd been able to ascertain she hadn't left him any lunch.

Like his wife, the Commander hadn't slept. Lying awake in the room next to hers, the episode with the boy had kept recurring to him, the sweat running on the boy's face and his hands protruding from the sleeves of the dog's-tooth suit and his voice making its extraordinary statements. When they had eventually managed to get him out of the house he'd helped her to carry the remaining dishes from the dining-room, a thing he never did. He'd repeated several more times that everything the boy had said was drunken nonsense. He'd said he was sorry the incident had occurred and had asked her if she'd like him to make her some Ovaltine. As far as he could remember, she hadn't replied to anything except to shake her head when he'd mentioned Ovaltine.

As he walked on the sand, the Commander attempted to reassure himself. He had often watched the cub scouts playing rounders on the beach. The Gedge boy, who apparently spied on the entire population of Dynmouth, had no doubt seen him. But there was nothing furtive or dubious about watching a crowd of lads playing a game on the sands, any more than there was about carting food to the elderly. The boy's unfortunately unsober condition and his inadequate ability to express himself had clearly made for confusion. Without a shred of evidence he had employed an innuendo when what he should have said was that any normal English person could not but approve of the sight of young English lads in their uniforms, and would naturally pause to observe how they played a game.

But with all this argument, contrived for his own reassurance and for retailing to his wife, the Commander failed in the end to convince himself. The truth kept poking itself up, like a weed in a garden. You pushed it away to the back recesses of your mind, but it crept and crawled about and then annoyingly broke through the surface again. The truth was that the unfortunate boy had somehow pried his way into an area that was private, an area that naturally didn't concern anyone else. Commander Abigail didn't even like the area: it caused him shame and guilt to consider it, he tried not to think about it. That occasionally it ran away with him was a simple misfortune, and was always distasteful in retrospect.

Progressing slowly, seeming older by years than he had seemed on this beach the day before, more bent and huddled, the Commander shook his head in time to the steps he took. It puzzled him beyond measure that the boy should have stumbled upon this private area. He racked his brain, he cast his mind back. Pictures he did not wish to see passed before him in dazzling procession. Voices spoke. He saw a figure that was himself, the villain of his peepshow. His own face smiled at him and then the pictures ceased. Again, more in control of matters, he cast his mind back.

When the boy had first come to the house he'd been more of a child and had naturally been treated as a child. Once or twice, when gesturing him into the dining-room for supper, he'd laid a hand on his shoulder. Once or twice, while the boy was squatting on the floor polishing the linoleum surround, he had playfully touched his head, as in passing one might pat the head of a dog. There was a game they'd played a few times when Edith was out of the house, a rough-and-tumble sort of thing, perfectly harmless. There was Blind Man's Buff, and a thing called Find the Penny, in which he himself stood like a statue in the center of the sitting-room while the boy searched him all over, rifling through his pockets for a hidden coin. A perfectly harmless little game it was, and had afforded both of them amusement. Naturally enough, they hadn't played it since the boy had entered adolescence.

That had been, and was, their innocent relationship. Yet the boy had insinuated so knowingly that the Commander had begun to wonder if perhaps he suffered from lapses of memory. Had rough-and-tumbles not been as he recalled, had their Blind Man's Buff ended differently? Or could it be that the boy had taken his spying into the Essoldo Cinema? He pushed that from his mind, and his mind filled instead with the face of a lad on a bicycle who'd once been friendly, and the face of another who didn't mind playing Find the Penny in the hut on the golf-course. There was the red-haired cub scout who liked talking about his badges.

He turned and walked, more slowly still, back towards Dynmouth.

Like Dynmouth's Essoldo, the Pavilion in Badstoneleigh was old. Swing-doors on either side of the box-office in the small foyer led to an inner foyer, carpeted and dimly lit. On brown walls there were large framed photographs of the stars of the thirties: Loretta Young, Carole Lombard, Annabella, Don Ameche, Robert Young, Joan Crawford. There were cigarette burns on the carpet, and here and there the brown of the walls had been rubbed away to reveal a pinkish surface beneath. There was a kiosk which sold confectionery.

The auditorium itself was rather similar, brown-walled and patchy. Lights were kept low, to cover a multitude of small defects. The upholstery of the seats had once been crimson: it had faded to a faint red glow, balding, springs occasionally exposed. Pale curtains with butterflies on them had once been a blaze of color but now were nondescript. The smell was similar to the Essoldo's smell: of Jeyes' Fluid and old cigarette smoke.

In the stalls Timothy Gedge sat three rows behind the children from Sea House, with the carrier-bag by his feet. Having eaten two packets of bacon-flavored potato crisps, he had purchased another tube of Rowntree's Fruit Gums, which he was now enjoying while waiting for the lights to

dim. Once Stephen looked round and Timothy
smiled at him.

The dim lights were dimmed some more, and
advertisements for local shops and eating places
began. There was a film about the construction
of a bridge in Scotland, two trailers, a list of
future attractions, and then *Dr. No.* The plot,
familiar to Timothy, presented no new depths on
a second investigation. Attempts were made to
destroy James Bond by shooting him, placing a
tarantula in his bed, poisoning his vodka, and
drowning him. Each attempt failed due to the
mental and physical inadequacies of its perpe-
trator. The story ended happily, with James Bond
in a boat with a girl.

The lights went up and a picture of the confectionery kiosk appeared on the screen. An attached message announced that sweets, chocolate
and nuts were available in the foyer.

Timothy rose when Stephen and Kate did, glad
that they had decided on refreshment. "Cheers,"
he said, standing behind them in a queue.

They knew him by sight. He was a boy who was
always on his own, often to be seen watching
television programs in the windows of electrical
shops. He always wore the same light-colored
clothes, matching his light-colored hair.

"Hullo," Kate said.

"I see you over Dynmouth way."

"We live in Dynmouth."

"You do." He smiled at them in turn. "Your
mum just married his dad."

"Yes, she did."

They bought packets of nuts, and Timothy
bought another tube of fruit gums. When he returned to the stalls he sat beside Kate. "Care for

a gum?" he said, offering them both the tube.
They took one each, and he noticed that they
nudged one another with their elbows, amused
because he had offered them fruit gums.

Diamonds Are Forever took the same course
as its predecessor. James Bond ran a similar
gamut of attempts to bring his life to a halt. He
again ended with a girl, a different one this time
and not in a boat.

"We'd easily get the half-five bus," Timothy
said, offering his gums again, blocking their passage and the passage of two elderly women who
were endeavoring to pass into the foyer.

"Come along then, please," an usherette, elderly
also, cried. "Move there, sonny."

In a bunch the women and the three children
passed through the swing-doors into the brown
foyer.

"We're going back by the beach," Kate said.

"Great." He blinked against the sudden glare
of sunshine on the street. He could see they were
surprised that he'd latched on to them, but it
didn't matter. He walked beside them on the pavement, three abreast, so that pedestrians coming
toward them had to step out into the street. He
swung the carrier-bag with the Union Jack on it.
It was hard to know what to say to them. He said:

"D'you know that Miss Lavant? She fancies the
doctor, Greenslade."

They'd seen Miss Lavant on the promenade
and about the town, always walking slowly, sometimes with a neat wicker basket. Kate had often
thought she was beautiful. She hadn't known she
was in love with Dr. Greenslade, who had a wife
already, and three children.

"She fancied the man for twenty years," Timothy said.

It explained Miss Lavant. There was a nervous quality about her, which was now explained also: her nerves were on edge as she slowly perambulated. Her eyes, always a little cast down, were being well-behaved, resisting the temptation to dart about in search of Dr. Greenslade.

"She's in a bedsitting-room in Pretty Street," Timothy said. "To the left of the hall-door." He laughed remembering again how he'd insisted that Miss Lavant was Mrs. Abigail's sister. "I looked in the window once and she was eating a boiled egg, with another boiled egg in an egg-cup across the table from her. She was chatting sixteen to the dozen, entertaining Greenslade even though he wasn't there. Three o'clock in the afternoon, everyone out in their deck-chairs."

He had a funny way of talking, Kate thought. Yet he made her feel sorry for Miss Lavant, a woman she'd hardly thought about before. It wasn't difficult to imagine the bedsitting-room in Pretty Street, on the left of the hall-door, and the two boiled eggs in two egg-cups.

Stephen felt sorry for Miss Lavant also, and resolved to examine her more closely. She never walked on the beach, and without ever thinking about it he had assumed she didn't because she didn't want to spoil her shoes. He thought he'd once heard someone saying that about her, but it now seemed that reason wasn't the right one: the beach was hardly the place to catch a glimpse of Dr. Greenslade, with his black bag and his stethoscope, which he sometimes wore round his neck on the street.

"I wouldn't mind a beer," Timothy said, adding

that the only trouble was that the Badstoneleigh supermarkets wouldn't serve a person who was under age. "There's an off-license in Lass Lane," he said, "where the bloke's half blind."

On the way to Lass Lane they told him their names and he said he was Timothy Gedge. He advised them not to come into the off-license with him. He offered to buy them a tin of beer each, but they said they'd rather have Coca-Cola.

"You eighteen, laddie?" the proprietor enquired as he reached down a pint tin of Worthington E. He wore thick pebble spectacles, behind which his eyes were unnaturally magnified. Timothy said he'd be nineteen on the twenty-fourth of next month.

"Gemini," the man said. Timothy smiled, not knowing what the man was talking about.

"You often get loonies in joints like that," he remarked on the street. "They drink the sauce and it softens their brains for them." He laughed, and then added that he'd been drunk as a cork himself, actually, the night before. He'd woken in a shocking state, his mouth like the Sahara desert.

They walked toward the seashore and sat on the rocks, beside a pool with anemones in it. They drank the Coca-Cola and Timothy consumed the Worthington E, saying it was just what he needed after being on the sauce the night before. When he'd finished he threw the beer-tin into the pool with the anemones in it.

They began to walk toward Dynmouth. The sea was coming in. There were more seagulls than there had been that morning, on the cliffs and on the sea itself. The same trawler was in the same position on the horizon.

"Are you at school then?" he asked, and they

told him about their two boarding-schools. He
knew they were at boarding-schools, but it was
something to say to the kids. He said he was at
Dynmouth Comprehensive himself, a terrible
dump. There was a woman called Wilkinson who
couldn't keep order in a bird-cage. Stringer, the
headmaster, was rubbish; the P.E. man went
after the girls. Sex and cigarettes were the main
things, and going up to the Youth Center to smash
the legs off the table-tennis tables. There was a
girl called Grace Rumblebow who had to be seen
to be believed.

"D'you know Plant?" he said. "Down at the
Artilleryman's?"

"Plant?" Stephen said.

"He's always hanging about toilets." He laughed.
"After women."

He explained to them what he meant by that,
about how he'd run into Mr. Plant in the small
hours, wearing only a shirt. He described the
scene he'd witnessed in his mother's bedroom,
during *A Man Called Ironside*.

They didn't say anything, and after a few
moments the silence hardened and became awkward. Kate looked out to sea, wishing he hadn't
joined them. She stared at the petrified trawler.

"Your mum on a honeymoon?" he said.

She nodded. In France, she said. Smiling, he
turned to Stephen.

"Your dad'll enjoy that, Stephen. Your dad'll
be all jacked up."

"Jacked up?"

"Steaming for it, Stephen."

He laughed. Stephen didn't reply.

His face was like an axe-edge, Kate thought,
with another axe-edge cutting across it: the line

of the cheek-bones above the empty cheeks. His fingers were rather long, slender like a girl's.

"Your mum has a touch of style, Kate. I heard that remarked in a vegetable shop. I'd call her an eyeful, Kate. Peachy."

"Yes." She muttered, her face becoming red because she felt embarrassed.

"He knows his onions, Stephen? Your dad, eh?"

Again Stephen didn't reply.

"Did you mind me saying it, Stephen? He's a fine man, your dad, they're well matched. 'It's great it happened,' the woman in the shop said, buying leeks at the time. 'It's great for the children,' she said. D'you reckon it's great, Kate? D'you like having Stephen?"

Her face felt like a sunset. She turned it away in confusion, pretending to examine the gray-brown clay of the cliff.

"Dynmouth people can't mind their own business," she heard Timothy Gedge saying. "They're always like that, gassing their heads off in a public shop. The best place for Dynmouth people is in their coffins." Laughter rippled from him, quite gently, softly. "D'you ever go to funerals, Kate?"

"Funerals?"

"When a person dies, Kate."

She shook her head. They progressed in silence for a moment. Then Timothy Gedge said:

"Ever read books, Stephen? *The Cannibal's Daughter* by Henrietta Man?"

He laughed and they laughed also, a little uneasily. In a woman's voice he said:

"When's it unlucky to have a cat behind you?"

They said they didn't know.

"When you're a mouse. See it, Stephen? Cross

an elephant and a kangaroo, Kate? What d'you get?"

She shook her head.

"Dirty great holes all over Australia, Kate." He smiled at her. He said he was going in for the Spot the Talent competition at the Easter Fête. "As a matter of fact," he said, "I'm looking for a wedding-dress. I have an act planned with a wedding-dress."

"You mean you dress up as a bride?" Kate said.

He told them. He told them about the bath in Swines' building yard. He repeated the information he'd passed on to the Abigails and to Mr. Plant: that George Joseph Smith had bought fish for the late Miss Munday, and eggs for Mrs. Burnham and Miss Lofty. They didn't comment on any of it.

"I often saw your dad about the place, Stephen," he said. "With a pair of field-glasses."

"He's an ornithologist."

"What d'you call that, Stephen?"

"He writes books about birds."

"Is your mum's wedding-dress in a trunk, Stephen?"

Stephen stopped, staring down at the sand. The toe of his right sandal slowly drew a circle. Kate looked from one face to the other, Stephen's screwed up with bewilderment, Timothy Gedge's smiling pleasantly.

"I saw your dad with it, Stephen." He spoke softly, his smile still there. "I was looking in the window of that Primrose Cottage."

They didn't say anything. Both of them were frowning. They moved on again and Timothy Gedge went with them, swinging his carrier-bag.

"You didn't mind me looking in at the window,

Stephen? Only I was passing at the time. Your dad was packing his gear up. He took the wedding-dress out of the trunk and put it back again. A faded kind of trunk, Stephen. Green it would be in its day."

There was another silence, and then they ran away from him, leaving him standing there, shocked to stillness by their abrupt movement. He couldn't understand why they were suddenly running over the sand. He thought for a moment that it might be some kind of game, that their running would cease as suddenly as it had begun, that they'd stand like statues on the sand, waiting for him to catch up with them. But they didn't. They ran on and on.

He took a fruit gum from what remained of the tube. He stood there sucking it, watching the seagulls.

6

"I think I'm going to try and cut the grass," Quentin Featherston said as he and Lavinia washed up the dishes after the Mothers' Union tea-party, which had been even more trying than usual. When Miss Poraway had mentioned a Tupperware party Mrs. Stead-Carter had gone much further than she'd ever gone before. She'd pointed out that it was stupid to talk about Tupperware parties as a means of raising funds since funds raised at Tupperware parties naturally went to the manufacturers of Tupperware. Miss Poraway said there were other parties of a similar nature, at which suede jackets and coats were modeled, and sometimes underclothes. In greater exasperation Mrs. Stead-Carter said she'd never heard anything as silly in her life: the Mothers' Union in Dynmouth had neither Tupperware nor suede clothes nor underclothes at its disposal, Miss Poraway's whole line of conversation was a waste of time. She failed to see, Mrs. Stead-Carter finally declared, why it was that Miss Poraway, who had never been a mother, should concern herself with the Mothers' Union in the first place. Miss Poraway had at once become tearful and Lavinia had had to take her to the kitchen. Mrs. Abigail, she'd told Lavinia, had called her a fool that morning just because she dropped a tin plate when they were doing Meals on Wheels. Dynmouth was becoming a nasty kind of place.

"Poor Miss Poraway," Quentin said as they washed the tea dishes, and Lavinia—not feeling agreeably disposed toward Miss Poraway—did not say anything. She wished she could say she was sorry now, not in the middle of the night when he was asleep. It wasn't his fault; he did his best. It wasn't easy for him, all those women bickering and only a handful of people out of Dynmouth's thousands ever setting foot in his church, and Mr. Peniket sighing over the decline of church life. She wished she could say she knew she was being difficult and edgy, taking it out on him because she'd been denied another child. But although she tried to speak, actually tried to form words and force them out of her mouth, no words came. They washed and dried in silence, and then the twins appeared with lemon cake all over them.

"Tidying," Susannah said.

"No, that's not true," Lavinia protested. "You've been eating cake."

"Tidying crumbs," Susannah said.

"I wish just once you'd tell the truth." Lavinia was angry. A day didn't pass now during which it failed to occur to her that she had borne two congenital liars. Jam fell like rain, cake had to be tidied on the floor. "Mouses making buns," Deborah had said the afternoon before when flour and raisins had been discovered in a corner. "Mouses can have party," Susannah had added. "And games," Deborah said. "Mouses can have games if they want to."

Lavinia, still scolding, wiped the crumbs from their cardigans.

"Twins didn't eat one crumb," Susannah assured her.

"Mouses did," Deborah explained. "Two mouses came out of the chair."

"You come and watch me cutting the grass," Quentin suggested, but the twins shook their heads, not understanding because such a long time had passed since there'd last been grass-cutting. They suspected, however, that whatever it was their father intended to do the activity would prove dull to watch. Watching wasn't often interesting.

Already Quentin had begun to tidy up the garden for the Easter Fête. He'd pulled up the first spring weeds from the flower-beds, little shoots of dandelion and dock and Scotch grass. He'd poked at the soil with a hoe to give it a fresh look.

He'd cleared away a lot of last autumn's leaves.

In the garage he examined a machine called a Suffolk Punch, a lawnmower that was now exactly ten years old. It had been lying idle since a Saturday afternoon in October, with begonia tubers in its grass-box and a bundle of yellowing newspapers balanced on its engine. The bundle was tied together with string and had been left there and forgotten one morning when Lavinia was in a hurry. She collected old newspapers and milk-bottle tops and silver paper for the girl guides.

Quentin hated the Suffolk Punch. He hated it especially now as he dragged it out of its corner in the garage, squeezed it between his Vauxhall Viva estate car and the twins' tricycles, and rolled it on to the uneven surface in front of the garage doors. He pulled at the starting device, a coil of plastic-covered wire that snapped obediently back into position after each attempt to engage the engine. No sound came from the engine, no promising little cough, and naturally enough no roar of action. You could spend all day pulling the plastic-covered coil, the skin coming off your hands, sweat gathering all over you. You could take the plug out and examine it, not knowing what you were looking for. You could poke at it with a screwdriver or a piece of wire and wipe it with a piece of rag. You could take it to the kitchen and put it under the grill of the electric cooker in order to get it hot, without knowing why it should be hot.

He pulled the coil of plastic-covered wire forty times, pausing between every ten or a dozen efforts. A smell of petrol developed, as it usually did.

"All right then, Mr. Feather?" the voice of
Timothy Gedge enquired.

The boy was standing there, smiling at him for
the second time that day. He attempted to smile
back at him, but found it difficult. The same uneasy feeling he'd experienced that morning returned, and he realized now why it came: of all
the people of Dynmouth this boy in his adolescence was the single exception. He could feel no
Christian love for him.

"Hullo, Timothy."

"Having trouble with the cutter then?"

"I'm afraid I am." In the garage there was a
kind of spanner, a hexagonal tube with a bar
going through it, that was designed to remove
plugs from engines. He went to look for it, remembering that he had used it a couple of times
since October, trying to take the plugs out of the
estate car. He disliked the estate car almost as
much as the Suffolk Punch, which was why he
preferred to make his way around the streets of
Dynmouth on a bicycle. He disliked the English
Electric washing-machine in the kitchen, especially the button which was meant to operate the
door-release and quite often didn't. He disliked
the transistor radio he'd saved up for to get
Lavinia for her birthday three years ago. No
sound had emerged from it for six months: spare
parts were hard to get, Dynmouth Hi-Fi Boutique
informed him.

To his surprise, he found the hexagonal spanner on the ledge in the garage where it was meant
to be. He returned to the lawnmower with it.
Timothy Gedge was still standing there. The way
he kept hanging about him, Quentin wondered if

he had perhaps decided to become a clergyman again.

"You find what you want then, sir? Only I spoke to Dass about the curtains, Mr. Feather."

"Curtains?"

"I mentioned curtains to you this morning, sir."

Quentin unscrewed the brass nipple on the end of the plug and disengaged the lead. He fitted the hexagonal spanner around the plug and turned it. The plug was wet with petrol and oil. There was a shell of carbon around the points. He never knew if there should be carbon there or not.

"Dass is going to donate them, sir."

"Donate?"

"A set of curtains, sir."

"Good heavens, there's no need for that."

He returned to the garage and tore a piece from one of the yellowing newspapers. He wiped the points of the plug with it. "I shall have to heat it up," he said.

Timothy watched him as he went hurriedly toward the house. He hadn't even listened about the curtains. For all the man cared, the competition mightn't take place, nor the Easter Fête either. He began to follow the clergyman into the house, and then changed his mind. No point in taking trouble with him; no point in explaining that he'd walked all the way up to the blooming rectory to set his mind at rest. Stupid it was, saying you had to heat up a thing out of a lawnmower.

Old Ape ambled past him on the way to the back door for his dinner and his scraps, carrying a red plastic bucket. Timothy addressed him, gesturing, but the old man ignored him.

"Hullo," a voice said, and then another voice said it.

He looked and saw the clergyman's two children, known to him from past association.

"Cheers," he said.

"We got cake," Susannah said.

"We ate lemon cake," Deborah said.

He nodded at them understandingly. Any cake they could get hold of he advised them to eat. He said they could have a picnic if they brought some cake out into the garden, but they didn't seem to understand him.

"We're good girls," Susannah said.

"You're good definitely."

"We're good girls," Deborah said.

He nodded at them again. He told them a story about a gooseberry in a lift and one about holes in Australia. "You're out with a blonde," he said, "you see the wife coming?"

They knew it was all funny because of the funny voice he put on. He was doing it specially for them.

"Ever read books?" he said. *Tea for Two* by Roland Butta?"

They laughed delightedly, clapping their hands together, and Timothy Gedge closed his eyes. The lights flickered in the darkness around him, and then the limelight blazed and he stood in its yellow flame. "Big hand, friends!" cried Hughie Green, his famous eyebrow raised, his voice twanging pleasantly into his microphone. "Big hand for the boy with the funnies!" All over Dynmouth the limelight blazed on Dynmouth's television screens, and people watched, unable not to. "Big hand for the Timothy G Show!" cried Hughie Green in Pretty Street and Once Hill and

High Park Avenue. Like a bomb the show exploded, the funnies, the falsetto, Timothy himself. Clearly they heard him in the Cornerways flats and in Sea House and in the Dasses' house and in the lounges of the Queen Victoria Hotel. From the blazing screen he smiled at the proprietor of the Artilleryman's Friend and at his mother and Rose-Ann and his aunt the dressmaker and at his father, wherever he was. He smiled in the Youth Center and in the house of Stringer the headmaster and in the house of Miss Wilkinson with her *charrada*. He smiled at Brehon O'Hennessy, wherever he was too, and in the houses of everyone in 3A. He thanked them all, leaning out of the blaze in order to be closer to them, saying they were great, saying they were lovely.

In the rectory garden the twins still laughed and clapped, more amused than ever because he was still standing there with his eyes closed, smiling at them. The most marvelous smile they'd ever seen, the biggest in the world.

Commander Abigail was not a heavy drinker, but after his gloomy morning walk he had felt the need of consolation and had found it in the Disraeli Lounge of the Queen Victoria Hotel. He had entered the lounge at twenty-past two and had ordered a sandwich and a large measure of whiskey, which he'd consumed quickly. He had attempted to obtain more whiskey, but was informed that the bar was now closed until five-thirty. Unable to face his wife in the bungalow in High Park Avenue and fearful of meeting her in one of the shops if he hung about the town, he set off for another walk along the beach, striking out this time in the opposite direction from the one he'd taken that morning. With the passing of time, he began to think that he'd taken far too glum a view of the situation. His foremost maxim—of never admitting defeat, of sticking to your guns through thick and thin—came to his aid and offered the first shreds of comfort since the unpleasantness of the night before. At half-past five he returned to the Disraeli Lounge and at ten to eight, his spirits further lightened by his intake of whiskey, he entered the bungalow, whistling.

"Where on earth have you been, Gordon?" she demanded as soon as he appeared in the sitting-room. She was half-heartedly knitting, with the television on, the sound turned low.

"Walking," he replied briskly. "I reckon I walked twenty miles today."

"Your dinner'll be as dry as dust." She rose, sticking her knitting needles into a ball of blue wool. Laughter emerged softly from the television set as a man hit another man in the stomach. She could smell the whiskey even though the length of the room was between them.

"I want to talk to you," he said.

"If you're drunk, Gordon—"

"I am not drunk."

"There's been enough drunkenness in this house."

"Are you talking about young Gedge?"

"I've been sitting here worried sick."

"About me, dear?"

"I've been waiting for you for six hours. What on earth am I to think? I didn't sleep a wink last night." •

"Sit down, my dear."

"I want to leave Dynmouth, Gordon. I want to

leave this bungalow and everything else. I thought
I'd go mad with that woman this morning."

"What woman's that, dear?"

"Oh, for heaven's sake, what's it matter what
woman it is? You've never displayed the slightest
interest in what I do. You've never asked me, not
once, how anything has gone, or where I've been
or whom I've seen."

"I'm sure I've asked about your Meals on
Wheels, dear, I remember distinctly—"

"You know perfectly well you haven't. You're
incapable of taking an interest in me. You're
incapable of having a normal relationship with
me. You marry me and you're incapable of performing the sexual act."

"That's not true."

"Of course it's true."

"You're sixty-four, dear, I'm sixty-five. Elderly
people don't—"

"We weren't elderly in 1938."

Her bluntness astounded him. Never in their
whole married life had she spoken like that before. No matter how tedious she was in other
ways, he had always assumed that it wasn't in
her nature to be coarse, and certainly she'd never
displayed evidence of the inclination. Prim and
proper had always been her way, and he'd appreciated her for it.

She returned to her chair and sat down. The
two sharp points of red that had come into her
cheeks the night before were there again. If he
wanted food, she remarked unpleasantly, it was
in the oven.

"We had a nasty experience last night, Edith.
We're both upset."

He crossed to the window table. The decanter,

diminished by Timothy Gedge, still contained a few inches of amber liquid. He poured some for them both, and carried her glass to her.

She took it from him and sipped at the sweet sherry, reminded by its taste that he bought it specially because she didn't like sweet sherry. It was at least fifteen years since he'd carried a glass across a room to her.

"Young Gedge didn't know what he was on about, Edith. I'll tell you one thing, he'll never enter Number Eleven High Park Avenue again."

"The drink you gave him brought the truth out, Gordon. He spoke nothing but the truth."

"Well, it's not our business—"

"It's our business what he said about you."

In the Disraeli Lounge he had planned what he'd say. He had prepared the sentences in his mind. He said:

"I didn't really notice that he said anything about me, dear."

"You know what he said, Gordon."

"As far as I could gather, what he was saying was some nonsense about the Easter Fête. Well, I dare say there's no reason—"

"Are you or are you not a homosexual, Gordon?"

He remained calm. Signals operated in his brain. Further prepared sentences came readily to his lips. He returned to the window table and poured himself the dregs of the sherry. He remained by the table, holding the edge of it with one hand because the hand was shaking.

"For young Gedge to say," he said quietly, "that he has seen a person watching boys playing rounders hardly makes that person a homosexual. I am a normal married man, Edith, as well you know."

"No, Gordon."

"I am not a passionate man, my dear. I prefer things in moderation."

"Thirty-six years' abstinence is more than moderation, Gordon."

Her voice was as soft and as deliberate as his. She shook her head and stared into the fire and then at the television screen. The program had changed: a collie dog was now gamboling about, apparently seeking aid for a distressed shepherd.

"I don't always feel well," he said, which was another statement he had prepared. He paused, searching his mind for something else to say, something that might move the emphasis away from himself. He said:

"I honestly didn't know you still had interests like that, Edith."

"I cannot remain married to a man who is known to be a homosexual."

He shivered. He recalled again the game of Find the Penny, and the face of the cub scout who liked to talk about his badges. Once in the Essoldo Cinema a lad had moved away when he'd done no more than offer him a piece of chocolate in the darkness. Once on the promenade a boy had laughed at him.

"It's not true what he said. I've no interest in cub scouts. I swear by almighty God, Edith."

She looked away from him, not wishing to have to see him. She said there was no need to discuss it: she wanted to leave Dynmouth and to leave him, that was all.

"I never did anything wrong, Edith."

She didn't speak. Still standing by the window, he began to weep.

His mother was out when he arrived back at
Cornerways, and so was Rose-Ann. In the small
grease-laden kitchen the dishes they'd eaten a
meal off were in the sink. On the draining-board
there was a piece of butter, half wrapped in its
original paper, with scrapings from toast adher-
ing to it. There were two tins, one that had contained peaches and the other half full of spaghetti. His mother would be at Thursday-evening
Bingo, Rose-Ann out in Len's car.

He knocked what remained of the spaghetti
into a saucepan, and placed four slices of Mother's
Pride bread under the grill of the electric cooker.
He hunted in a cupboard for another tin of
peaches—or pineapples or pears, he didn't mind.
He knew he wouldn't find any. He wouldn't even
find a tin of condensed milk, because his mother
always opened tins on the day she bought them.
In Mrs. Abigail's cupboards there were tins and
jars of all sorts of things, fruit cocktail, chicken-
and-ham paste, steak-and-kidney pie, Gentleman's
Relish. He poked through a jumble of dusters
and Brasso, a broken electric iron, clothes pegs
and a jelly mold. Finding nothing edible, he
closed the cupboard door.

He went on thinking about Mrs. Abigail. When
he'd finished eating the spaghetti he'd call round
and see her. He'd explain that in the kerfuffle
last night he hadn't been paid for the jobs he'd
done. He'd say he was sorry for the kerfuffle,
which was what she'd want to hear. He'd blame
it all on the beer and the sherry, he'd say with
a laugh she'd been right to tell him not to take
any. Then he'd raise the subject of the dog's-tooth
suit.

The spaghetti sizzled in the saucepan, the toast

flared beneath the grill. Unlike his mother and
Rose-Ann he didn't object to burnt toast, so he
buttered it as it was, not pausing to toast the
other side of it. He poked at the spaghetti with a
knife, separating the congealed orange-and-white
mess.

The Abigails were still in their sitting-room
when the doorbell rang. The Commander, having
ceased to weep, was sitting on the sofa. Mrs.
Abigail was in her armchair. The television set,
still turned low, continued to perform.

On hearing the doorbell, the Commander's re-
action was affected by the events of the day and
the matter they had just been so emotionally dis-
cussing: irrationally, he believed he was being
visited by the police. Mrs. Abigail, similarly affected, believed that what she'd been dreading
all day had now come about: the parents of some
child had arrived at the bungalow.

"I'd better go," she said.

"No, no. No, please—"

"We can't just sit here, Gordon."

She rose slowly. She passed close to him as she
crossed the room, averting her eyes. He had
sobbed like a child. Tears had run on his cheeks
as she had never seen tears coming from an adult
man before. He had collapsed on to the sofa,
holding his face with his hands, shrunken-looking.
She hadn't said anything. She'd even felt quite
calm, only thinking that in the oven his dinner
would be in cinders now.

In the hall she dreaded the advent of a parent
less than she had dreaded it earlier. It was less
terrible because her marriage was over. She had
spoken and he, by his tears, had confessed:

everything was different. She felt as though she had regained consciousness in a hospital bed after some physical calamity, that because of injury and loss she must now map out a new existence for herself.

"Cheers," Timothy Gedge said when she opened the hall-door.

The sight of him dismayed her. Some of the strength she had gained through coming to terms with the truth oozed out of her. She attempted to be brisk, but could not.

"Well?" she said, and then cleared her throat because her voice was croaking.

"I come up to say I'm sorry, Mrs. Abigail. If there was any inconvenience, due to the sherry and the beer—"

"The Commander and I would rather you didn't return here, Timothy."

"I was trying to play a joke on you, dressing up and that. I thought we were on for charades. I didn't mean to cause a kerfuffle."

"It would be better if you went." She shook her head at him. She tried to smile, attempting to indicate that she knew it wasn't his fault, that he hadn't known what he was doing. "The Commander and I are upset, Timothy."

She heard a sound in the hall behind her and then Gordon was pulling at the hall-door, opening it wider and shouting. In a high voice he used expressions she'd never heard before. His face had reddened. His eyes had a wildness about them, as though he might attack the boy, who was looking at him with his mouth open.

"The kind of person you are, Gedge," the Commander shouted, "you should be locked away. You're a bloody young devil. You can't mind your own business. Can you, Gedge?" shrieked the Commander. "Can you mind your own business?"

"I do the best I can, sir."

"You can't tell the truth, Gedge. You're trying on a blackmail attempt. You can be had up for blackmail, you know."

"We'll keep the secret, Commander. No harm at all. Easy as skinning a cat, Commander."

"You deserve to be birched. You spy on innocent people. You tell nothing but lies."

"I wouldn't ever tell a lie, sir."

"You bloody young pup!" screamed the Commander.

There was silence then. A door opened in a bungalow across the avenue. A figure stood in the rectangle of light, attracted by the noise. The Commander was quietly weeping.

"It's all right, Gordon," she said in a flat, emotionless voice. "It's all right, dear."

She tried to close the door but he was grasping the edge of it, supporting himself against it. He moaned and sobbed, clinging to the door. He said he thought he would commit suicide.

The boy didn't go away. She couldn't understand why he didn't turn and go.

"Lies," her husband sobbed, in a voice that was now so soft it could scarcely be heard. Spittle was running down his chin and dripping on to his clothes. His fingers still gripped the edge of the door, his small body was pressed against it. He'd been shy and fair-haired the Sunday afternoon he'd asked her to marry him, without any confidence in those days. She'd wanted to mother him. She'd wanted to press him to her and to stroke the thin, vulnerable nape of his neck. He had asked her to marry him because he was ashamed of himself, because he wanted to hide. For thirty-six years she had been convenient for this purpose. "Lies," he whispered again. "All lies about me."

"I was wondering about the cash that was owing," the boy said. "I was passing and I looked in. I was wondering if you'd agree to loan me the suit." He smiled at her, and then he mentioned the money and the suit again.

She prised her husband's fingers from the edge of the door and pulled him into the hall. He was weeping more noisily now. She banged the door, pushing at it with her foot because her hands were occupied. After a moment the bell rang again, but this time neither of them answered it.

He didn't mind. It wasn't polite of them not to answer the door, knowing that he was standing there, but it didn't really matter. Tomorrow or the next day he'd call in again and she'd hand him over the money and the suit. Just like Dass would get hold of a pair of curtains.

In the small car-park of the Artilleryman's Friend he waited by a Vauxhall that had been abandoned there ten months ago. The public house was closed. All the other cars had been driven away.

From the back-yard came the sound of bottles rattling as Mr. Plant stacked crates on top of one another. He whistled as he did so.

Timothy crossed the car-park, glad that the publican was whistling since it suggested good humor. He passed through an opening in a wooden fence into the yard, which was lit only by the light from within the house. Mr. Plant was

in his shirt-sleeves. His three-legged dog was eating a cork.

"Cheers, Mr. Plant," Timothy said.

Bent over a crate of bottles, with his back to
Timothy, Mr. Plant gave a startled grunt. He
turned and peered into the shadows where Timothy was standing.

"Who's that?"

"It's me, sir. Young Timothy."

Mr. Plant took a bottle from the crate and
advanced toward his visitor with it. He spoke in
a low voice, saying a man could have a heart
attack, being crept up on like that.

"Get off my property, son. I warned you this
morning."

"I thought maybe you'd have time to think it
over, Mr. Plant."

"Keep your bloody voice down. Are you stupid
or something? No one messes me, son. Clear off
immediately."

The voice of Mrs. Plant called out from behind
a lighted upstairs window, wanting to know whom
her husband was talking to.

"I don't want to cause you any kerfuffle, Mr.
Plant. We'll keep the secret—"

Mr. Plant drove the base of the bottle at Timothy's stomach, but Timothy side-stepped away
from it.

"Mrs. Plant," Timothy said quite softly, and
Mr. Plant whispered that if he issued another
sound he would thump him to a pulp. He drove
the bottle in the direction of Timothy's stomach
again and he reached out with the fingers of his
other hand in order to grasp the back of Timothy's
head.

"Mrs. Plant," Timothy said again, a little louder than before.

"For God's sake!" whispered Mr. Plant, and without further argument he agreed to convey the tin bath from Swines' yard to the rectory garden on the morning of Easter Saturday. "Hop it," he whispered furiously. "Get to hell out of here now."

As Timothy went he heard the voice of Mrs. Plant again, demanding more sharply to know whom her husband was conversing with. The publican replied that he'd been talking to his dog.

All during supper, eating a pork chop and cauliflower and mashed potatoes, Stephen had wanted to be alone. He'd pushed forkfuls of food into his mouth, chewing it mechanically, drinking water to make swallowing easier. If he'd left it Mrs. Blakey would have made a fuss, she'd have wanted to take his temperature, she'd have asked questions he couldn't answer.

In bed it was easier to think. He'd never even seen the wedding-dress the boy had mentioned. His mother had shown him lots of things, photographs and even odds and ends she'd had as a child, but she'd never shown him her wedding-dress. It seemed strange that it should still be there, in a trunk. It seemed too strange to believe. Surely it was a lie that the boy had looked through a window of Primrose Cottage and seen it? Surely it was part of a make-believe, like imagining you were playing number 3 for Somerset? Timothy Gedge was a horrible sort of person, talking about honeymoons like that, saying Kate's mother was peachy. Of course it was all lies.

He fell asleep, but hours later he woke up and

felt again—as he'd felt for a moment in the hall
when he'd arrived—that he shouldn't be in this
house. There was something wrong, there was
something the matter. He felt it, not knowing
what it was, like a feeling in a dream. He remembered now the faded green trunk the boy had
mentioned. He could see it quite clearly when he
thought about it. He could see his father lifting
the lid and taking out the wedding-dress, not
knowing what to do with it now that he was getting married again. In the warmth of his bed
Stephen shuddered. When he tried to think he
was unable to, as though he didn't want to think,
as though he was afraid to. "Mummy died," his
father said again, and there seemed to be something wrong with the way he said it.

The Dynmouth Hards rode into the town that
night and took away the telephone from the kiosk
in Baptist Street. In the promenade bus-shelter
they broke the window they hadn't broken the last
time they'd visited it. With their paint-guns they
sprayed messages on the bonnets of four parked
cars. They had hoped to find the Pakistani on his
way back from night work in the steam laundry,
but the Pakistani successfully avoided them. They
swerved in front of Nurse Hackett's Mini.

The men of Ring's Amusements still worked
in Sir Walter Raleigh Park, but the Dynmouth
Hards knew better than to engage these men in
any form of combat. They bought the last chips
that were available in Phyl's Phries and at one
o'clock they drifted apart, not satisfied with their
night out. Girls were dropped off at the ends of
the roads where they lived, motor-cycles were
pushed into front gardens and covered with PVC

sheeting. The engines became quieter, purring quite ordinarily as they approached these resting places. In the yard of some lock-up garages one couple uncomfortably made love, their mock-leather garments still mostly in place. The girl, who happened never to enjoy this activity, ground her teeth together. "Lovely," she whispered through them, thankful when the youth had finished.

In their parents' houses the Dynmouth Hards crept upstairs and into bedrooms in which other people slept, considerate because in their homes they were required to be. One of them dreamed that he was the mayor of a town in Australia. A girl who was a hairdresser gave Princess Elizabeth of Yugoslavia a blue rinse.

A better day today, Miss Lavant wrote in her diary, *quite a bit of sunshine. Out shopping this morning. Mock's have a new chap on the bacon counter. Apparently Mr. Tares retired at the end of last week. Easter eggs in all the windows now, extremely expensive. The nuns from the convent have bought a van. I was admiring it and one of them said it was a Fiat—Italian, which is suitable. While standing there I noticed Dr. Green-slade drive by.*

Miss Vine's budgerigar Beano died that night, and so did old Miss Trimm, a favorite teacher once in Dynmouth Primary, whose declining years had tricked her into believing she'd mothered another son of God. She died in her sleep while dreaming that she was teaching geography, her mind quite lucid again. Beano died without dreaming about anything.

7

He clambered over the shingle at the bottom of the cliff and then up the cliff itself, arriving at the eleventh green. He was carrying the carrier-bag with the Union Jack on it.

He passed through the archway in the garden wall of Sea House, opening the white iron gate and leaving it open. He walked between shrubs and empty flower-beds, past the monkey-puzzle beneath which, in his confusion, he had stood the night before last, thinking about the wedding-dress. He'd had an addled idea that he wanted to stand there all night, so that first thing in the morning he could approach the kids and explain to them what it was he was after. As he paused by the monkey-puzzle now the dogs came running at him, barking and jumping, sniffing at his feet.

Mr. Blakey came out of a distant glass-house, beyond lawns and flower-beds. He called at the dogs, but they paid him no attention. Timothy stood still, not wishing to be bitten by the animals.

"I was wanting to see the kids," he said when Mr. Blakey came closer. The man was known to him by sight and by name; he had nothing against him. "Nice day, Mr. Blakey," he said.

Mr. Blakey seized the dogs by their collars. He pointed at the house and ordered them to go toward it, which they obediently did.

"I was talking to the kids yesterday," Timothy explained, giving Mr. Blakey a smile. The man was staring at him, he noticed.

"You came into this garden in the night," Mr. Blakey said eventually.

Timothy, still smiling, shook his head. He said he was always in bed at night. He laughed companionably. "I think you had a dream, sir."

At this point the children came through the drawing-room French windows. After a moment of hesitation they walked towards Timothy Gedge. Mr. Blakey returned to his glass-house.

"What d'you want?" Stephen said.

"I was thinking about the wedding-dress." He held out the bag with the Union Jack on it. "I have a carrier here for it."

"We haven't got a wedding-dress," Stephen said quickly. "We don't know anything about it."

"Is there a price on the wedding-dress, Stephen?"

Stephen didn't reply. He began to walk back towards the house. Kate followed him, and Timothy followed, also.

"Your dad'd have no use for it, Stephen. It's still in the trunk, no good to anyone." He said he wished he could be friends with them. He reminded them that yesterday he'd bought them two tins of Coca-Cola.

"We don't want to be friends with you," Stephen said angrily. "Leave us alone."

"You're older than us," Kate explained.

"Fifteen."

"We're only twelve."

They had halted in their walk. Within the house, passing by the landing window, Mrs. Blakey paused, surprised to see this older boy in the garden. It was odd that he should be there. Vaguely she wondered if Kate and Stephen had been up to mischief.

"Your mum has no use for it either, Stephen."

"Stephen's mother—"

"Stephen's mother's dead, Kate."

Stephen began to walk away again. Kate said: "It upsets Stephen, talking about his mother."

She moved on, but Timothy Gedge moved with her. He remained silent until they had reached a flight of three stone steps between one lawn and a higher one, where Stephen was waiting. Then he said:

"It's no joke when your mother's dead. It's no joke for a kid, it could happen to any of us." He nodded at Stephen and Stephen stood still, waiting for him to turn and go, staring at him and frowning.

"Plant's going to convey the bath for me in his van, Stephen. Plant says the act'll bring the house down."

"It's all lies what you're saying." Stephen's face was flushed. He glared at Timothy and Timothy nodded at him, as if he'd misheard what had been said. He smiled at Stephen. He said:

"Only I definitely need the wedding-dress."

"Well, you can't have it. You're stupid and pathetic. We don't want to have anything to do with you."

Mrs. Blakey, recognizing that something was wrong, rapped sharply on the landing window and beckoned at the children. Timothy waved at her, endeavoring to indicate that nothing was the matter.

"I saw you at the funeral, Stephen. I saw your dad. I saw your mum, Kate." He spoke keenly and with even greater friendliness than before. "Your mother's finished with the dress, Stephen."

They looked at him smiling his smile, one hand hanging limply by his side, the other grasping the carrier-bag. Then Stephen walked on towards the open French windows, and Kate walked beside him. When he'd said he'd seen Stephen at the funeral she'd felt afraid of him for a moment. Something in his voice had made her feel afraid, she didn't know what.

He walked beside her and she knew he was still smiling. She could hear him sucking at a fruit gum.

"D'you know the Abigails, Kate?"

She didn't reply.

"And the Dasses?" He laughed. "They have a house called Sweetlea."

"Please go away now." She put her head on one side, trying to make him understand from the look in her eyes that Stephen had been upset by the references to his mother's death. He nodded at her. He said to Stephen:

"A person can't help himself, Stephen."

At the landing window Mrs. Blakey frowned. The boy looked strange, loose-limbed and broad-shouldered, with his very fair hair. The children seemed quite tiny beside him, Stephen even frail. He kept grinning at them as though they were all three the very best of friends, but clearly that wasn't quite so. He was so very familiar on the streets of the town, with that zipped yellow jacket and his jeans, yet he looked like something from another world in the garden. He didn't belong in gardens, any more than he belonged in the company of two small children. His presence puzzled her beyond measure.

"A person has temptations. You could argue like that, Stephen."

It seemed to them that he said anything that came into his head. His head was like a dustbin, with all sorts of rubbish mingling in it, and all of it eventually spewing out of his mouth.

"Only the Commander was upset with nerves on account of a remark I made the other night. D'you understand what I'm referring to, Kate?"

"How could she?" Stephen cried. "How could she possibly make head or tail—"

"The Commander's gay as a grasshopper, homo-ing all over the joint. Out after cub scouts, lads in the Essoldo, anything you like. Up on the golf-course, down on the beach, in and out the windows. The wife never guessed."

He smiled at Kate because she was frowning, seeming bewildered and even put out. "The wife didn't guess till it slipped out when I was on the sauce the other night. She married a gaylord, Kate."

Stephen shook his head, not believing that. There'd been a master at Ravenswood, a man called Funny Stiles who'd been given the sack because he'd made boys presents of whistles and fountain-pens. But Commander Abigail wasn't like Funny Stiles. It couldn't possibly make sense for a man who was married to go homo-ing about.

They had reached the French windows. It wouldn't take two minutes to slip up to the attic, Timothy Gedge said.

"I often saw your dad," he said, "out with the field-glasses. The day I saw him at her funeral I said to myself he was a fine man. I saw him standing there getting wet all over him and I said to myself he was a fine person. I said it

afterwards to the clergyman. The way he stood,
I remarked to the Reverend Feather, the way he
bowed his head down over the loss of your mother,
Stephen. There's some stand any old how, you'd
be really ashamed of them. You'd want to go up
to them and tell them to do better."

"You're half mad," Stephen said quietly, with
anger just beneath the surface of his voice.

Timothy shook his head. "I thought the same
thing the night I saw him with her wedding-
dress. Not like Plant or Abigail, I remarked to
myself. Not like Dass or the clergyman. I'd say
your father looks a different kettle of fish, Stephen, and isn't that the way to keep it? Any
trouble your father might have we can hide under
wraps. D'you get the picture, Stephen?"

Stephen stepped through the French windows
and when Kate was in the drawing-room with
him he stood in the opening, one hand on the
frame of the window, to prevent the older boy
from entering. "Don't ever dare to come into the
garden again," he ordered, with the same violence
in his voice. "Clear off and don't come back."

He closed the window and latched it.

"Whatever's going on?" Mrs. Blakey said.
"Whatever's Timothy Gedge want?"

He'd lost a penknife on the beach, Kate said.
He was wondering if they'd found it.

There was a spinney they'd made their own,
by the river. They went there in the middle of
that morning, passing through the gate in the
garden wall and along the cliff-path for a few
hundred yards and then on to the golf-course.
Rapidly they crossed fairways, by greens and
bunkers and tees. They passed behind the club-

house, leaving the golf-course behind them. They went through a field where sheep grazed, and then through bracken that sloped down steeply to the River Dyn. They wore Wellington boots, their corduroy jeans and the same jerseys as yesterday, Kate's red, Stephen's navy-blue.

Stephen walked ahead of her on the river bank. He led the way around the edge of a marsh and then through drier land, with limestone boulders on it. Ferns grew among the boulders, and further on the spring undergrowth was already dense. At a twist in the river lay the spinney, a clump of birch saplings sprouting through a thicket of bramble. It wasn't large and never attracted other people. A stream ran through it to the river.

In the middle of the undergrowth, unseen either from the river or the bank on the other side, they had built a hut with lengths of fallen wood and some corrugated iron they'd found. It was a private lair, and though they'd often wished to have a fire they'd never done so—not because they feared for the dry wood of the spinney but because they knew that rising smoke would sooner or later be investigated.

They crawled into their hut. Outside, the sun glanced through a lacing of branches and bramble and scattered light in patches. Inside it was almost dark. They didn't speak. Kate's arms were clasped around her knees in an attitude she often took up. Stephen lay flat, gazing out at the patterns of sunlight, his chin resting on the backs of his hands. They hadn't spoken to one another about Timothy Gedge, either last night or since Stephen had closed the French windows in his face, several hours ago. They hadn't said to one another that they couldn't understand his talk about the

Abigails and the Dasses and Mr. Plant of the Artilleryman's Friend. They had attempted to visualise his world, as they had so often visualised each other's boarding-schools. But they knew too little about him and what they knew was bewildering. They tried to imagine him acting in a comic manner the part of a man who had murdered three wives in a bath. They tried to imagine people watching this gruesome comedy.

"He's making it up. The wedding-dress isn't even there." Kate spoke softly, shaking her head in denial.

"I don't know. I don't know if it's there." He remembered waking up in the middle of the night, and then he remembered Miss Tomm walking into the dormitory and saying that the headmaster wanted to see him and Cartwright saying: "Eee, what's Fleming done?" He remembered his father in his tweed overcoat in the Craw's study, his father saying later how it had happened, and then the funeral in the rain. Timothy Gedge had said he'd seen him there. He'd said the best place for the people of Dynmouth was in their coffins.

Stephen suddenly wanted to hit him. He wanted to hit him all over the face with his fists, to smash away his stupid smile, to stop him talking.

"I think we should tell Mrs. Blakey," Kate said.

"No." He shook his head, still gazing at the patterns of sunshine on the grass outside the hut. "No," he said again, closing the subject.

They made a dam on the stream, which was something they often did when they came to the spinney. They could feel the chill of the water through the rubber of their Wellington boots. Their hands, piling up stones, became red with cold.

Kate watched him, glancing sideways without turning her head. In the garden that morning she'd thought he was going to cry because of the memory of his mother's death. She'd thought he was going to turn his back on Timothy Gedge and on herself and run into the house so that they wouldn't see his tears. She'd felt his unhappiness and she felt it now. She wanted to say that he'd feel all right when a little time had passed, just like you did at school when you were homesick at the beginning of term. But she didn't because she didn't know that that would happen. She didn't know what would happen, she didn't know what was happening now.

They ate the sandwiches they'd made before they'd left the house, and then they lay in their shelter and read two paper-backed books they'd brought with them. In the middle of the afternoon they decided to walk back to Dynmouth. There was an army display on for one day only, Mrs. Blakey had said at breakfast: the car-park behind the fish-packing station had been taken over for it.

"Hullo there," a sergeant said. "Come to see for yourselves, then?"

Boys were playing with machine-guns, swiveling them this way and that, peering through the sights. Bored soldiers were showing how various mechanisms operated and explaining the rate at which bullets could be discharged. Other boys climbed in and out of tanks or queued outside a caravan which advertised a film about combat in the jungle. A second caravan contained an exhibition of recruitment leaflets and in a third one there was an exhibition of army rations for

Antarctic expeditions. Amplified pop music was playing.

"This looks the best," Kate said, determinedly leading the way to the rations caravan. "Look, tinned rice pudding. And Spangles. Imagine taking Spangles to the Antarctic!"

There was meal to make porridge with in the Antarctic, and sugar and powdered milk, and biscuits and powdered soup, and tinned stew.

"Whatever next?" Kate tried to giggle, reading out the directions on the stew, but nothing seemed funny. "I think they're pampered," she said lamely.

They went to the recruitment caravan, and to the film about combat in the jungle, which they left before it was over.

"Cheers!" Timothy Gedge said, coming up behind them.

His presence wasn't a surprise. They didn't reply to his greeting. He was carrying the same carrier-bag and for some reason they found it impossible not to stare at it. It swung lightly in the air, the Union Jack gay against his pallid clothes, seeming imbued with his own anticipation.

He walked away from the army display with them, offering them fruit gums and chattering. In his woman's voice he repeated two conversations between waiters and men ordering plates of soup. He drew their attention to the goods in shop windows, to the cooking-stoves and washing-machines in the windows of the electricity show-rooms. These electrical gadgets were all good value, he said, nodding his head repeatedly: the South-Western Electricity Board was an honest organization. "If your mum's after a washer," he advised Kate, "she'd best move in while the sale's on." In everything he said there were wisps of mockery.

"Why are you following us?" Stephen asked, knowing the answer to the question.

"I need the dress for my act, Stephen."

He smiled his smile at them. They stopped, waiting for him to walk on, but he didn't.

"We've told you we're not going to get a wedding-dress for you," Kate said.

He began to whistle beneath his breath, a soft sound without a tune, as if he were attempting to imitate the rushing of wind through trees. He ceased it in order to speak again.

"It's great being friends with you," he said. He pointed at meat in a shop window and said it was good value. "Did you ever notice," he said to Kate, "Miss Lavant has bad teeth?"

They walked on, not speaking, not reacting to what he was saying. He asked them why elephants didn't ride bicycles and explained that it was because they hadn't any thumbs to ring the bell with. George Joseph Smith, he told them, had spent a night in Dynmouth one time, at the Castlerea boarding-house, still in business.

"Were you ever in Tussaud's, Kate? They have the bath set up on the floor there, you can reach a hand out and touch it. They have Christie in Tussaud's, Kate. And this bloke called Haigh that sent his clothes in to the model-maker so's they wouldn't have the trouble of faking them. And another bloke that used to drink his own Number One." He laughed. He'd read up about George Joseph Smith, he said, after he'd got his idea for a show. "I read up about a lot of them, Kate. This Maybrick woman who finished her hubby off with fly-papers. And the Thompson woman who was administering glass for eight months, only it didn't take, so Freddie Bywaters had to stick a knife into the man near Ilford Station. And this Fulham woman who was administering arsenic, only all that was happening was her hubby was getting a tingling in his feet." He laughed again. A lot of it was comic, he explained, you definitely had to smile. You'd go mad if you couldn't smile at things, you'd go mad without a sense of humor.

"You should see a psychiatrist," Stephen said.

"Freddie Bywaters definitely stuck the knife in, Stephen."

"I'm not talking about Freddie Bywaters. We think you're insane."

"Did I mention the Dasses to you?"

"We don't want to hear about them." Stephen's voice had risen, as it had that morning in the garden, and again Kate thought that he was trying not to cry. He was afraid of Timothy Gedge.

"Let's go in here, and I'll show you that bath."

They were passing a builder's yard. *A. J. Swines*, it said on high brown doors that were standing open so that lorries could pass in and out. *Builders and Plumbers*, it said.

"It's just there. Behind the timber sheds."

It would not be there, Kate thought. It would be like opening the trunk and the wedding-dress not being there. He would lead them into the yard and behind the sheds, and then he'd point at nothing and say there it was. It would at least be an explanation, a confirmation of his madness. Stephen hesitated and then followed the other two.

They passed a cement-mixer that was being

operated by two men with cement dust on their caps and dungarees. Timothy Gedge smiled at the men and said it was a nice day. He led the way behind some sheds in which planks of timber were stored. "There," he said, pointing. "How's about that then?"

It was badly chipped and covered with rust marks. Timothy Geodge said it was made of tin. Quite light really, he explained, lifting up one end, not like a cast-iron one. "I thought you'd like to see it," he said as they left the yard. "Shall we walk up to the house now?"

They didn't answer. He said again that it was great being friends with them.

"We're not your friends," Stephen replied hotly. "Can't you get it into your head? We don't like you."

"I often go up, Stephen. I go up to the place it happened: to remember the way it was, actually."

They didn't ask him what he meant. They were in Fore Street now, busy with afternoon shoppers. As in Badstoneleigh yesterday, he pushed his way through them.

"I witnessed it," he said. "I was there in the gorse."

They knew what he was referring to, and Kate resolved that whether Stephen liked it or not she was going to tell Mrs. Blakey. She'd tell her every single thing, all he'd said about Commander Abigail and all about the bath and the wedding-dress and what he was saying now, about witnessing the accident. Mrs. Blakey would immediately tell her husband and Mr. Blakey would immediately go to wherever it was this boy lived and warn him that if he didn't stop the police would be informed. And that would be the end of it.

They turned into Lace Street, walking by the side of the Queen Victoria Hotel. They crossed a zebra-crossing when they came to the promenade and turned right, leaving the harbor and the fish-packing station behind them. Ahead of them was Sir Walter Raleigh Park and in the distance, the highest point on the cliffs, Sea House. Miss Lavant, with her wicker shopping basket, was out for her afternoon turn on the promenade, prominent among the other strollers, in scarlet. The beach, stretching endlessly away beneath the cliffs, was a narrow strip of shingle now, for the sea was fully in.

"Tipped," Timothy Gedge said, the word appearing to have been chosen at random.

"Listen, will you shut up?" Stephen cried. "Will you shut up and go away? Will you clear off?"

"I witnessed it, Stephen. I saw her tipped down that cliff."

Stephen stared at him, ceasing to walk. He frowned, unable to think, unable to grasp immediately what was being implied.

"Tipped?" Kate repeated after a moment.

"What d'you mean, tipped?" Stephen demanded, not intending to ask the question. "What're you talking about?"

He said the council had put up a wire fence at the place on the cliff-path. After the tragedy a couple of men had gone up with concrete posts: he'd watched them at it. The place was supposed to be dangerous because the path was too narrow between the gorse bushes and the edge: it stood to reason, she stumbled over in the wind. He put a fruit gum in his mouth. The truth was, all that was a load of rubbish. "Your dad tipped her down, in actual fact."

Stephen tried to shake his head, but found it hard to do so. It was meant to be some kind of joke. It was meant to be funny.

"You shouldn't say things like that," Kate said. Her voice was shaky, her eyes had become round and dull with astonishment. It didn't seem to her that Timothy Gedge was trying to make a joke, yet it was amazing that he was saying all this just to pay them back for not being friendly or because he wanted a wedding-dress they wouldn't give him, or for any reason at all.

"She was shouting out your mum's a prostitute, Kate. Then he tips her down and she's screaming her head off. I was there in the gorse, Stephen. I followed them up."

"That's not true," Kate cried. "None of it's true."

"My mother's death was accidental. She was alone. She went for a walk alone."

"It's horrible what you're saying," Kate cried.

"We'll keep the secret, Kate. He tipped her down because he was head over heels on your mum and she was calling your mum a prostitute. There's always a reason why a person performs the murder act. They were on the job, see, your mum and Stephen's dad. He was black as thunder when she said your mum was a pro. You'd be black yourself, Stephen, if someone said the same thing about Kate."

Stephen began to walk on again. Kate said they'd tell the Blakeys and the Blakeys would go to the police.

"Ever read books, Stephen? *Clifftop Tragedy* by Eileen Dover?"

In a sudden jerk of anger Stephen turned and kicked at his shins, but the blows didn't hurt because of Stephen's Wellington boots. What was more painful were Kate's fists smacking into his stomach, blow after blow. She hit him so savagely that a woman with a pram told her to calm down.

Kate took no notice of the woman. "You leave us alone," she shouted at Timothy Gedge. "Just get away with your lies."

Her voice was quivering beneath the pressure of tears. She blinked her eyes in an effort to hold them back.

"Don't you dare speak to us again," she cried. "Don't you dare ever speak to us."

They left him standing there and this time he didn't follow them. The woman with the pram asked him what all that had been about. He smiled at her even though his stomach was paining him. He said they were just kids. He said it was just fun.

They walked on, towards and then past Miss Lavant, and past the other strollers on the promenade. Miss Lavant's scarlet coat was of fine tweed, her skin had the poreless look of porcelain. She smiled as they passed her by, and they saw revealed what Timothy Gedge had claimed: her beauty was marred by discolored teeth.

Stephen agreed that they must tell Mrs. Blakey. If they didn't tell Mrs. Blakey he would continue to follow them with his carrier-bag, talking. You could kick him and hurt him, you could hit him on the face and on the eyes so that he couldn't see, but he'd still manage to torment you. His conversation would never cease. He'd smile and say it was great being friends with you. He'd go on telling lies.

"He's a horrible person," Kate cried with re- newed vehemence, and looked behind her as if contemplating a continuation of her assault. He was standing where they had left him, a long way back now, gazing after them. It was too far to make out his smile, but she knew the smile was there.

"Come on, Kate."

As she turned to walk on she shivered, af- fected by a chilliness that seemed to be an ex- pression of her revulsion.

"We'll only say," Stephen said, "he keeps following us about. We'll say he wants clothes to dress up in. No need to tell her everything."

Kate agreed with that. There was no need to tell Mrs. Blakey everything because so much of it just didn't make sense.

The men of Ring's Amusements whistled and shouted, still preparing the machinery in Sir Walter Raleigh Park. Fifty yards ahead a bus, in shades of silver, slowly drew up. A man who happened to be passing with a camera took a photograph of it.

The sea slurped over green rocks, at the bottom of the promenade wall. It was beginning to go out again, calmly withdrawing, orderly, as though trained. "Look," his mother had said, making him watch with her while a tide spent itself. She had loved watching the sea. She'd loved walking by it. She'd loved the stones it smoothed, and its wild- ness when it flung itself over the promenade wall, scattering gravel and driftwood. Like anger, she'd said.

Elderly people climbed slowly out of the silver

bus, women in brown or cream or gray, old men in overcoats and hats. They stood uncertainly on the promenade, as if alarmed. They murmured to one another, and then they laughed because the bus-driver leaned out of his cab and made a joke. The man who'd taken a photograph of the bus asked if he might photograph the old people also, and the bus-driver told him to wait a minute. He put aside a newspaper he'd been going to read and jumped out of his cab. "Everyone for the gentleman's photograph," he shouted, lining the elderly people against the side of the bus. "Cheese please, Louise." All the elderly people laughed.

"It's called harassing," Kate said. "You harass people by not leaving them alone. I'd say it was against the law."

Stephen nodded, not knowing if it was against the law or not, and not much caring. The clothes of people who died were naturally left behind; he hadn't ever thought of that. He hadn't wondered where her clothes were when he'd returned to Primrose Cottage at the end of that autumn term. Other things had still been there, lots of her things. But even without looking he'd known that her clothes—all her dresses and her coats and her cardigans and her shoes—were no longer in her wardrobe or in the chests of drawers she shared with his father in their bedroom.

"What happens to dead people's clothes, d'you think?"

She said she didn't know. His father wouldn't burn them. It would be cruel to burn them since people needed clothes, refugees in India and Africa. His father was too nice and too charitable. She thought that but did not say it. His father would have given them to Oxfam, or to a jumble sale.

"But not the wedding-dress?"

"You wouldn't give a wedding-dress."

"You wouldn't put it on a bonfire, either."

"It wouldn't be right to do that."

The wedding-dress was in the faded green trunk, just as he'd imagined it in the night. It was as real as the bath behind the timber sheds. She'd stowed it away there, his father had found it. The boy had seen because he was always looking to see what people were doing.

They had almost reached the end of the promenade. Behind them the elderly people poked their way about in twos and threes, careful on the concrete surface. Farther behind, the scarlet figure of Miss Lavant moved past the façade of the Queen Victoria Hotel, toward the harbor and the fish-packing station. Timothy Gedge was nowhere to be seen.

At the end of the promenade they could take a flight of steps down to rocks that were slippery with seaweed, and clamber over them until they reached the shingle. They could make their way over that and eventually up the cliff to the eleventh green of the golf-course, to the gate in the garden wall. Or they could fork to the right, up Once Hill, past the rectory and on to the steep, narrow road that wound over the downs to Badstoneleigh, off which the entrance gates of Sea House opened. They were considering this choice when they were abruptly aware of Commander Abigail.

He made his way down the narrow road, huddled like a crab within his familiar brown overcoat. But his step was not his familiar jaunty one, nor did he carry his rolled-up towel and swimming-trunks. He moved as the elderly people from the bus moved, but without their caution because a red Post Office van had to swerve to avoid him. He stood for a moment on the promenade in the same huddled way, and then he made his way slowly toward a green-painted seat and sat slowly down on it.

They walked by him, looking at him because they couldn't help themselves. But their staring didn't matter because he didn't notice it. His face was parched. His eyes were dead, as if the Post Office van had mowed him down and killed him. His hands were clasped together as if to comfort one another. There was a chalkiness about his lips and his eyelids. His ginger moustache was vivid.

It was true, they thought, still looking at him: he was a married man who went homo-ing about, who had been exposed to his wife when Timothy Gedge was drunk. All that was easy to believe now, it was easy to imagine the drunkenness, and Timothy Gedge letting the facts slip out because he didn't care, because he'd find it enjoyable, even better than going to a funeral.

They left the promenade and on the sleek tarred surface of the road Stephen walked in front, Kate behind him. He changed his mind about telling Mrs. Blakey. He said they mustn't, not adding that the sight of Commander Abigail on the green-painted seat made all the difference. And as he hadn't at first referred to the wedding-dress, last night or until they'd reached the spinney that morning, so he didn't refer now to the fantasies of Timothy Gedge that were turning out not to be fantasies at all.

They sat in the kitchen at teatime, an awkward occasion, with Mrs. Blakey's beaming face puzzled by their silence. If he were possessed by devils, Kate thought, it would be a simple explanation. In her first term at St. Cecilia's there'd been a girl who'd had the gift of levitation, a disturbed girl called Julie who had been able to float eight feet above the ground, whom Miss Scuse had eventually had to have removed. Girls often had gifts like that, Rosalind Swain had said at the time, especially in adolescence. A girl called Enid could hypnotize other girls with the aid of a silver-colored fountain-pen top. Another girl could read a whole page of a newspaper and immediately repeat it. Rosalind Swain said she wouldn't be able to when she'd finished growing up. Adolescence was mysterious, Rosalind Swain explained. Adolescents often harbored poltergeists.

Mrs. Blakey kept on asking them what they'd done that day. As if he hadn't heard her, Stephen didn't answer. Kate said they'd gone to the army display and mentioned the rations that were taken on Antarctic expeditions. If he were possessed by devils, you couldn't fight against him: devils could possess people in the same way as other people were made to harbor poltergeists or were haunted by ghosts. Were they like vapors that rustled through him, devils owning him while he was unaware, making him smile his smile? Did he know what he was doing?

"Is Stephen all right, dear?" Mrs. Blakey asked her as they cleared the plates from the table, when Stephen had gone. Kate pointed out that Stephen was always a little on the silent side.

"You've gone silent yourself, Kate." Mrs. Blakey spoke in a sudden, laughing kind of way, seeming relieved because she'd received an answer of a kind. Would she have collapsed into a heap if she'd learned that Stephen was silent because he was wondering if his father had murdered his mother? His father who mended the broken wings of birds, his mother who had loved him for his gentleness? Was it really true? Had his mother shouted and screamed on the edge of a cliff, calling her own mother a prostitute? People quarreled horribly. People were cruel, like her father had been before the divorce, like Miss Shaw and Miss Rist were to Miss Malabedeely. Yet of course it wasn't true. Of course she hadn't screamed like that.

In the drawing-room of the house that because of death and marriage had become his home Kate watched him while he, in turn, watched the colored rectangle of the television screen. His intensity was contrived; already he had closed himself away from her. Like a physical presence, she could feel that between them.

Bullets ricocheted off the surface of a boulder, chipping pieces out of it but missing Kid Curry and Hannibal Hayes, alias Smith and Jones. Dismally she thought that nothing would be the same again. After all this ugliness, like a slime around them, he would resent her because she knew about it, because in sharing it she'd become part of it. She closed her eyes, wanting to cry but preventing herself.

"You're Hannibal Hayes," the voice of a sheriff roared from the television drama, and the voice of the cowboy quietly retorted, denying that he was. When she opened her eyes the cowboys were no longer crouched by the boulder. They were astride a single horse, tied back to back,

being led along a skyline by the sheriff's posse.
Still hiding in pretended concentration, Stephen
watched as though his life depended on it.

Ghosts were exorcised, there was a special
service. There was the casting out of devils, which
sounded similar. If the devils were cast out of
Timothy Gedge, would everything miraculously
be different? Would she and Stephen be sitting
just as they were now and be suddenly unable
to remember anything that had happened because
nothing would have been real? Would the idyll
she had dreamed of be there again, not smashed
to pieces as it seemed to be?

It had been smashed to pieces because Timothy
Gedge had followed them. Timothy Gedge, with
his hollow cheeks and his gawkiness, had picked
on them even though he didn't know them, even
though they'd done him no harm. Did he hate
them because they lived in Sea House, because
there was the garden and the setters, because
they were friends and he had no friends himself?
Or did he really just want a wedding-dress? Had
she really screamed like that?

~~~~~~

8

The sun trickled around the blinds in Kate's bedroom, falling in narrow shafts over the poppies
on the wallpaper and on the orange-painted
dressing-table. It was warm in the room when she
awoke and for some seconds she was aware of
pleasurable anticipation, before the revelations
of the day before came flooding in on her. Hig-
gledy-piggledy they came, without rhyme or reason. Unwillingly she marshaled them into order,
beginning with the moment when she and Stephen
had stepped out of the French windows, appre-
hensive because Timothy Gedge was in the garden. Stephen had been friends with her then. He
had been friends while they talked in the spinney,
and while they made the dam on the stream and
read their paper-backed books after they'd eaten
their sandwiches.

She got up, pulling back the bedclothes and
releasing the blinds on both windows. The sea
was calm. No breeze disturbed the budding magnolias or the tree mallows, or the azaleas for
which the garden was noted. Mr. Blakey stood
among his cropped rose-beds, pondering something. In their favorite morning resting place,
warm in the sunshine by the summer-house, the

setters reclined with dignity, like sleepy lions. In Dynmouth the clock of St. Simon and St. Jude's chimed eight. She took her night-dress off and quickly dressed.

That day, a Saturday, was a horrible day. They didn't leave the house. In Kate's room, hardly speaking, they played draughts and Monopoly and Rickety Ann and Switch and Racing Demon. She hated the silence and felt subdued by it, and in the end defeated. When she tried to be cheerful she ended up flustered and red-faced, clammy all over. At lunchtime in the kitchen she tried to cover the silence up by chattering about anything that came into her head, but her chattering made the silence more obvious. Stephen didn't say a single word. Mrs. Blakey became worried, and it showed.

They watched a Saturday-afternoon film on television, *All This and Heaven Too.* Afterward they read. They played Monopoly again. From the window of Kate's room they watched Mrs. Blakey on the distant seashore throwing driftwood for the setters. They watched her returning, passing through the gate in the archway of the garden wall, the setters' mouths drooping open from excitement and fatigue.

They were still at the window when Timothy Gedge appeared a few minutes later. He peeped through the white ornamental iron-work of the gate. He looked up at the windows of the house.

Days went by like that, Sunday and Monday and Tuesday. On Saturday their parents would be back.

On all these days Timothy Gedge appeared at

the gate in the garden wall. On the Monday and
the Tuesday he came to the front of the house
and rang the hall-door bell. "There's that Gedge
boy wants you," Mrs. Blakey said in a puzzled
way on each occasion, and on each occasion they
replied that they didn't wish to see him. When he
came again Mrs. Blakey said he must not return.
The children hadn't found his penknife, she said.

For Kate, the passing of time made the silence
chillier, until it felt like an icy shroud around her.
For Stephen, time was a tormentor. Thoughts
formed in his mind, images occurred. In the
newspapers there'd been an army officer's wife
who'd disappeared while the army officer was
engaged in a liaison with a woman in the army
catering services. This woman had become the
army officer's second wife. His first wife had gone
to Australia, he had claimed in the dock, but
there was doubt about that. There'd been photographs of these people's faces in the newspapers,
but Stephen had forgotten what the faces looked
like. New faces appeared in his mind, with features that were grotesque in their exaggeration
of innocence and evil.

There was another face then, which didn't have
to be invented: a moustached face that had recently and endlessly appeared on the television
news, the face of a man who was accused of
battering to death the nanny of his children, of
attempting to do the same to his wife. "A kind
and generous person," a woman on the news
said. "He loved people for what they were." He
was missing and wanted for murder. His car was
found with bloodstains on the steering-wheel.
"He couldn't possibly do a thing like that," his

best friend said. In France and South Africa, all
over the world, the police were looking for him.
Had he, too, mended the broken wings of birds?

His father had the same seriously intent eyes
and the delicate look that Stephen had. But he
was brown-haired and his smile was different.
His smile came slowly, beginning at the corners
of his mouth and creeping all over his face,
wrinkling the flesh of his cheeks, lighting up his
eyes. Stephen's smile was jerky and nervous,
coming quickly, in flashes, and quickly evaporat-
ing. His father had a way of losing himself in
some private absorption, of not hearing when
people spoke to him, and then of apologizing
concernedly. He would watch the movements of
birds for hours through his binoculars without
ever assuming that this activity could be interesting to other people, without ever promoting it as
a topic of conversation. His privacy in this matter,
and in others, had thrown Stephen and his mother
together. That had seemed natural to Stephen, the
way things should be: his father working and
then emerging from his work, all three of them
walking on the beach, or walking to Badstoneleigh
to go to the Pavilion, or having tea on Stephen's
birthday in the Spinning Wheel, or going to see
Somerset play.

It was impossible not to remember, after what
Timothy Gedge had said. With his father and his
mother, he'd often walked along the cliffs, by
the golf-course. Dozens of times they'd gone in
single file when they came to the narrow place,
made narrow by a growth of gorse. "Careful,
Stephen," they both seemed endlessly to have
said. Often on the beach, when he'd run on ahead

looking for flat pebbles to skim over the sea, he'd glanced back to find them walking with their arms around one another. "No one's nicer than Daddy," his mother had once said.

On these walks, when Stephen was much younger, his father used to tell him stories about a family of moles he'd invented, elaborate adventures that went on for miles. On his mother's birthday they didn't go to the Spinning Wheel but to the Queen Victoria for lunch, because his father insisted. She'd sit there in the place of honor, black-haired and rather thin, beautiful on her birthday, as his father used to say. She'd laugh at things. She'd reach out toward them both and put her hands on theirs, smiling with her very white teeth. He always liked it when she wore a certain shade of lipstick, coral, not cherry. He liked it when she wore her green dress, with the belt that had a brass buckle.

His father insisted on the whole day being given up to her birthday, taking trouble, making her laugh. "Funny, being a bird-watcher," a boy called Cosgrave had once said and Stephen had made him take that back, twisting his arm until he agreed to. Once when he was alone with her he'd said it would be nice to have a brother, but she'd explained that it wasn't possible. She'd hugged him, saying she was sorry. "Dear Mummy!" his father said all of a sudden in the Queen Victoria, while the waiter was standing there spooning out peas.

Such memories crowded him. They came briefly, as moments rapidly hurrying, one bundled away by the next. But they were sharp as splinters, each stabbing on another's wound. He

clenched himself against them, tightening himself, determined not to be taken unawares. He
wanted to be silent.

"Now, don't be silly, Kate," Mrs. Blakey said
firmly when Kate was helping her to make lemon
meringue pie. "The boy don't behave like a zombie
for nothing. You're both behaving queerly. D'you
think I'm stupid or something?"

"We don't mean to, Mrs. Blakey."

"If you've done something, tell me. If you've
broken something—"

"We haven't broken anything."

"I can't know if you don't tell me, Kate."

"There's nothing to tell."

Mrs. Blakey pressed her lips together. She said,
coolly, that she could manage on her own in the
kitchen now.

"I don't mind helping."

"You just run along now." She had been given
a telephone number in France: Cassis 08.79.30,
Les Roches Blanches, a hotel. It had been given
to her in case an emergency arose, but it seemed
to Mrs. Blakey that the atmosphere which had
developed in the house couldn't be called an
emergency. She wouldn't know how to put it in
any case, she wouldn't be able to explain since it
was all so hard to pin down. And it would cause
a worry, ringing up France like that. For a start,
it would cost a fortune.

"Stephen," Kate called outside the closed door
of his bedroom, but he didn't answer.

He stayed awake and after midnight he went
to the room which Kate's mother had set aside
for his father to write about birds in. It was on

the ground floor, at the back of the house. A
single window reached almost to the floor, looking
over the garden. Against a faded wallpaper,
striped in red and pink, were cases of butterflies
and moths. In the corner by the door there was
a small grandfather clock; from the mantelpiece,
beneath a dome of glass, an owl stared. His
father's four mahogany filing-cabinets from Primrose Cottage were there, in pairs against two
walls, between glass-fronted bookcases that had
always been in the room. There was a green-
shaded lamp on his mahogany desk, and a small
white Olympia typewriter. There was a blotting
pad with blue blotting-paper, and a wooden bowl
with pencils and paperclips and a fountain pen
in it.

Stephen pulled down the blind and sat at his
father's desk, opening one drawer after another.
He discovered notes on the Sand Martin and the
Rufous-sided Towhee and the Isabelline Wheatear
and the Whiskered Tern. A professor in the Un-
iversity of Pennsylvania had written to ask about
the distribution of the Upupidae Hoopoe in Britain. There was a bill from a firm of removals
people, Messrs Hatchers Worldwide, and the final
telephone account at Primrose Cottage, and the
final electricity account, including the charge for
disconnection. There were letters from solicitors
and insurance people, and at the bottom of a
drawer, tied together with string, there were letters of condolence.

There were other letters, tied together also, old
letters that his mother had written in 1954, and
in a stained buff envelope there were some his
father had written to her. They were full of love

and promises, and references to the future. Stephen read bits of them and then replaced them.

In another drawer, set aside from everything else, he found other letters that were full of love. They, too, referred to the future, to being at last together, and to happiness. There were fewer of them and they were shorter than his mother's and none of them was dated beyond giving a day of the week. *It's hard to wait*, one protested. *Nothing makes sense without you*, said another. These, too, he left as he had found them.

Light from the desk-lamp fell on his hands spread out on the blue blotting-paper, thin hands with thin fingers, only half the size they would become. His face in the gloom outside the glow of light was pale beneath his smooth black hair, his eyes intent yet empty of expression. He rose from the desk and turned on another light in the room. There was a book that had always been in Primrose Cottage, a thick book with a torn green dust-jacket. *Fifty Famous Tragedies*, it said on the jacket. He'd never seen his mother or his father reading it, but once he had opened it himself. He knew the kind of tragedies they were.

All the people Timothy Gedge had spoken of were there: Freddie Bywaters and Edith Thompson, Mrs. Fulham, the beautiful Mrs. Maybrick, Christie and Haigh and Heath, George Joseph Smith. There was Irene Munro, who had improved her complexion with Icilma cream before being battered to death for her handbag on a beach. There was a girl called Constance Kent, who had confessed to the murder of her small brother, fifty years ago, in a house not far from Dynmouth. On August 2nd, 1951, 48-year-old

Mrs. Mabel Tattershaw was spoken to by the man next to her in the Roxy Cinema, Nottingham. "I am," her murderer later remarked, "quite proud of my achievement." Owen Lloyd, a nine-year-old boy, drowned a four-year-old friend. "I won't do it again," he promised at his trial. A man called Wilson murdered a Mrs. Henrichson because she refused to rent him a room. Charlie Peace complained about the quality of the bacon at his execution breakfast. A chicken farmer called Edmund James Thorne fed the flesh of his wife to his fowls. In Brighton in 1934 the torso of a woman was found in a plywood trunk, wrapped in brown paper and tied with blind cord. Her murderer was never discovered. In Earl's Colne on January 20th, 1961, Linda Smith went out to buy a newspaper and was later found strangled eighteen miles away, in a field, by a hawthorn hedge. Her murderer was never discovered, either.

Murder was committed in order to silence people, and out of jealousy and revenge and anger, and simply for its own sake. There was murder within marriage because a husband or a wife wanted life to be different and for one reason or another could find no other way to bring that about. There was murder for gain, and for the most trivial and pointless reasons, often for hardly any reason at all. Two adolescent girls in New Zealand had killed with a brick the mother of one of them just because they wanted to. A child of eight had killed for sweets. In Hull a man had poisoned his wife because she'd refused to sew buttons on his clothes.

Stephen turned the main light off and returned

to his father's desk. He sat in front of the white typewriter, listening to the ticking of the clock in the corner by the window. The fountain-pen in the wooden bowl was blue, a small slim pen that had been hers. He remembered her using it, writing Christmas cards with it, and shopping lists.

In the room she seemed real. She felt quite close to him, as though her specter might appear, but he didn't feel afraid of that. He touched the fountain-pen and then held it in his hand. It seemed warm to him, as the handle of a spoon or a fork had often been, passed from her hand to his, after she'd mashed up something on a plate for him when he was younger.

He tried to remember if his parents had quarreled the holidays before she died, but couldn't remember that they had. It had been a fine summer. His father had been busy writing about shore larks. They'd gone to see Somerset playing Essex, Virgin 70 not out.

The more he thought about that summer the pleasanter it seemed. He remembered one Thursday morning walking with his mother from Primrose Cottage to a place called Blackedge Top, an old quarry on a hill. They'd gone to see another hill, which had been a Roman fort, covered in ferns now. He remembered having supper in the garden of Primrose Cottage, his parents seeming fond of one another, not quarreling or even disagreeing. They'd sat there for hours, until nine o'clock at least, until the small garden became shadowy in the dusk. There'd been a smell of roses, and of coffee. There'd been pink wine, Rosé Anjou 1969 on the label, celebrating the com-

pletion of the first half of his father's book on the
Shore Lark. He'd had Ribena with ice in it himself, and he could remember now, quite distinctly, thinking how horrible it must be for Kate,
not to have a father, nor ever to have an occasion
like this.

Yet all the time it must have been different.
His father had wanted things to be different, as
Edith Thompson had, in love with Freddie Bywaters, as Mrs. Maybrick had, and Mrs. Fulham.
They had sat there that night, after he'd gone to
bed, and their faces had changed. They had
stopped smiling because it wasn't necessary to
pretend any more. They had sat there hating one
another, quarreling in bitter voices, not wanting
to look at one another. As he thought about it,
creating the scene as it must have been, his
father shouted at her that she was useless and
silly. His father was quite unlike himself. Nothing
she ever did was any good, he said. The strawberry jam she'd made hadn't set, she couldn't
even take a telephone message. It sounded stupid
the way she went on about loving the sea. It was
no good pretending, his father said, it was no
good having birthday celebrations in the Queen
Victoria Hotel just so Stephen wouldn't know.

He left the room and in his bed he wept with
a violence he had never known before, spasm
following spasm. It was as though she had died
again, only it was worse, and he felt guilty that
he hadn't wept properly when she'd really died.
He felt that if he had all this would somehow not
have happened. He pressed his face into the pillow
to conceal the sound of a sobbing he could not
control. He wished he could destroy himself, as

she had been destroyed. He wished he might die. He fell asleep still wishing that.

He dreamed of the saintly Constance Kent cutting the throat of her baby brother in a quiet country house not far from Dynmouth. And of the beautiful Mrs. Maybrick soaking the arsenic from fly-papers in order to poison her husband. And of Irene Munro improving her complexion with Icilma cream, and of the torso in the plywood trunk. His mother slept in a deck-chair, near a fuchsia hedge, her black hair like polished ebony in the sun. A bundle flapped in the wind, a rust-colored headscarf, her rust-colored coat. Screams came from the bundle as it fell, turning twice in the air against the gray-brown cliff-face. The sea washed over her, swirling the headscarf into foam that was crimson already. The flesh of her face was rigid: taut, icy flesh that no one would touch. The setters rushed toward the sea and then pulled up short, barking at the waves. "Come on, come on," he called, but they took no notice. The sun was setting, making the dogs pink, like the pink wine that had been there on the table.

The setters ran away, sniffing the air excitedly. In the far distance they stopped, sniffing again, at a pink lump on the sand. It wasn't her, it was Commander Abigail in his swimming-trunks. His lips were drawn back in a snarl of pain, his skinny white limbs were like a frozen chicken's.

"She's over here," a voice shouted from the top of the cliff. He looked up. His father was pointing down at the rocks. The sea had gone out, his father shouted, but it hadn't taken her with it because she hadn't wanted to go. "She just wanted to lie there," his father said, beginning to laugh. She had only herself to blame.

And then Mr. Blakey stood among his rose-beds with his shears dripping blood, and her head lay in the soil. Her body without it walked away toward the house, staggering from side to side, blood flowing from the stump that had been her neck.

She had only herself to blame: she said that herself too, waking up in her deck-chair. She'd been silly, getting into an argument on the edge of a cliff and saying the wrong thing. But Stephen said it didn't matter, it didn't matter in the least if her strawberry jam didn't set, no matter what his father said. In his dream he felt relief because she hadn't died, because it had all been some other dream, because she was smiling in the sunshine.

Kate sat by the summer-house with the setters, hugging them and whispering to them, seeming small beside them. She brushed them with a brush that was kept in the summer-house, making them stand still, with their heads up. She wished people were like dogs, she said to them, and they looked at her knowledgeably with their big, drooping eyes. She sat between them on the steps of the summer-house, their chins on her knees, warmed by the heat of their bodies. It would be nice to breed dogs, she thought, and imagined setters running all over the garden, like the dalmatians in *The One Hundred and One Dalmatians*. She imagined living alone in Sea House, being quite old. She imagined puppies in the hall and a row of kennels at the side of the house, and people ringing the doorbell because they wanted to buy one of a litter. She would never have married because she couldn't marry Stephen. She might even be like Miss Lavant. People would tell other people the story of the woman in Sea House who lived alone with dogs. They'd tell of a tragedy on the cliffs, a death that wasn't what it had seemed to be. You couldn't blame Stephen for hating Dynmouth, people would say, for going away from it and all its horrible reminders.

But later, in a different mood, she knocked again on his door. The future she'd visualized was silly, puppies and a row of kennels and being alone. It was probably all right in its silly way, it was probably acceptable enough. But it wasn't a happy ending.

She could hear him in the room, yet he didn't answer. Something dropped to the floor, there was a rattle of paper. He was causing these noises deliberately, so that she'd know he was there, so that she'd know he didn't want to talk to her. His face had become cold and hard, like a face that could not smile and never had.

She knocked again, but still he didn't answer.

Stephen wished she wasn't always there. He wished she wasn't for ever tapping on the door of the room that was meant to be his, calling out to him when he didn't answer. She was there every morning as soon as he left the room, on the stairs or in the hall. A sloppy look kept coming into her face. She was sorry for him.

"Well, what are you two going to do today?" Mrs. Blakey had a way of saying, annoying Stephen because of the implication that everything

they did had to be done together. She said it in
the kitchen, on the Wednesday of that week, looking round from the Aga where she was frying
bacon. She put the bacon on to two warmed plates
and placed the plates in front of them. She asked
again what they were going to do.

"Shall we play Monopoly?" Kate suggested, as
though to please him.

"Oh, now, wouldn't you go outside?" Mrs.
Blakey cried. "Go on one of your tramps, why
don't you? Make yourself sandwiches, dears."

"Shall we?" Kate asked, looking at him.

He wanted to say that she should make sandwiches for herself and go on her own for what
Mrs. Blakey called a tramp. There was nothing
stopping her. If she was stupid enough not to
realize that Timothy Gedge would be waiting for
her it wasn't anyone's business except hers. He
returned her look, not saying all that. He wished
he could be alone, he tried to say with his own
look.

"There's bananas there for sandwiches, see."
Mrs. Blakey was already bustling about, taking
butter from the fridge and putting it on the edge
of the Aga to soften, taking a sliced loaf from
the bread-bin. "Chicken-and-ham paste, Stephen?
Liver-and-bacon? Sardine? Tomato? Apricot
jam?"

He wanted to pick up something from the
breakfast table and throw it on to the floor, the
plate from which Mr. Blakey had eaten his fry,
the apricot jam, the tea-pot, the bundle of knives
and forks that Kate had collected and put on top
of the pile of green cereal bowls. Why did she
collect the knives and forks and clear the table?

She didn't want to, nobody in their senses would want to: she did it because it was something her mother usually did. The feeling of anger increased, a choking in his throat. She'd stopped looking at him. She carried the cereal bowls and the knives and forks to the sink. She was about to wash them.

"No, leave them, dear," Mrs. Blakey said. "You make your sandwiches. And take apples. Granny Smiths in the cold room, Stephen."

"I don't think Stephen wants to go out."

"Oh, Stephie, why ever not?" Mrs. Blakey cried.

He left the kitchen without replying. He passed through the green-linoleumed passage and into the hall. There was a smell of polish. There were daffodils in bowls. The fire hadn't been lit yet, but soon it would be. The flames would flicker on the glass of the brass-framed pictures, enlivening the theatrical characters, making everything cozy.

He went to his bedroom and closed the door. He looked to see if there was a key in the lock, knowing there wasn't because he'd looked before.

"Essoldo Cinema, good morning, madam," a woman's voice said.

"Good morning," Mrs. Blakey said into the telephone. "Who's that, please?"

"Essoldo box-office here. We'd like to speak to the kids, madam."

"Is that Timothy Gedge?"

"Essoldo Cinema, madam. The kids was anxious about forthcoming attractions. Only we have a message to ring—"

"You've a message to ring nowhere. D'you think

I'm stupid or something? What do you want with them?"

"Forthcoming attractions, as requested yesterday A.M. Could you get hold of the kids, please? Only there's a queue forming."

Mrs. Blakey replaced the receiver. In the hall of Sea House she stood by the telephone, looking at it. She felt quite shaky. It had happened before, last night and yesterday morning. She hadn't guessed then that the woman's voice was Timothy Gedge's. She'd gone and found the children and they'd refused to come to the telephone, which had surprised her. The calls had come from a call-box because there'd been the call-box signal before the money was put in. Yet yesterday it hadn't occurred to her that there was anything wrong with such a sound coming from the Essoldo Cinema box-office.

As she stood in the hall, the recollection of the high-pitched voice seemed almost eerie to Mrs. Blakey; so did the fact that she hadn't bothered to think about the call-box signal. It was all absurd that she hadn't guessed straightaway, and absurd that he should be standing in a telephone booth somewhere, talking about a queue forming. But the absurdity had something else woven through it, some sort of reality, sense of a kind. Because it was Timothy Gedge, with his loitering and his telephoning, who had caused the silence in the house. She'd sensed something when he'd first stood in the garden with the children; she'd sensed it when she'd opened the hall-door to him.

"That boy'd give you the creeps," she said, still shaky in the glass-house where her husband was working.

Mr. Blakey raised his head from his seed-boxes. With soil-caked fingers he drew a handkerchief from a pocket and blew his nose. He did not say that a week ago the boy had been standing under the monkey-puzzle in the middle of the night, looking up at the windows of the house. It would have alarmed her if he had. She suffered slightly from blood pressure: there was no point in aggravating that. He said some kind of game was probably going on between the children and Timothy Gedge. "It'll be nothing," he said. "Children have their ways."

"They're not playing no game," Mrs. Blakey said, her grammar lapsing as it did when she was distressed. She wanted to remain in the earthy warmth of the glass-house, watching him pricking out seedlings. She didn't want to go back to the lies Kate told whenever she asked her what the matter was, to the telephone ringing and the queer, high-pitched voice insisting it was the box-office of the Essoldo Cinema.

"Essoldo Cinema, good morning," it said again, as soon as she picked up the receiver in the hall.

Stephen walked about his room, thinking about the house he was in, about the garden and the brick wall that surrounded it, and the white iron gate in the archway, and the setters and the summer-house. He hated all of it. He hated the room he'd been given as his own, with the picture of Tony Greig that someone had taken from his room in Primrose Cottage and pinned up on the wall, and the pictures of Greg Chappell, who'd once played for Somerset, and Brian Close. He hated the kitchen and the elegantly curving stair-

case and the Egyptian rugs on the stone floor
of the hall. He hated the big drawing-room, with
its French windows. He wanted the days to pass
so that he could be back at Ravenswood School,
safe in the dining-hall and his classroom. He
wanted to be in bed in his dormitory, in the bed
between Appleby's and Jordan's.

"We can't stay in for ever, Stephen. We can't
not ever go down to the beach again, or to the
spinney."

Akbar's tomb at Sikandra, he read, *was com-
pleted in 1613 and is one of the most important
monuments of its kind in India.*

"You go down. You do what you like." He spoke
without taking his eyes from the print. *The Maus-
oleum combines Hindu and Moslem art forms in
a remarkable manner*, he read, lying on his bed.

The evening before, the carrier-bag had been
at the foot of the monkey-puzzle, propped up
against the trunk, facing the house. It had been
placed there when Mr. Blakey had finished in the
garden. Stephen had seen it from the window
of his room, its red, white and blue vivid in the
twilight.

"If we told the Blakeys," Kate began to say, "if
we just said—"

"Are you insane or something?" He was shouting, suddenly glaring at her. His face was flushed.
He looked as though he loathed her. "Why d'you
keep saying it?"

"Because we can't just stay here. Because it's
silly to stay locked up in a house just because
you're afraid of someone." She was angry herself.
She jerked her chin up. She glared back at him.

"I'm not afraid of him," he said.

"Of course you are. He's a horrible person—"

"Oh, for God's sake, stop saying he's a horrible person!"

"I'll say it if I like, Stephen."

"Well, don't say it here. This is my room. It's meant to be private."

"There's no need to quarrel."

"What's it like for me, d'you think? Locked up in a house—"

"You're not locked up. There's no need to be locked up."

"Locked up in a house with people I don't even like."

"You do like us, Stephen."

"I don't like you and I don't like your mother. Everything was perfectly all right until your mother came along."

"She didn't come along. My mother was there all the time—"

"She came along and the trouble started. I don't want to talk about it to you."

"We have to talk about it, Stephen. We can't just leave it there, hanging there."

"Nothing's hanging there. I don't want to talk to you."

"You can't just not talk to me."

"I can do what I bloody like. This is my room. I'm reading a book in it."

"You're not reading a book. You're lying there pretending."

"I am reading a book. Sikandra is five miles from Agra if you want to know. The entrance to Akbar's tomb is of red sandstone with marble decorations."

"Oh, Stephen!"

"I want to be left alone. I don't like you. I don't like the way you're so bloody silly."

She began to say something else and then changed her mind. She said eventually:

"Don't let it upset you."

"Nothing's upsetting me."

"You know what I mean."

"I don't know what you mean and I don't want to. We don't have to do everything together. I'm sick of Mrs. Blakey talking about Granny Smiths. I'm sick of everything."

"You don't have to hate me."

"I'll hate you if I want to."

"But you don't and I don't hate you—"

"I don't mind if you hate me."

She looked at him lying on his bed, pretending to read. She wanted to cry and she imagined the tears flowing down her cheeks and dripping on to her jersey and how he'd probably say that she should go somewhere else to cry. She felt silly standing there. She wished she was grown-up, brisk and able to cope.

"You do mind if I hate you," she said.

He went on pretending to read and then he suddenly looked up and stared at her, examining her. His face was cold, that same unsmiling face, pinched and thin, his dark eyes cruel, as if he dared not let them be anything else.

"You're always going red. You go red for the least little thing. You'll be fat like Mrs. Blakey."

"I can't help going red—"

"You're ugly, even when you're not red you're ugly. You're unattractive. It's just silly to think you're going to grow up and be pretty."

"I don't think that."

"You said so. You said you wanted to be pretty. I don't care if you want to be pretty. I don't know why you tell me."

"I said I'd like to be. It's not the same—"

"Of course it's the same. If you'd like to be it means you want to be. It's stupid to say it doesn't."

"I didn't mean it like that."

"Why don't you say what you mean then?"

"I do say what I mean," she cried with sudden anger. "Why are you being so horrible to me? Why d'you keep away from me? Why can't you even speak to me?"

"I've told you."

"I haven't done anything."

"You're boring."

He returned to his encyclopaedia. She had to pause before she could speak because there were tears behind her eyes, her voice would be clogged with them. Blinking, she fought them back, aware of their actual withdrawal. It was horrible to be called boring. She said:

"I'm going down to the beach."

"You don't have to tell me."

"Stephen—"

"I don't care where you're going."

She went away, and after a minute or two he got up from his bed and went to the window. She was in the garden with the setters on their leads. He watched while she approached the gate in the wall, while she went through it and then passed out of sight. Ten minutes later she appeared on the distant seashore. As he watched her, he suddenly thought how childish it had been to imagine you could play number 3 for Somerset just because you'd once made seventeen in an over off the indifferent bowling of Philpott, A. J.

He took the carrier-bag from a drawer. He opened the door and paused for a moment, listening for sounds of Mrs. Blakey. He crossed the landing and mounted the narrow stairs to the attics. When he opened the faded green trunk the wedding-dress was there, at the very bottom, beneath clothes that were familiar to him.

On the seashore Kate threw two balls for the dogs, the red one and the blue one. She kept wanting to cry, as she had with Stephen, as she had for so much of the time since Timothy Gedge had come into their lives. The dogs bounded about her, obstreperously wagging their tails. Again she felt—and more vehemently now than she had felt it before—that Timothy Gedge was possessed.

"I missed seeing you," he said, coming from nowhere.

She told him then, unable to help herself: he was possessed by devils. He reveled in the idea of murder, he wanted to glorify the violence of murder in a marquee at the Easter Fête. He wanted people to applaud because harmless women had been killed. It would give him pleasure to make jokes that weren't funny while he was dressed up in the wedding-dress of a woman he claimed had been murdered also. He went to funerals because he liked to think of people being dead in coffins. There was nothing about him that wasn't unpleasant.

"Devils?" he said.

"You don't know what you're doing. You don't know the unhappiness you cause."

He shook his head. He didn't smile, as she'd expected he might. He said he only told the truth.

He followed her when she moved toward the cliffs and began to climb up the path that curved and twisted on the cliff-face. She asked him not to follow her, but he took no notice. He said:

"At half-past eleven on a Thursday morning I had the idea in Tussaud's."

He was talking nonsense. He was mocking and pretending, even though he wasn't grinning any more. His act with the brides in the bath was an excuse. His wanting a wedding-dress was an excuse for saying all the things he'd said. Nothing was as it appeared to be with him.

"Devils?" he said again. "D'you think I have devils, Kate?"

She didn't reply. The setters walked sedately on the cliff-path, beside the eleventh green. Ahead of them the weathered brick of the garden wall, touched with Virginia creeper, looked warm in the morning sun.

"Devils," he murmured, as if the sound of the word pleased him. He'd thought he'd die himself, he said when they came to the white iron gate, he'd thought he'd die when he'd heard the woman's scream, sharp as a blade above the whine of the wind and the rain. Kids should be protected from stuff like that, he said. You read it in the papers: it could ruin you for life, witnessing a murder.

〰〰〰〰〰〰〰〰〰〰〰〰〰〰

9

The Holy Week that had passed so harshly for
the children in Sea House had passed less fear-
fully in Dynmouth itself. The saints' days had
been noted by Quentin Featherston, St. Walter's,
St. Hugh's, St. Bademus's. St. Leo the Great, that
year, claimed Maundy Thursday.

The town has changed since Easter last year,
Miss Lavant wrote in her diary, *but only in small
little ways, not worth recording. Out walking this
morning I noticed Dr. Greenslade on his rounds.
Mrs. Slewy has been in trouble for taking the
cancer-box from the counter in Mock's.*

The orphans from the Down Manor Orphanage
progressed each day of that week in a crocodile
from Down Manor to the beach. In pairs, the
nuns from the convent walked on the promenade.
Old Ape received his Thursday hand-out at the
rectory. The Dynmouth Hards rampaged by night,
wives were swapped on the Leaflands Estate, old
Miss Trimm was buried. A niece of Miss Vine's
bought her a new budgerigar.

In the house which their son had accused them
of boringly christening Sweetlea the Dasses continued the lives which he'd said were boring also.
Mrs. Dass read two further novels by Dennis
Wheatley, and was unaware of the statements

made to her husband by Timothy Gedge. Her
husband lived uneasily with the statements. It
upset him, as much as it would have upset his
wife, to know that the boy had eavesdropped on
this most intimate family moment. The fact
gnawed at him, haunting him while he cleaned
out the sitting-room fire or made tea or used the
Electrolux. It was accompanied by an image:
Nevil standing in the dining-room and saying
what he had said, the boy peeping and listening.
Time, by passing, had soothed some of the harsh-
ness of the occasion. Yet for no apparent purpose
the painfully healing wound had been maliciously
opened.

But there was a purpose and he was reminded
of it, a purpose which seemed to Mr. Dass to be
so petty that he hadn't at first been able to take
it seriously. Then, while shopping in Fore Street
one morning, he was approached by Timothy
Gedge, who smiled at him as though nothing un-
toward had occurred between them and asked if
he had come to a decision about donating the
curtains. The boy walked beside him from the
Post Office to Lipton's, talking about the secret
that was safe between them, pursuing him into
the shop itself. "My God!" Mr. Dass cried, screw-
ing his eyes up as though seeking to peer into
the boy's brain. He had a wire basket in his left
hand, in which he had placed two tins of pine-
apple cubes. The bowl of his pipe hung from the
top pocket of his tweed jacket. "All right then,
Mr. Dass?" the boy said, going away at last.

Mr. Dass couldn't understand how a set of
curtains for the stage at the Easter Fête could
have driven a boy to such ends. Yet while his
wife slept one afternoon he found himself looking

in cardboard boxes in the attic for blackout curtains which he remembered from the War. "Yes,
I've found some," he said the next morning, approached again by the boy, as he'd known he
would be. He'd been down to the coke-cellar
beneath the church, where the stage was stored,
and with the assistance of Mr. Peniket he'd tried
the curtains for size. He'd left them in the
Courtesy Cleaners: they'd be ready in time for
Easter Saturday.

"You didn't mind me mentioning them, Mr.
Dass?" the boy said, smiling at him. Mr. Dass
did not reply, for there was nothing he felt he
might have said. In the eyes of this boy he and
his wife were probably ridiculous, she lying on a
sun-chair, he old and out of touch with the world.
They probably seemed as ridiculous to the boy
as they'd seemed boring to Nevil, who had been
right to say they had harmed him with their indulgence and from whom they would willingly
now have asked forgiveness. But they had done
no harm to Timothy Gedge, and if they seemed
ridiculous they couldn't really help it. Unable to
help it either, Mr. Dass ended by hating the boy.

In High Park Avenue life fell together. During
the first days of that Holy Week Mrs. Abigail
continued to believe that she could not endure a
marriage that was a travesty, and that she could
no longer endure life in Dynmouth. But as the
days went on the truth became less difficult to
live with than it had threatened to be, and she
knew that she would never leave her husband
because she, too, was to blame. The truth acquired a logic and an ordinariness, until in the
end her blindness to it in the past became puz-

zling to comprehend. Increasingly, she wondered
if in some unconscious way she had not simulated naivety since the first weeks of her marriage,
if she had not—through her uncontrollable self-
lessness—permitted a skin to grow instead of
probing beneath it. Married or unmarried, he
would not have had the courage of his pro-
clivities: he needed the pretense there had been
because pretense was everything to him.

Even within the handful of days of Holy Week,
further pretense modestly began its growth. The
Commander did not cease to deny the accusations
of Timothy Gedge, while at the same time seeking
his wife's foregiveness in a general way. She
recognized that he could not bear openly to
confess, yet that he wished to in order to pro-
nounce the mending of his ways. A message, un-
spoken, was there between them: he was to be
a new man, there was to be a new relationship.
But beneath the surface of resolution she knew
he would regain his former self and enjoy again
the shame of his surreptitious ways. He perked
up during that Holy Week, little by little, hour
by hour. He took up the daily routine of his swim
again, and one afternoon when he was in the sea
there was a visit to the bungalow by Timothy
Gedge.

"Fifteen p," the boy said, explaining that that
was the amount outstanding since the night he'd
cleaned the oven and left the tapioca saucepan
to steep.

She left him in the hall while she went to fetch
her purse. When she returned with the money he
brought up the matter of the dog's-tooth suit. He
asked if she'd had time to think about it. The
Commander never wore it, he pointed out. He

smiled at her, but the concern she'd once felt for him had wholly dissipated. "For the Easter Fête," he said. "I mentioned it."

She'd once been to the Easter Fête. She'd bought a pot of raspberry jam that had turned out to be bad. The talent contest had taken place in a marquee. *Spot the Talent!* a notice had said, but she hadn't chosen to do so.

"All right then?" he said, smiling again, his head a little on one side, a gesture he'd had as a small boy. "O.K. to have the suit, is it?"

"Of course not, Timothy." But while actually speaking she changed her mind. Quite suddenly it seemed fitting that the suit of her husband should garb a man who had slaughtered his brides: there was in that, somewhere, a gleam of relevance. It didn't matter to her that Timothy Gedge intended to enact monstrous scenes in a rectory garden. It would have mattered once, she'd once have attempted to prevent him: for his own sake, she would have said. Instead, again, she told her visitor to wait.

Her husband's naval uniform hung neatly in his mock-mahogany wardrobe, retained with pride. Next to it was a suit in plain gray worsted and then a mustardy one, a brown pinstripe, and the dog's-tooth. She could remember the purchase of each, standing about herself in Dunne's or Burton's, going from one branch to another. She remembered his tetchiness with shop assistants, which presumably had been simulated. No doubt he'd enjoyed this association with young men, trousers and jackets endlessly tried on in curtained booths. "Oh, we can alter that, sir," a youth would pleasantly promise. "Nice young chap," he'd say casually afterward, in Oxford Street or somewhere.

She found a flat cardboard box in the bottom of the wardrobe and placed the dog's-tooth suit in it. She didn't try to disguise the gap it left behind by drawing the other suits together. He'd notice and wouldn't mention it because mentioning would bring everything in the open again. He'd know what had happened to the suit, and it seemed right that he should: this small tribute to the truth that had been exposed seemed at least her due. She left the doors of the wardrobe open.

"Do not ever come back here," she said in the hall.

The boy had supplied her with facts. She should have been grateful. Yet as long as she lived she hoped she would never be obliged to exchange another word with him. She closed the hall-door while he stood there, shutting him for ever away from her.

In the rectory Lavinia Featherston's edginess reached a new proportion.

"He gives me the creeps," she angrily cried, protesting about Timothy Gedge as Mrs. Blakey had. She'd come across the twins propped up against the garage doors, applauding and screaming with delight at a patter delivered in a woman's voice. She'd snatched them away as if they were in danger, and afterward burst into Quentin's study to have her scene. She glared accusingly at him, investing him with all the blame for Timothy Gedge's presence in the garden. Furiously, she again spoke of Old Ape coming and going with his red plastic bucket, and Mrs. Slewy denying she'd ever touched a cancer-box in her life, and Miss Poraway and Mrs. Stead-Carter and old Miss Trimm, now mercifully dead. None of them at least had ever bothered the children. "He's not to come back," she snapped, banging the study door.

"We think you're too old," Quentin said, "to play with the twins, Timothy."

10

He was possessed by devils, Kate said, and then wept and could not contain herself. If you believed he was possessed, she whispered between her sobs, everything was explained.

In the kitchen Mrs. Blakey comforted her and Mr. Blakey sat at the scrubbed table stirring sugar into a cup of tea. Possessed by devils put him in mind of a case in the north of England: a man had become worse than ever apparently after clergymen of two denominations had attempted an exorcism ceremony. He'd seen on television once an exorcism ceremony, a clergyman's hands on the head of the afflicted person, the clergyman jerking about with spasms, perspiring and disheveled. Afterward the clergyman had said he could feel the devils leaving the body of the afflicted person, like an electrical current seemingly. And then the evil was meant to flow into his own body, where it could do no harm because of the presence of God. A lot of malarkey, Mr. Blakey had considered; clergymen on television looking for publicity. The man in the north of England had clearly been a nutcase. Extremely harmful it had been, meddling with him like that.

Kate's sobbing subsided and ceased. She sipped some of the cocoa Mrs. Blakey had made for her. She said she wanted Timothy Gedge to stop looking up at the windows of the house. She'd gone down to the seashore with the dogs and there he'd been, following her. He was an awful person.

"Say things, does he?" Mrs. Blakey asked as casually as she could, pushing a packet of wafer biscuits toward Kate.

"He says horrible things."

She ate a biscuit and drank more cocoa, Mrs. Blakey asked what kind of things, and she said just horrible things, things about people having secrets. He looked in people's windows, like Miss Lavant's. He followed people about. He listened to people's conversations. He harassed people with jokes that weren't funny.

She would not go into the detail that Mrs. Blakey urged her towards. "Unless you explain to us, dear," Mrs. Blakey began. "Unless you could say—"

"He's possessed, he's not a normal person: you can tell that when you're with him." She told them about the disturbed girl at St. Cecilia's, the girl called Julie who performed feats of levitation, and about the girl who could read a page of a newspaper and remember it, and Enid who could hypnotize with a fountain-pen top. She repeated what Rosalind Swain had said about odd things happening in adolescence, about adolescents harboring poltergeists. Devils could get into children because children were weak and didn't know what was happening to them. In the past there'd been cases of children who were witches.

Mrs. Blakey, only a little less skeptical than her husband of this line of talk, nevertheless recalled how Timothy Gedge had affected her when he'd come on to the telephone with a woman's voice, and her bewilderment when the silence had first begun in the house. Yet it was hard to believe that the explanation for all this was that a school-boy was in the hands of devils. Hypnosis and levitation and poltergeists were all very well, and so was remembering the page of a news-paper, but what on earth did devils mean? A hundred years ago they might have made sense, due to ignorance: like the child said, there'd been talk of witches. In Africa they were probably believed in even today, because of drum-beating and that. When she thought about them, she saw devils as small creatures with hooves and a tail, horned and two-legged and yet at the same time resembling tadpoles. It was extremely difficult to imagine an assocation between such creatures and a Dynmouth boy.

Yet Mrs. Blakey continued to sense the unease she'd been aware of on the telephone, which she'd first of all sensed when she'd looked out of the landing window and seen the boy with the chil-dren in the garden. The boy had waved at her. In retrospect his yellow clothes had seemed, just for a moment then, an outward sign of some disorder.

"It had nothing to do with a penknife, had it, Kate?"

"Penknife?"

"You said he'd lost his penknife."

Kate shook her head. Mrs. Blakey smiled encouragingly. It would help to know in what way precisely he maligned people, but the child remained as mum as a mute, one hand gripped tightly into a fist, the other holding the mug of cocoa. "Don't tell Stephen," was all she'd say. "Don't tell him I told you."

"Stephen went off with a carrier-bag, dear."

"Yes, I know."

"Has it to do with Timothy Gedge? The carrier, Kate?"

Kate shook her head again, saying she didn't know, and Mrs. Blakey was aware she wasn't telling the truth. You always knew when a child was lying, by the light in the child's eyes, as she'd discovered twenty-seven years ago with her own Winnie.

Kate finished her cocoa, listening to Mr. Blakey breathing while he drank his tea beside her. She wasn't sorry she'd told them what she said. "I missed seeing you," Timothy Gedge's voice said again, as it had on the beach. It had echoed after she'd left him, as she'd turned into the archway in the wall and passed through the shrubbery of azaleas and magnolias and tree mallows, as she'd passed through the drawing-room and the hall. "I missed seeing you," it had kept saying, just like it was saying now.

"Mr. Blakey'll speak to him," Mrs. Blakey said. "Mr. Blakey'll read the riot act if ever he shows his face again."

Kate nodded, but didn't feel reassured. What good were riot acts being read? What could you say to a person who was possessed since being possessed was a mystery? You couldn't know anything about a person who was possessed. All there was was the voice, going on like a weapon, confusing and tormenting.

There was a secret, Mrs. Blakey said, they were keeping a secret. "Won't you tell us, dear?" she pleaded, but Kate said it wasn't her secret to tell.

That night in bed, not able to sleep, she remembered she'd once knocked on Miss Malabedeely's door and when Miss Malabedeely hadn't answered she'd just gone in. Miss Malabedeely had been kneeling by a chair, praying, and Kate had thought immediately that she'd been asking God to stop Miss Shaw and Miss Rist being so unpleasant to her. Miss Malabedeely had looked embarrassed, discovered on her knees like that, but it hadn't mattered because of her niceness.

Kate remembered all that, and then she said to herself that she had been meant to remember it. She began to pray to God herself, seeing God quite clearly, as she always did when she said prayers, a robed, long-haired, bearded figure, partly obscured by clouds. She hadn't thought of praying before. For all the week that Timothy Gedge had been tormenting them it hadn't once occurred to her, which surprised her as she prayed now. She began to go through the whole thing in her prayer and then realized that God of course would know anyway, so she simply asked if it could be that Timothy Gedge was possessed by devils. The bearded face went on staring at her, the eyes not blinking, the lips not moving. But Kate knew she was being told she was right, that Timothy Gedge was possessed by devils and that before anything else could happen the devils must be taken out of him. Everything would be different if the devils were taken out of Timothy Gedge because God could do anything. He could perform miracles. He could turn what had happened into a dream. She could wake up and find that it was still the night of their parents' wedding, that only that afternoon she and Stephen had been on the train. She could lie there thinking about a most unpleasant nightmare, thanking God that it wasn't true.

She closed her eyes and communicated again with the figure. She promised that the devils would be cast out of Timothy Gedge, as it said in the Bible. When she concentrated, urging a reply, she was certain she was told that in return for her promise the facts of the last week would be altered, that yes, of course, a miracle was possible.

He smiled when Stephen came to him. He nodded and smiled, not reaching for the carrier-bag, waiting for Stephen to hold it out to him. He was sucking a gum. His sharp-boned face was lit with pleasure.

"I'll never forget it," he said, "the sound of your mum going over that cliff, Stephen."

~~~~~~~~~~~~~~~~~~~~~~~~~~~~~~~~~~~~~~~

11

It being Good Friday, the shops in Dynmouth were mostly closed. Fore Street and East Street were quiet, Pretty Street and Lace Street deserted. No one was about in the suburban roads and avenues.

In Sir Walter Raleigh Park, however, the activities of Ring's Amusements were reaching a crescendo: tomorrow afternoon, at one forty-five, the booths and stalls and whirligigs would welcome the public. The shouting of the dark-faced men was louder, the bustle more urgent, the dismantled machinery for the most part back in place again. A dozen or so extra men had made their appearance in Sir Walter Raleigh Park, with wives and children who now assisted with the preparations. Lines of washing hung between the caravans, transistor radios played loudly. There was a smell of frying.

The Queen Victoria Hotel and the Marine, the Duke's Head and the Swan were livelier with visitors than they had been. The Queen Victoria was full for the Easter weekend, the others nearly so. Some of these visitors strolled along the promenade; a few penetrated to the beach; none ventured on to the cliffs. Children eyed the closed Essoldo; a handful of golfers moved briskly on the

golf-course. Quentin Featherston cut the grass of
the rectory lawns again. It hadn't grown much
since he'd cut it a week ago, but he wanted the
lawns to have a shaved appearance for the Easter
Fête.

As he operated the Suffolk Punch, his thoughts
wandered idly, in and out about his parish,
through the poverty in Boughs Lane, among the
inadequate children of Mrs. Slewy. He'd woken
up at a quarter-past four that morning to find
Lavinia awake beside him, as often she was now
in the middle of the night. She said she was sorry
she'd been so cross about Timothy Gedge. She
worried about the twins, she said. The twins had
wandered out of the rectory garden and had been
missing for twenty minutes. They'd played with
matches in their room, lighting a fire in the garden of their dolls' house. All children, he'd begun
to say, but she'd cut him short. Another thing,
she didn't feel she was good any more at running
the nursery school. Indignantly, he'd told her
what nonsense that was. Her nursery school had
a waiting list a mile long. Everyone said it was
better than the Ring-o-Roses, where there was no
discipline of any kind whatsoever. And the playgroup that the WRVS ran was stodgy. In the end,
to his own surprise, he had quite successfully
smoothed away her early-morning blues, and she'd
returned to sleep without having mentioned once
the child she'd lost.

As he walked behind the lawnmower he didn't
care for, he remembered the first time he'd ever
seen her. He'd met her on the beach walking with
a dog, a wire-haired terrier called Dolly which
had come sniffing up to him. He'd told her he'd
come to Dynmouth to help old Canon Flewett.

He'd loved her immediately, without any hesitation.

He loved her still, with just the same passion. "You're to be good with Mummy," he'd commanded the twins after breakfast. "Do you understand now?" He'd regarded them unsmilingly, as ferociously as he could. If there was trouble of any kind whatsoever that day, either the lighting of fires or leaving the rectory garden for a single instant, they would not be permitted to attend the Easter Fête. They would be put in two separate rooms, with the curtains drawn. Humbly they had promised to be good.

He emptied the grass-box, depositing the cuttings in a corner. He said to himself that there was nothing wrong with cutting grass on Good Friday. There'd been services in St. Simon and St. Jude's every day this week. There'd been Holy Communion at eight this morning, and afternoon prayers. Later there'd be evensong. Yet a few of his older parishioners, passing by the rectory wall and hearing the engine of the Suffolk Punch, might consider it odd that grass should be cut by a clergyman on the day of the Crucifixion. Mr. Peniket would certainly consider it odd and would again recall the days of old Canon Flewett. Nothing would ever be said, but the activity would be seen as part of a clerical decline. It would sadden Mr. Peniket and the older parishioners, and it saddened Quentin to think it would, but he saw no point in sitting in a chair and meditating all day.

His name was called, and he turned his head and saw Lavinia waving at him from the porch. Beside her stood a child, not either of the twins.

He turned the engine of the lawnmower off and waved back. He began to walk toward them.

The child was a girl, wearing corduroy jeans and a red jersey. Lavinia was wearing a tartan skirt and a green blouse and cardigan. He apologized when he was close enough, because he guessed he hadn't been able to hear Lavinia calling to him above the noise of the Suffolk Punch. The child had brown hair, curving about a round face, and eyes that were round also.

"Kate wants to speak to you," Lavinia said.

She must have once been a child of the nursery school. He looked more closely at her, remembering her: she was the child from Sea House, her parents were divorced. She didn't come to church, or to Sunday school. Faintly, he remembered Lavinia once saying that the little girl from Sea House was going to come to the nursery school next term. Before the twins were born it would have been, seven or eight years ago, the nursery school's earliest days.

"Well, Kate?" he said in his study, a small room with a cross over the mantelpiece. He was alone with the child because Lavinia didn't ever remain when a visitor came to see him. "It's that boy, Timothy Gedge," Lavinia had said, and then had called out to the twins, who were clamoring for her upstairs somewhere. "I'm here in the hall," she'd shouted as Quentin closed the study door.

It was a rigmarole, a muddled torrent of words, not easy to follow and yet startling. Timothy Gedge had looked through the window of Miss Lavant's bedsitting-room and had seen her pretending to give Dr. Greenslade a meal. Timothy Gedge had met Mr. Plant half undressed in the middle of the night. Timothy Gedge had become drunk in the Abigails' bungalow. He'd been annoying the Dasses. He'd said to Mrs. Abigail that her husband went homo-ing about the place. The act he'd devised for the Easter Fête was a black mass. Timothy Gedge was possessed.

"Possessed?" He was sitting behind his desk. Beside him there was a calendar with a square red frame around yesterday's date. He moved the red frame and felt its magnetic base gripping the surface again. "Possessed?" he repeated, as calmly as he could.

She didn't answer. She was facing him across his desk, sitting on the dining-room chair that was specially placed for visitors with troubles. She said that the act Timothy Gedge had devised had to do with the Brides in the Bath. He planned to dress up as each bride in turn and also as their murderer. It was all only an excuse. It was because he liked the idea of death, because he wanted to talk about it. The place for the people of Dynmouth, he'd said, was in their coffins.

The child had begun to cry. He went to her and bent over her, giving her a handkerchief. He put an arm around her shoulders and kept it there for a moment. Then he returned to his desk and sat behind it. He thought of the funerals Timothy Gedge hung around. "Really good," he'd said again, in the vestry, after Miss Trimm's. The child said he claimed to have witnessed a murder, and had been affected by it. Stephen's mother hadn't fallen from the cliff-path in a gust of wind: she had been pushed by Stephen's father.

"I love Stephen," she said, and then she repeated it, her tears returning. "I can't bear it, seeing Stephen so frightened."

He knew who Stephen was. He remembered

him at the funeral of his mother. He remembered speaking to him, saying he'd been brave. The parents of these children were now married. The man was an ornithologist.

"There's no need for anyone to be frightened, Kate."

She said she had prayed because it was impossible for people to live in a house like that, with lies everywhere, as there would have to be. In desperation she had prayed. She said:

"You have to exorcise devils. Could you exorcise the devils in Timothy Gedge?"

He was taken aback, and more confused than he'd been a moment ago. He slightly shook his head, making it clear he didn't intend to exorcise devils.

"When I prayed," she said, "I promised. I said, if it wasn't true, then the devils would be exorcised. I promised God."

"God wouldn't want a promise like that. He doesn't make bargains. I can't just exorcise a person because he tells a lie."

"Lie?"

"Stephen's father wasn't in Dynmouth the day the accident happened. He came back from London and someone had to tell him at the station. He was actually on a train when it happened."

She looked at him, her eyes opening wider and then wider. Tears still glistened on one of her cheeks. Her lips parted and closed again. Eventually she said:

"I prayed and He changed things."

"No, Kate. Nothing has changed. Before you prayed it was true that Stephen's father was not here that day."

"You must exorcise Timothy Gedge, Mr. Featherston."

He tried to explain. He didn't believe in the idea of people possessed by devils, because it seemed to him that that was only a way of trying to tidy up the world by pigeon-holing everything. There were good people, and people who were not good: that had nothing to do with devils. He tried to explain that possession by devils was just a form of words.

"I told him he had devils," she said.

"You shouldn't have, Kate."

"I promised God. God wants it, Mr. Featherston."

She cried out, her tears brimming over again, red in the face. The brown hair that curved in around her cheeks seemed suddenly untidy.

"I promised God," she cried again.

She was still sitting down, leaning forward in her chair, burning at him with her round eyes. It was like being in the room with Miss Trimm yet again confiding that she'd mothered another Jesus Christ. Miss Trimm had talked about her son as an infant, how he had blessed the fishermen on Dynmouth Pier, how he had emerged from her womb without pain. In her days as a school-teacher she'd been known for the quickness of her wit and her clarity of thought. But in her lonely senility her eccentric belief had been un-shakable, the world had become impossible without the closeness of God. This child in her distress appeared to have discovered something similar.

Yet he was unable to help her, unable even properly to converse with her. God's world was not a pleasant place, he might have said. God's world was cruel, human nature took ugly forms.

It wasn't God who cultivated lily-of-the-valley or
made Dynmouth pretty with lace and tea-shops
or made the life of Jesus Christ a sentimental
journey. But how on earth could he say that, any
more than he could have said it to Miss Trimm?
How could he say that there was only God's insis-
tence, even though He abided by no rules Himself,
that His strictures should be discovered and
obeyed? How could he say that God was all vague
promises, and small print on guarantees that no
one knew if He ever kept? It was appalling that
Timothy Gedge had terrified these children, yet it
had been permitted, like floods and famine.

"He'll do something terrible," she said, weeping
copiously now. "It's people like that who do terrible things."

"I'll talk to him, Kate."

Faintly, she shook her head. She was huddled
on her chair, her small hands clenched, pressed
against her stomach, as though some part of her
were in pain, her face blotched. He felt intensely
sorry for her, and useless.

"He loves hurting," she said. People had done
him no harm, the Dasses, the Abigails. He
laughed when he mentioned the name of the
Dasses' house. "Mrs. Abigail didn't know about
her husband. He went and told her. He got drunk
on beer and sherry—"

"So you said, Kate."

"He thinks it's funny."

"Yes."

"He thinks it's funny to do an act like that."

"His act won't be permitted."

"He made us think a murder had been committed. We both believed it. Don't you see?" she
cried. "We both believed it."

"I do see, Kate."

"They'd have driven a stake through him. They'd have burnt his bones until they were cinders."

"We're more civilized now."

"We couldn't be. He wouldn't be alive if we were more civilized."

"Kate—"

"He shouldn't be alive. It's that that shouldn't be permitted." She screamed the words at him. He let a silence fall. Then he said:

"You mustn't say that, Kate."

"I'm telling you the truth."

There was another silence, only broken by her sobbing. She wiped her face with his handkerchief and then held the handkerchief tightly, squeezing it in her fists. He said there was a pattern of grays, half-tones and shadows. People moved in the grayness and made of themselves heroes or villains, but the truth was that heroes and villains were unreal. The high drama of casting out devils would establish Timothy Gedge as a monster, which would be nice for everyone because monsters were a species on their own. But Timothy Gedge couldn't be dismissed as easily as that. She had been right to say it was people like that who do terrible things, and if Timothy Gedge did do terrible things it would not be because he was different and exotic but because he was possessed of an urge to become so. Timothy Gedge was as ordinary as anyone else, but the ill fortune of circumstances or nature made ordinary people eccentric and lent them color in the grayness. And the color was protection because ill fortune weakened its victims and made them vulnerable.

While he spoke, he saw reactions in the child's

face. She didn't like what he said about shades
of gray, nor the suggestion that villains and
heroes were artificial categories. It cut across her
child's world. It added complications she didn't
wish to know about. He watched her thinking
that as he spoke, and then he saw everything he'd
said being summarily dismissed. She shook her
head.

She spoke of an idyll and said that God would
not permit it now. She would go back to Sea
House and tell Stephen that his father had been
on a train at the time of his mother's death. The
nightmare was over, but in its place there was
nothing. They would be friends again, but it
wouldn't be the same.

"I can't explain," she said, quite recovered now
from her passion and her tears.

She meant he wouldn't understand. She meant
it wasn't any good just talking, sitting there beneath a cross that hung on a wall. She meant he
might at least have promised to have a go at shaking the devils out, even if he didn't quite believe
in them; he might at least have tried. No wonder
clergymen weren't highly thought of. All that was
in her face, too.

She walked away from the rectory, up Once
Hill and then on to the narrow road that wound,
eventually, to Badstoneleigh. If they'd told the
Blakeys a week ago the Blakeys would have said
what the clergyman had said: that Stephen's
father could not have been responsible. She kept
thinking of that, of their telling Mrs. Blakey in
the kitchen and Mrs. Blakey throwing her head
back and laughing. They'd all have laughed, even
Mr. Blakey, and then quite abruptly Mrs. Blakey

would have said that Timothy Gedge deserved to be birched.

"You like a cuppa, Mr. Feather?"

Quentin declined the offer. The boy was alone in the flat in Cornerways. He'd explained that his sister was on the pumps at the Smiling Service Filling Station, even though it was Good Friday. His mother was over in Badstoneleigh for the day, seeing her sister, the dressmaker. He led the clergyman into a room that had the curtains drawn. Deanna Durbin was singing on the television screen.

"I wanted to talk to you," Quentin said.

"Is it about the competition, Mr. Feather?"

"In a way. The little girl from Sea House came to see me. Kate."

Timothy laughed. With annoying irrelevance it occurred to Quentin that the name of the film on the television screen was *Three Smart Girls*, which he'd seen about thirty-five years ago, when he was a child himself.

"Do you mind if we have the television off, Timothy?"

"Load of rubbish 's matter of fact, sir. TV's for the birds, Mr. Feather." He turned it off. He sat down without drawing back the curtains. In the gloom he was only just visible, the gleam of his teeth when he smiled, his pale hair and clothes.

"You've upset people, Timothy."

"Which people had you in mind, Mr. Feather?"

"I think you know."

"There's some upset easy, sir. There's Grace Rumblebow down at the Comprehensive—"

"I'm not talking about Grace Rumblebow."

"I give her a prick with a needle. You'd think

I'd cut her foot off. D'you know Grace Rumble-bow, Mr. Feather?"

"Yes, I do, but it isn't Grace Rumblebow—"

"Unhealthy she is, the size of her. She's ob-sessed on doughnuts, did you know? Forty or fifty a day, three gallons of beer, drop dead one of these days—"

"Why have you caused this trouble, Timothy?"

"What trouble's that, Mr. Feather?"

"Those two children."

"They're tip-top kids, sir. Friends of mine."

"Timothy—"

"The three of us went to the flicks, over Bad-stoneleigh way. James Bond stuff, load of rub-bish really. I bought the kids Coca-Cola, Mr. Feather, as much as they could drink. I explained to them about the act I've got."

"I've been told about your act. I'm afraid it isn't suitable for the competition, Timothy."

"You haven't seen the act, sir."

"I've heard about it."

"That kid's talking through her umbrella, sir. It's a straight routine, sir, it'll bring the place down. D'you ever watch Benny Hill, Mr. Feather?"

"What happened to those three women wasn't funny."

"It's a long time ago, Mr. Feather."

"I'd like you to give me the wedding-dress you got from the children."

"What wedding-dress is that, sir?"

"You know what I mean. You terrorized those children, you bullied them into getting a wedding-dress for you."

"I got a dog's-tooth off the Commander. Dass come up with the curtains, they're down in the

Courtesy Cleaners. I have Plant coming up with a bath."

"You've been telling lies."

"I definitely told the truth, Mr. Feather. The Commander's gay as a grasshopper, old Dass's son walks in and tells them they make him sick to the teeth. I only reminded Dass about that, sir. I only explained I was listening in at the time. I didn't make anything up."

"That boy imagined his father was a murderer. You made him imagine that. For no earthly reason you caused him to believe a monstrous lie."

"I wouldn't say it was a lie, Mr. Feather. George Joseph Smith—"

"It has nothing to do with George Joseph Smith. The child's father was on a train. He was nowhere near that cliff when his wife was killed. Nor were you, Timothy."

"I was often in the gorse, Mr. Feather. I like following people about."

"You weren't in the gorse then. And a murder did not take place."

"I heard them having a barney, Mr. Feather. A different time this is, if you get me. She's calling the girl's mum a prostitute. I heard her, sir: 'Why don't you throw me down?' she says. He told her not to be silly."

"Timothy—"

"I'd call it murder, Mr. Feather. If the man was on two thousand trains I'd call it murder."

"She fell over a cliff."

"She went down the cliff because he was on the job with the other woman. He was fixing to get rid of the first one in the divorce courts. I was up at Sea House one night, looking in through the window—"

"I don't want to know what you were doing."
He shouted angrily. He jumped up from the chair
he was sitting on and knocked something on to
the floor, something that must have been on the
arm.

"You knocked over an ash-tray, Mr. Feather."

"Look, Timothy. You told those children terrible lies—"

"Only I wouldn't call them lies, sir. I'm afraid
of what she'll do,' the man says when I was
looking in through the window, and then the
other woman goes up to him and starts loving
him. She's stroking his face with her fingers, a
married man he was, and then the next thing
is—"

"That doesn't concern us, Timothy."

"The next thing is, sir, I was there in the gorse
again. She was crying and moaning in the wind,
sir, up there on her owny-oh with nobody giving
a blue damn about her. She went down the cliff
when a gust of wind came."

"Timothy—"

"They pushed her, Mr. Feather. D'you get what
I mean? She was fed up with the carry-on."

"You don't really know, Timothy. You're guessing and speculating."

Timothy Gedge shook his head. It had upset
him at the time, but you had to get over stuff like
that or you'd go to the wall. He smiled. You had
to keep cheerful, he said, in spite of everything.

"That wedding-dress must be returned. I've
come for that, Timothy."

"I was thinking maybe that Hughie Green
would be in Dynmouth, Mr. Feather. Only I heard
of stranger things. I was thinking he'd maybe
walk into the marquee—"

"That's nonsense and you know it. Your act has been an excuse to torment people. You had no right to behave to those children as you did."

"I can do a woman's voice, Mr. Feather, I had them in stitches up at the Comprehensive. I had your own two kiddies in stitches." He laughed. "The *charrada* of the clown, Mr. Feather, if ever you've heard of it."

Quentin sat down again. He told Timothy he lived in fantasies. His act had been devised, he said again, so that people could be shocked and upset. To his surprise he saw Timothy nodding at him through the dimness, before he'd finished speaking.

"As a matter of fact, it was for the birds, sir." There was a silence. Then he added:

"I often thought it was maybe for the birds. The only people who liked it was your kiddies."

"I'd like to help you, you know."

"I'm happy as a sandboy, Mr. Feather."

"I don't think you can be."

"I put a lot of thought into that act. I used to walk around the place, thinking about it. And all the time it was a load of rubbish. Kids' stuff, Mr. Feather." He nodded. He explained, as he had to everyone else, how his act had come about: Miss Wilkinson's charades, the visit to Madame Tussaud's. He explained about how the philosophy of Brehon O'Hennessy had remained with him, even though at the time Brehon O'Hennessy had seemed to everyone to be a nutter.

"The kid remarked I had devils." He laughed. "Do you think I have devils, Mr. Feather?"

"No, Timothy."

"I fancied the idea of devils."

"Yes."

"The sexton doesn't care for you, does he, Mr. Feather? That Mr. Peniket?"

"I'm afraid I've no idea."

"Does he think you're laughable, Mr. Feather?"

Quentin did not reply. Timothy said:

"If you want the wedding-dress you can have it, sir."

"I'd like it."

The boy left the room and on the way he turned the light on. He returned with an old, torn suitcase and a flat cardboard box. He opened the suitcase and took from it the carrier-bag with the Union Jack on it. He handed this to Quentin. The wedding-dress was still in it, he said, he hadn't even taken it out. "There's this," he said, holding out the cardboard box. "Abigail's dog's-tooth." He suggested that Quentin might like to return the suit to the bungalow in High Park Avenue, since he was returning the wedding-dress. There were other things in the suitcase, he explained, but they had nothing to do with his act. He'd known he wouldn't be putting on the act as soon as the boy had handed him the carrier. He'd said to himself as he walked away with it that all along the act had been a load of rubbish.

"You must leave those children alone now."

"They're no use to me, Mr. Feather." He laughed. "Opportunity won't knock, sir. I'll get work in the sandpaper factory. I'll maybe go on the security. My dad scarpered. Like Dass's son." He laughed, and Quentin realized that the Dasses' son was one of the people whom Timothy had had conversations with on the streets of Dynmouth. He recalled the rather unhealthy appearance of Nevil Dass, the hot-house appearance of a youth too heavily cosseted.

"I gave him the idea," Timothy said, "when I told him about my dad. 'You just walk out,' I told him. 'Don't ever come back.' He was down in the Queen Victoria for two hours, plucking up courage on Double Diamond."

"Timothy—"

"There was just the thing about the entrance fee, sir. Fifty p I give Dass."

Quentin gave him the coin, apologizing because he'd forgotten about it. Timothy said it didn't matter. He began to talk again about Stephen handing him the wedding-dress, how he'd walked away with it and had then sat down on a seat on the promenade, not wanting to go on with his act any more. Miss Lavant had passed by and had smiled at him.

"She gave me a sweet one time when I was a kid, a bag of Quality Street she had. She's always had a smile for me, Mr. Feather."

Quentin nodded, preventing himself from saying that Miss Lavant's sweets and smiles were beside the point.

"It never occurred to me till yesterday, sir. She gave birth to his baby."

"I'd like to help you," Quentin said again, and Timothy laughed again.

"Did you ever hear it said, sir, that Miss Lavant and Dr. Greenslade—"

"Timothy, please."

"Only she gave birth to his baby, sir."

"That isn't true, Timothy."

"I'd say it was, sir. She gave birth to it, only she couldn't keep the kid by her because of what Dynmouth people would say about it. She removed herself from the town for the birth. The doctor goes with her, saying he was in Yorkshire on medical business. The next thing is they get the kid fixed up with a Dynmouth woman so's they can see it growing. D'you get it, Mr. Feather?"

"That's the purest fantasy, Timothy."

"D'you get the picture, though? Forty or fifty a week the Dynmouth woman's paid."

"Oh, don't be silly now. You know as well as I do a child was never born to Miss Lavant. Dr. Greenslade is a happily married man—"

"It never occurred to me till yesterday, Mr. Feather, when I was sitting on the seat and she smiled at me. She was scared out of her skin the time I was walking along the wall of the prom. 'Come down, please,' she says in that voice of hers, holding out the bag of Quality Street. It's like something on a television thing, *Crossroads* maybe, or *General Hospital*, or the one about the women in a prison."

"You're talking nonsense, Timothy."

"The man walks into this room, Mr. Feather, and the baby's there on the table. He takes one look at it and the next thing is he's shouting. It's not his baby is what he's saying, no more than it's hers. He's not going in for any pretending over a baby unless he comes in for a share of the cash, bloody ridiculous it is. She goes up to him and tells him to stuff himself and in a flat half-minute he's belting the old lorry up the London road. Isn't that the way it happened, Mr. Feather? Isn't it true?"

"Of course it isn't true."

"If you close your eyes you can see it in this room, the two of them standing there, rough kind of people. She's an awful bloody woman, as a matter of fact."

"That'll do, Timothy. And if you go bothering Miss Lavant—"

"We have the secret between us, sir. I wouldn't mention it to another soul. I'd quicker burn than mention it to Miss Lavant. I wouldn't embarrass her with it."

"You watch too much television, Timothy."

"There's good stuff on the telly. D'you watch it yourself ever? Does Mrs. Feather tune in at all? Only there's women's programs on in the afternoon, cooking hints, what to do with a fox-fur, anything you'd name. There's educational programs, not that Mrs. Feather needs education. Only there's good stuff for the ignorant. You know what I mean, sir?"

"Forget the story you've made up about Miss Lavant, Timothy. It's childish, you know."

"When she smiled at me yesterday I could see a resemblance. Did you ever notice the doctor's cheek-bones? He has sharp cheek-bones, like a person I could mention not a million miles away."

"Please, Timothy."

"If you tell me to forget it I will, Mr. Feather. I'll put it out of my mind. I'll promise you that, sir."

"Thank you."

"Easy as skinning a cat, sir. All right then, Mr. Feather?" He moved toward the television set. He waited with his hand on a knob, politely.

"I'm always there," Quentin said, and Timothy laughed. He turned the light out as the clergyman left the room.

He secured the flat cardboard box on the

carrier of his bicycle with a piece of string that
was tied to the carrier for such a purpose. He
hung the bag with the Union Jack on it from
the handle-bars.

He cycled to High Park Avenue and rang the
bell of Number Eleven. When Mrs. Abigail answered the door he handed her the box, saying he
believed it was her property. He was sorry, he
said, unable to think of anything better to say.
He was sorry Timothy Gedge had been a nuisance.
With some reluctance Mrs. Abigail took the box
from him. It didn't matter about Timothy Gedge,
she said, as long as he never came to the bungalow again.

He cycled to Sweetlea and there, too, said he
was sorry that Timothy Gedge had been a nuisance. It was very kind to have supplied curtains
for the stage. "Curtains?" Mrs. Dass exclaimed
softly, from her sun-chair in the bow window,
and her husband confessed that he'd found an
old set of blackout curtains that were just about
right for size.

It wouldn't be necessary, Quentin told Mr. Plant,
to convey the bath from Swines' yard to the
rectory garden: Timothy Gedge's act would not
be included in the Spot the Talent competition
because it wasn't suitable. Mr. Plant seemed
doubtful when he heard that. He'd promised the
boy, he said, he never liked to break a promise.
"I've talked to the boy," Quentin said. "I'm sorry
he was a nuisance, Mr. Plant." But Mr. Plant
denied that Timothy Gedge had been a nuisance
in any way whatsoever. He liked to do his bit,
he said, for the Easter Fête or for any other good
cause. If a bath needed moving he was only too

willing; if it was to stay where it was, no problem either.

"I think this is yours," Quentin said in Sea House, handing Stephen the bag with the wedding-dress in it.

He felt foolish, doing all that. He saw himself: an ineffectual clergyman on a bicycle, lanky and gray-haired, a familiar sight, tidying up. He remembered the child's face when he'd tried to explain to her about devils. Timothy Gedge had used him to practice a fantasy on.

"Almighty God, we beseech Thee graciously to behold this Thy family," he said in his church, murmuring the words in the presence of a small congregation. There was a smell of prayer-books and candle-grease, which he liked. "For which our Lord Jesus Christ was contented to be betrayed, and given up into the hands of wicked men, and to suffer death upon the cross."

It was true, it had the feel of truth: the woman hadn't just fallen over a cliff. Yet what good came from knowing that a woman had killed herself? The children who had suffered a trauma would survive the experience, scarred by it and a little flawed by it. They would never forget that for a week they had imagined the act of murder had been committed. They would never see their parents in quite the same way again, and ironically it was apt that they should not, because Timothy Gedge had not told lies entirely. The gray shadows drifted, one into another. The truth was insidious, never blatant, never just facts.

"God be merciful to us," he said, "and bless us: and show us the light of His countenance."

The boy would stand in court-rooms with his smile. He would sit in the drab offices of social workers. He would be incarcerated in the cells of different jails. By looking at him now you could sense that future, and his eyes reminded you that he had not asked to be born. What crime would it be? What greater vengeance would he take? The child was right when she said it was people like that who did terrible things.

The church was without flowers because of Lent. Old Ape was in the shadows at the back, Mrs. Stead-Carter looked impatient at the front.

"The peace of God," he said, "which passeth all understanding, be with you and remain with you, tonight and for evermore."

Their heads were bowed in prayer and then they slowly raised them. They shuffled off, Mrs. Stead-Carter brisker than the others, Miss Poraway waiting to say goodbye. Mr. Peniket collected the prayer-books and straightened the hassocks.

As he disrobed in the vestry, Quentin paused more than once, glancing at the closed door, as though expecting the boy to appear with his smile. He thought he might because evening prayer on Good Friday was in a way a funeral service. But the boy didn't come. Quentin took his black mackintosh from a hook and put it on.

In the empty church more truth nagged, making itself felt. It didn't belong in the category of murder, or of suburban drama with sex or filial rejection. Yet it seemed more terrible, a horror greater than the Abigails' marriage or the treatment of the Dasses by their son, greater even than the death of Stephen's mother because Stephen's mother had sought peace and at least had found it. It filled his mind, and slipped through the evening streets of Dynmouth with him as he rode his bicycle back to his ivy-clad rectory. It kept him company on Once Hill and as he pushed the bicycle into the garage and leaned it against the Suffolk Punch.

In the sitting-room Lavinia listened.

"Horror?" she said, bewildered by her husband's emotion. He stood with his back to the sitting-room door, leaning against the door-frame. His bicycle-clips were still around his ankles. "Horror?" she said again.

Two people had derived a moment of pleasure from the boy's conception. The mother you could see about the place, hurrying on the streets of Dynmouth, a woman with brass-colored hair who sold clothes in a shop. The father was anonymous. The father had probably been unhappy with his wife; he'd probably set up another family somewhere. The boy had become what he was while no one was looking. The boy's existence was the horror he spoke of.

Lavinia wanted to say she was sorry for Timothy Gedge, but did not because it didn't seem true. An image of Timothy Gedge hovered, smiling in his irritating way. She knew what the child had meant, saying he had devils in him. She remembered how he had given her the creeps.

"I should have been honest with that child this morning."

"Of course you were honest, Quentin."

He shook his head. He said he should have said that morning that if you looked at Dynmouth in one way you saw it prettily, with its teashops and lace; and that if you looked at it in another way there was Timothy Gedge. You could even drape prettiness over the less agreeable aspects of Dynmouth, over Sharon Lines on her kidney

machine and the world of Old Ape and Mrs.
Slewy's inadequate children and the love that
had ruined Miss Lavant's life. You could make it
all seem better than it was by reminding yourself
of the spirit of Sharon Lines and the apparent
contentment of Old Ape and the cigarette cocked
jollily in the corner of Mrs. Slewy's mouth and
the way in which Miss Lavant had learned to
live with her passion. But you couldn't drape
prettiness over Timothy Gedge. He had grown
around him a shell because a shell was necessary.
His eyes would for ever make their simple statement. His eyes were the eyes of the battered
except that no one had ever battered Timothy
Gedge.

"But surely," Lavinia said, beginning some
small protest and then not continuing with it.
"Come and sit down," she urged instead.

Existence had battered him, he said, remaining
where he was, seeming not to have heard her:
there'd been a different child once. He paused
and shook his head again. What use were services
that recalled the Crucifixion when there was
Timothy Gedge wandering about the place, a far
better reminder of waste and destruction? What
on earth was the point of collecting money to
save the tower of a church that wasn't even
beautiful? He was a laughable figure, with his
clerical collar, visiting the sick, tidying up.

"You're not laughable, Quentin."

"I can do nothing for that boy."

He took his black mackintosh off, and his
bicycle-clips. He came and sat beside her, saying
that the story of Timothy Gedge seemed to be
there to mock him. The story wasn't fair. You
couldn't understand it and mockingly it seemed

that you weren't meant to: it was all just there,
a small-scale catastrophe, quite ordinary although
it seemed not to be. Wasn't it just as neat and
unlikely to blame the parents as it was to talk
about possession by devils? Were the parents so
terrible in their sins? Didn't it seem, really, to be
just bad luck?

She didn't understand. "Bad luck?" she said.

"To be born to be battered. To be Sharon Lines
or Timothy Gedge."

"But surely—"

"God permits chance."

Lavinia looked at her husband, looking into his
eyes, which contained the weariness that his
words implied. It wasn't easy for him, having to
accept that God permitted chance, any more than
it was easy for him to be a clergyman in a time
when clergymen seemed superfluous. He would
pray for Timothy Gedge and feel that prayer
wasn't enough in a chancy world.

"It depresses you," he said, and felt as he spoke
that he'd be better employed packing fish in the
fish-packing station than in charge of a church.
His house of holy cards had collapsed through
his own ineptitude. The opinion of the child that
morning, and of Timothy Gedge, was an opinion
shared by the greater part of Dynmouth: there
were the shreds of a traditional respect for his
calling, and then impatience, occasionally con-
tempt.

It was hard to comfort him. Awful things happened, she said, feeling the statement to be lame;
yet people had to go on. It was impossible to
know the truth about Timothy Gedge, why he
was as he was; no one could know with certainty.
The Easter Fête would take place. They'd hope

for a fine day. He had a wedding at half-past ten and another at twelve. He should go to bed, she said.

"He's pretending he's Miss Lavant's child."

"Miss Lavant's? But Miss Lavant—"

"Miss Lavant's and Dr. Greenslade's. A child that was given to Mrs. Gedge to bring up."

"But where on earth did he get that idea?"

"It replaces his fantasy about going on a television show."

"But he can't believe it."

"He does. And more and more he will."

There was a silence for a moment in the sitting-room, and then Lavinia said again that he should go to bed.

He nodded, not moving, not looking at her.

"You're tired," she said, and added that there was no point in gloom because gloom made everything worse. There were the good things, too, she reminded him. There were children who were loved and who were lovable. There were his own two children, and thousands of others, in Dynmouth and everywhere. It was only the odd one who grew a shell like Timothy Gedge's.

He nodded again, turning to look at her.

"I'm sorry I've been so dreary lately," she said. "I'm sorry."

"You're never dreary, Lavinia."

They went to bed and when Lavinia woke in the night it was Timothy Gedge she thought of, not her lost child. Was it really impossible to know the truth about him? She wondered how he would be now if he'd been brought up in the Down Manor Orphanage. She wondered how he'd be if his father had not driven off or if his mother had shown him more affection. How would he be if

on one of those Saturday mornings when he'd
hung around the rectory she'd recognized herself
the bitterness beneath his grin?

She couldn't believe that the catastrophe of
Timothy Gedge was not somehow due to other
people, and the circumstances created by other
people. Quentin was wrong, she said to herself.
She was certain he was wrong, certain that it was
not just bad luck in a chancy world; but she did
not intend to argue with him. And doubting her
husband on this point, she wondered if Timothy
Gedge's future was as bleak as he had forecast.
She thought about it without finding any kind of
answer, and then she thought about the futures
of her nursery-school children and others among
the children of Dynmouth. What men would her
own two children marry, if they married at all?
Would they be happy? Would the children of Sea
House be happy? Would Stephen ever discover
that Timothy Gedge had not entirely told lies?
She did not visualize Kate as Kate had visualized
herself, alone in Sea House, a woman like Miss
Lavant. Quentin had said that for a moment Kate
had reminded him of Miss Trimm, and for another moment Lavinia imagined that: Kate at
eighty-two, passionately involved with God. That
might be so, or not. Kate, and Stephen too, must
be left suspended because children by their nature, with so vast a future, had to be. Little Mikey
Hatch she thought of, suspended also, dipping
his arms into water at the nursery school, and
Jennifer Droppy looking sad, and Joseph Wright
pushing, and Johnny Pyke laughing, and Tracy
Waye being bossy, and Thomas Braine interrupting, and good Andrew Cartboy, and Mandy Goff
singing her song. Their faces slipped through

her mind, round faces and long faces, thin, fat, smiling, somber. A whole array of faces came and went, of children who were at her school and children who had been there once. Would little Mikey Hatch become, like his father, a butcher? Would Mandy Goff break hearts all over Dynmouth, as people said her mother had? Would Joseph Wright in time become a Mr. Peniket, or Johnny Pyke a Commander Abigail, or Jennifer Droppy a Miss Poraway? Would Thomas Braine, indulged by his parents already, one day turn on them, as the child of the Dasses had? Would Andrew Cartboy, so tiny and sallow, become a Dynmouth Hard? Would Tracy Waye's bossiness turn into the middle-aged bossiness of a Mrs. Stead-Carter?

The future mattered because the future was the region where their stories would be told, happy and unfortunate, ordinary and strange. Yet it was sad in a way to see them venturing into it, so carelessly losing innocence. The future was like the blackness that surrounded her, in which there weren't even shadows. She stared into the blackness, and the faces and limbs of children, her own and others, again slipped about in her mind. And Timothy Gedge smiled at her, claiming her, or so it seemed. His face remained when the others had gone, sharp-boned and predatory, his eyes hungry, his smile still giving her the creeps.

12

On the morning of Easter Saturday the marquee, borrowed for the Easter Fête through Mrs. Stead-Carter, arrived in the rectory garden and was erected by the men who brought it, as it always was. The twins watched. They could remember the Easter Fête last year. It was a glorious occasion.

At half-past ten Mr. Peniket arrived, with the stage for the Spot the Talent competition on a trailer behind his car, the timber boards and the concrete blocks and the landscape of Swiss Alps on hardboard. Then Mr. Dass arrived with his lights and the blackout curtains that had been cleaned by the Courtesy Cleaners.

Chairs and benches and trestle-tables were delivered, borrowed from another firm through the offices of Mrs. Stead-Carter. Mrs. Keble arrived to set up her tombola and Mrs. Stead-Carter with cakes for her cake-stall. Miss Poraway told the men who were unloading the trestle-tables that she would require a good one, because she ran the book-stall and always had. They'd made thirty-five pence last year, she said, which was considered good. Mrs. Trotter set up her jewelry-stall, and Quentin and Mr. Goff arranged the hoopla, the coconut shy, the bran tub, and the Kill-the-Rat. In the rectory kitchen Lavinia and Mrs.

Blackham and Mrs. Goff buttered buns and cut up sponge cake and ginger cake and fruitcake, and arranged oatmeal fingers on plates. Dynmouth Dairies delivered forty pints of milk.

People arrived with jewelry for Mrs. Trotter and cakes for Mrs. Stead-Carter and prizes for the tombola. People came with books for Miss Poraway, tattered green-backed Penguins, *Police at the Funeral* by Margery Allingham, *Surfeit of Lampreys* by Ngaio Marsh, half of *Why Didn't They Ask Evans?*, the greater part of *Death and the Dancing Footman*. Someone brought an old Cook's Continental Timetable and *VAT News No. 4* and *VAT News No. 5*. Someone else brought fifty-two copies of the *Sunday Times* color supplement.

"Susannah help with books," Susannah said. "Susannah can."

"Deborah can," Deborah said.

"Oh now, how kind you are!" Miss Poraway cried, and one by one the twins took volumes from a carton that Mrs. Stead-Carter had carried from her car. "We sell them for a penny each," Miss Poraway explained. "Some real bargains there are. *Cow-Keeping in India*," she read from the spine of a volume that had suffered from damp. Never judge a book by its cover, she warned the twins. "*Practical Taxidermy*," she read from the spine of another.

In the kitchen Mrs. Blackham said Lavinia looked a little tired and Lavinia said she was, a little. Being upset about Timothy Gedge had made her tired, but she was glad she'd been upset, for at least it made sense, not like moping over a baby that couldn't be born.

That afternoon, on the loudspeaker system of Ring's Amusements, Petula Clark sang "Downtown." All over Dynmouth she could be heard because the volume had been specially turned up, the first indication that Ring's were once again open for business.

Even though it was daylight the strings of colored bulbs were lit up in Sir Walter Raleigh Park. The voices of the stall-holders jangled against one another, urging and inviting, different from the voices of the stall-holders at the Easter Fête. The Ghost Train rattled, amplified screams came from a record in the Haunted House, and amplified laughter from the Hall of a Million Mirrors. Yellow plastic ducks went round and round, inviting hoops to be thrown over them. Wooden horses and kangaroos and chickens went round and round also, a few of them with children on their backs. Wooden motor-cars and trains went round and round, more slowly. Empty chairs with harnesses swung violently through the air, high above people's heads. Motor-cycle engines roared in the pit of the Wall of Death. "Just listen to the music of the traffic in the city," sang Petula Clark. "Linger on the sidewalks where the neon-signs are pretty."

Mrs. Blakey heard the voice of Petula Clark, a faint whisper in the kitchen of Sea House. The atmosphere had gone from the house. At lunchtime the children had been normal, Stephen quiet but no longer looking drawn, Kate chattering about their parents' return. She would not say anything, Mrs. Blakey decided as she collected around her the ingredients of a steak and kidney stew for everyone's supper. She wouldn't mention the boy who'd made trouble unless for some

reason she happened to be asked about him, and
she felt she would not be. She hummed quite
happily again, her two red cheeks exuding her
interrupted cheerfulness.

Kate and Stephen went on the dodgems and then
bought candy floss. They watched the Dynmouth
Hards performing at the rifle range, their black-
frilled girls loitering beside them, seeming bored.
They watched Alfonso and Annabella on the Wall
of Death. They walked through the Haunted
House. They looked at themselves in the Hall of
a Million Mirrors. They traveled on the Ghost
Train.

They left Sir Walter Raleigh Park and walked
to the rectory garden. Stephen won a coconut.
Kate bought two tickets in Mrs. Keble's tombola.
They paid to enter the marquee to see the Spot
the Talent competition. It was due to start at four
o'clock, but didn't begin until twenty past due to
a hitch. Last year's carnival queen sang "Tie a
Yellow Ribbon round the Old Oak Tree." Stout
Mrs. Muller, in her national costume, sang. The
Dynmouth Night-Lifers, with electric guitars,
sang. The man called Pratt who'd come to the
Dasses' house on a motor-cycle did his imitations
of dogs. Mr. Swayles did his conjuring. The manager of the tile-works played the mouth-organ.
Miss Wilkinson did her Lady of Shalott. Mrs.
Dass came on in a fluffy magenta dress and
awarded the first prize to last year's carnival
queen and the second to Mr. Swayles and the
third to Mrs. Muller.

The children left the marquee. They saw Miss
Lavant in a suit with buttercups on it, strolling
about among the stalls, her downcast eyes occasionally glancing up. But Dr. Greenslade was

not at the Easter Fête. They saw Commander Abigail, with his rolled-up towel and bathing-trunks under his arm, buying cake from Mrs. Stead-Carter. Timothy Gedge's sister, Rose-Ann, was there with her boyfriend, Len. His mother was there, her hair freshly styled, hurrying round the stalls with her sister the dressmaker, whose hair looked smart also. Mr. Plant and his wife and children were there, but when he met Mrs. Gedge face to face near the hoopla they passed as if they were strangers. Mrs. Slewy slipped a bottle of sherry, third prize in the raffle, into a plastic hold-all.

The Easter Fête was for the birds, Timothy Gedge said. The Spot the Talent competition was a load of rubbish again. As he spoke, Kate could feel the devils. She could feel them coming toward her from his eyes and his smile, but they were different now, quieter, triumphant. He had won a victory. God had changed things but God had been defeated: she would believe that for ever, she would go on repeating it to herself and to anyone else who ever wanted to know. A miracle had happened but the miracle had fallen flat because you couldn't have miracles these days, because nobody cared, not even a clergyman. He'd see them around, Timothy Gedge said, but they knew from his tone of voice that they were of no further use to him. "Cheers," he said, not following them when they moved away.

They looked at Miss Poraway's books. *Practical Taxidermy* had not yet been bought. "Such a lovely fête!" Miss Poraway said. Susannah handed Stephen a book about bridge, grinning at him. Deborah handed Kate *Cow-Keeping in India*. "Only a penny!" Miss Poraway cried, but Kate explained that Indian cow-keeping didn't much interest her.

They left the fête and wondered for a moment about returning to Ring's. While they paused on Once Hill, Mr. Blakey approached in the Wolseley, on his way to Dynmouth Junction to fetch their parents from the station. He stopped when he saw them and asked if they wanted to come with him. They got into the back of the car.

He drove slowly, with old-fashioned care, easing the Wolseley through the Saturday shoppers in the center of the town. Two nuns lifted cartons of groceries into the back of their new Fiat van. The Down Manor crocodile chattered in Lace Street, the orphans on their way to the Easter Fête and the Amusements. A waiter came out of the car-park of the Queen Victoria Hotel. People loitered outside the Essoldo Cinema, examining photographs that advertised *The Wizard of Oz.* Old Ape rooted in the dustbins outside Phyl's Phries.

In the kitchen of the rectory Lavinia and Mrs. Goff speedily washed cups and saucers which were immediately used again. Now that the Spot the Talent competition was over teas were being served in the marquee. Mrs. Stead-Carter had sold her cakes and was hurrying between the kitchen and the tea-tables. So was Mrs. Keble, who'd taken eight pounds odd on the tombola. Mrs. Blackham was buttering more buns.

He would come regularly to the rectory now, Lavinia thought. Not to play with the twins, not for solace or scraps or to complain about the social security man, but simply to be a nuisance since being a nuisance was his way: to say again that he was the child of Miss Lavant. He would take the place of the rectory visitor who had died, mad Miss Trimm, and the place of the child which had not been born. After her long wakefulness in the night there was no escaping that thought, there was no escaping the suggestion of a pattern: the son who had not been born to her was nevertheless there for her. Believing still that the catastrophe had been caused by other people and the actions of other people, believing it as firmly as Kate believed that it had been caused by devils and Quentin that it was part of God's mystery, Lavinia saw a spark in the gloom. It was she, it seemed, not Quentin, who might somehow blow hope into hopelessness. It was she who one day, in the rectory or the garden, might penetrate the shell that out of necessity had grown. As she changed the water in her washing-up bowl, the feeling of a pattern more securely possessed her, the feeling of events happening and being linked, the feeling that her wakeful nights and her edginess over her lost child had not been without an outcome. Compassion came less easily to her than it did to her husband. She could in no way be glad that Timothy Gedge would come regularly to the rectory: that prospect was grim. Yet she felt, unable to help herself, a certain irrational joyfulness, as though an end and a beginning had been reached at the same time. You could not live without hope, some part of her woman's intuition told her: while a future was left you must not.

Coming into the kitchen, Quentin saw these thoughts reflected in his wife's face and said to himself that no matter what else had recently happened in Dynmouth, Lavinia had at least re-

covered from her discontent. His faith, to a de-
gree, had dissipated his own, imbuing with a
little fresh strength his run-down role. It was a
greater task to be as he was in his given circumstances than among God-fearing people: in that
fact itself there was an urge toward determina-
tion, and a hint of comfort. From across the
kitchen Lavinia smiled at him as though to reassure him, as though stating again that he did
not seem laughable. He slightly shook his head,
hoping to imply that it wasn't important how he
seemed.

"More butter, have we, Mrs. Featherston?" Mrs.
Blackburn inquired, and Lavinia said there were
half-pounds in the door of the fridge.

On the loudspeakers of Ring's Amusements
Petula Clark sang her song again. Everything was
waiting for you, she pointed out, and everything
was going to be all right.

"Dynmouth's livening up," Timothy Gedge remarked, falling into step with an old-age pensioner
on the way down Once Hill, smiling and laughing. Things always livened up, he went on, when
Ring's opened; things got set for the season. The
Whitsun visitors would follow the Easter ones;
in no time at all the hotels would be jammed to
the doors. He told the old-age pensioner two jokes.
He revealed that he'd been intending to do an
act at the Easter Fête but had abandoned it because he'd decided it was a load of rubbish. He
asked the old man if he'd ever worked in the
sandpaper factory and added that he'd probably
be going to work there himself when he'd finished
at the Comprehensive. He wasn't sure, he said,
you never could tell. He asked the old man if he

knew Miss Lavant, if he'd seen her at the fête, in clothes with buttercups on them.

His companion, who'd attempted to interrupt before, successfully did so now: it was no use trying to have a conversation with him because his deaf-aid had fallen to pieces.

Timothy Gedge nodded sympathetically. It was a beautiful story, he said, the story of Miss Lavant and Dr. Greenslade. It was beautiful, two people loving one another all these years and Dr. Greenslade being too much of a gentleman to leave his wife and family, and Miss Lavant giving birth to a baby and the baby being handed to a Dynmouth woman. It was beautiful how they'd laid it down that the baby should be brought up in Dynmouth so that they could always see it about the place. Miss Lavant looked great in all the different clothes she had, her scarlet outfit and her green and her blue, the beautiful buttercup thing she was wearing today. Fifteen years ago they'd decided to be circumspect, they'd brought their love affair to an end because the baby had been born. He was an elegant man, Dr. Greenslade, a handsome man in his gray suits and his smooth gray hair, not at all run to fat, like Cary Grant almost. If you closed your eyes you could imagine them together on the promenade, arm-in-arm like they should be, the doctor with a silver-knobbed stick, loving one another in a public place.

He raised his voice even though the old man continued to indicate that he could not hear him. It would always be a secret: even if the doctor's wife died and the doctor married Miss Lavant it would still be a secret about the child that had been born, because they'd never want it to be known out of respect for the dead. It would be a secret carefully kept, never mentioned by the people it concerned. It would just be there, like a touch of fog. He had said to the clergyman that opportunity wouldn't knock, but you never knew and you definitely had to keep your spirits up or you'd go to the wall. One minute you discovered you could do a falsetto, the next that there was a reason why a woman had given you a sweet. Everything was waiting for you; for a start you could get money left to you in a will. He smiled at the old-age pensioner and wagged his head. "Really good," he said, referring to the voice of Petula Clark.

The old-age pensioner could not hear it, but for everyone else it continued to throb with the promise of its message, drifting over Dynmouth on the breeze that blew gently from the sea.

"How can you lose?" sang Petula Clark. "Things will be great."